SIX
CROOKED
HIGHWAYS

SIX CROOKED HIGHWAYS

A NOVEL BY

WAYNE JOHNSON

HARMONY BOOKS NEW YORK

Published by Harmony Books, 201 East 50th Street, New York, New York 10022. Member of the Crown Publishing Group.

Random House, Inc. New York, Toronto, London, Sydney, Auckland

www.randomhouse.com

HARMONY BOOKS is a registered trademark and Harmony Books colophon is a trademark of Random House, Inc.

Printed in the United States of America

Design by Barbara Sturman

Library of Congress Cataloging-in-Publication Data

ISBN 0-609-60459-7

10 9 8 7 6 5 4 3 2 1

First Edition

FOR KAREN, THE ONE WITH WINGS

Those who travel by water control the waters;
makers of arrows make arrows straight;
blacksmiths temper their steel;
and the holy watch over their souls.

— NODINA'KWOD
Clouds filled with Wind

The heart is half a prophet.

— Folk proverb

ACKNOWLEDGMENTS

I am grateful to the many people who helped make this book possible, among them: Terry and Matt Cullen, Carole and Ron Stronach, Shirley Vonterharr, Betty Ann Schermann, Kim Benton and the Dyersville Library crowd, T.N.R. Rogers, Patsy and Martin Tracy, Sibashton Little Thunder, Ed and Hwi-ja Canda, Augusta Good Strike, Vik and Raj Vohra, Kevin Cooklin, H. Clay Bedford, Chris Tossberg, Gerald Davey, and Mike and Mary Farrell.

I extend a special thanks to my wife, Karen, for providing perspective, intuition, and humor when most needed; and to the Spirit, be whatever its name, to whom I owe a debt of gratitude immeasurable.

Finally, I give my thanks to two outstanding women: Shaye Areheart, my editor, who has brought out the best in my work, in everything from line edits to cover art; and Wendy Hashmall, who has provided right-on-the-mark critical commentary, worked with great cheer and enthusiasm, and been an advocate in all aspects of this process.

Miigwech! Thanks!

SIX
CROOKED
HIGHWAYS

ONE

Dead of night, the boat came up the lake from the south, at first no louder than a mosquito, that signature outboard whine, then closer, louder, until with an insistent grinding the boat went by the lodge docks and out onto the bay, passing us, to my relief—but there, instead of going farther north, through the buoys and up the channel, instead of going on to Barney's Ball Lake, or to the Northwest Outfitters, or Halbert's to bother someone else, now, whoever it was, made a hard, sharp turn, that outboard chuttering and whining at it, coming at us.

In bed, I lay on my back, staring into the dark, willing myself to stay put.

It's nothing, I told myself. They would keep going, they were just getting their bearings. Still, I had reason to be awake in the middle of the night waiting.

I reached for the clock on the nightstand; the arms glowed bright green in the dark. Four ten. A visit this time of night could be nothing but trouble, I thought, though maybe these were just a couple overzealous fishermen playing early bird, or lost?

But even as I was thinking it, there was a distinct, watery splash, which I knew could be nothing but someone going overboard.

I very nearly laughed at it, relieved.

I looked at my wife, Gwen, beside me, hair blue black on the white pillowcase, beautiful, and didn't want to wake her, or our daughter, Claire, just two and in her crib in the other room, so hesitated.

Propped on my elbow, I thought, Why get up? They'll be gone by the time I'm out of bed.

The boat went into a third circle of the bay, and I thought, happily, kids. That's what it was. Kids, wilding. Making a nuisance of themselves. It had to be that. But it wasn't even near Hump Night, when the resort help got crazy before heading down to White Earth and logging, wouldn't be that time for another two months.

I was waiting for a second splash—the motorman, taking a dive, too. But that didn't come. That was the old trick: steal a boat, run it around the lake, bang it to hell on things, and when dawn was on your tail, dump the boat.

I swung my legs around to put my feet on the floor.

The boat made a fourth, then fifth circle right offshore of the island.

Gwen turned on her side toward me; opened her eyes, trying to wake herself.

"What are they doing out there?" she said.

I touched the side of her face, kissed her hair, smelled lilac.

"Nothing," I said. "It's just kids."

Still, that did it. I shook myself, yanked on pants, shirt, cinched my belt—thought, shit! the belt was onto that third hole, shore lunch fat—scuffed on my shoes.

I bolted out of the cabin, ran to the bluff overlooking our docks; there, in the bay, the moon was reflected in a wash of cream on blue-black water, the boat cutting around it, a fine, hydroplaning arc, a perfect circle.

And no one behind the wheel.

I ran up along the bluff, closer to the water, the path to the boathouse and dock to my right, scanning the lake, and that's when I saw it.

A line of ripple leading to the north, not from the boat, but from the swimmer, who, drunken, I supposed, had left a veritable wake behind him, slapping at the water. The moon caught on the shadowy figure of someone going up and into the trees on Snowbank Island, opposite us. And just like that, like *pakwene,* smoke—

he was gone, the boat turning yet another perfect circle.

LATER THAT MORNING, in the kitchen, I was hunched over the phone talking to Charlie Groten, Pine Point's finest, our constabulary in blue, my now on-again off-again pal and splinter in my foot. It seemed we were always arguing over something. Now it was the boat.

I wanted Charlie to pick it up, so I could get on with my day, but he was telling me he needed to look into a floater some guide had found offshore of the Angle.

I thought it was all a hedge, an excuse not to make the trip out, until he said, chuckling,

"Guy dropped it off'd nearly have to fly to make it down to the Angle, right?"

I asked him what he was getting at.

"Bunch of BCA cops are turning the lake inside out, trying to find the boat he was in."

I felt the skin prickle at the back of my neck. The BCA was the Minnesota Bureau of Criminal Apprehension, serious stuff.

"My name come up?" I said.

"Did you do something so it would?"

"Jesus, Charlie."

"Didn't lose your temper with any of the tribal council people, make any threats or—"

"Why—somebody say I did?"

He mentioned talking to someone at the Rambler's, a bar and grocery where I did business, but wouldn't say who, and when I asked him what I'd supposedly said, his voice trailed off until I couldn't make out what he was saying at all—I couldn't tell if for shame, or that he didn't want this new girl he'd got to play secretary in the office to hear.

Suddenly it was oppressively noisy in that kitchen, hot.

"Hang on, dammit!" I said, and, holding my hand over the phone, turned to Mardine.

Mardine was running the KitchenAid, mixing more pancake batter, while twelve already sizzled on the grill. Substantial, dark-skinned as strong tea, her braids bound in blue cloth, Mardine had gotten bigger, and when she bent down to take her muffins out of the oven, she butted me over, teasing.

I must have given her a nasty look, because she glared right back, said, *"Sit down* and let me finish here, you want people to eat breakfast."

I squeezed into the desk between the kitchen counter and the wall, one of those school deals, an apron of Mardine's tossed over the hump of junk on the writing surface, as if that tidied things up.

The mixer was even louder there, thwoking away. I held the phone out to Mardine, pointed to it.

"I can't go any faster," she said.

Hugh, a tall, good-looking Noka clan kid who'd been after me to have a hand in management, winked in my direction and snatched up one of Mardine's muffins, bit wolfishly into it and ducked out of the kitchen when Mardine took a swing at him with her spatula.

Gwen went by the counter, in a cobalt blue dress, balanced on her forearm the plates Mardine prepared. I smiled for her, and she frowned slightly—she could see it was some trouble or another now—then directed the new girl, Josette, to do the same, and went out.

Mardine reached for the KitchenAid and it stopped its frenetic thwacking of batter.

"No appliances for two minutes, all right?" I told Mardine. "And don't let anybody in here." Mardine gave me a so-you-want-to-ruin-my-breakfasts? shrug, stacked the last of the pancakes on a platter, and bustled into the dining room.

I took my hand off the phone. "So what are you trying to tell me?"

"What, you got 102nd artillery in the kitchen?"

"Cough it up, Charlie," I said. I wasn't about to have him put me off.

"Who knows about the boat?"

"Just Gwen," I said.

"Put it where nobody'll see it," Charlie said. "Just until I get out there, all right?"

I knew all too well what he was asking me to do, and that it could cause me serious trouble.

"Why?" I said.

There was that radio hum on the line, ominously loud now for Charlie's silence, then the rasp of a match, Charlie lighting a cigarette.

But I knew, all too well, what he was implying, through his silence.

Late August, two years earlier, shortly after our closing season dinner, two men and I had taken a Chris Craft powerboat up the channel through the buoys, each steel, seventeen feet in length, half of that under water, and weaving between them, the driver had lost control, the boat striking the eighth buoy, killing the two men in front and badly injuring me.

How the driver had lost control, that's what Charlie, my cop friend, thought he knew, that the two men had meant Gwen and me some real harm—had already done worse, had been instrumental in my son's death the autumn of the year before—and that as a last, and desperate, measure, I'd caused the boat to hit the buoy. Charlie had talked with the FBI after the accident, given his version of it. All that we had between us.

"Charlie," I said.

"Just *do it,* okay? I'll get out there when I can," he said, and hung up.

I let my head drop back, stunned at it, set my elbow down on that mess of a desktop, on Mardine's apron, and hit something hard but springy.

Our answering machine came on—

You've reached—
home of Minnesota's finest pike and
walleye fishing.

I lifted Mardine's apron off the desk. Here was the answering machine, duct-taped to the desktop, no doubt Mardine's solution to the space problem.

Clever, I thought, angrily.

I bent over the machine, wound so tight I was tempted to smack it, stop it right then and there. I didn't need anymore complications—much less from a machine.

That machine had caller ID, line switching, so people could leave messages for me, Gwen, or our help, and fifteen other features I'd been too busy to learn how to use. I hated the damn thing, and hadn't wanted it in the first place, and especially not in the kitchen, where as often as not it was noisy.

I jabbed at the buttons, was about to yank the plug out of the wall, when the machine shifted, playing a message left during the night:

Market value is all it's worth.
Offer it, but don't hang things up with
waiting. Are we clear on that?

There was a pause, and two voices started up on the other end, a conversation in a dialect of Ojibwemowin I didn't quite understand. It was a woman and a man, and they both laughed.

Our . . . Pawn, the man said, *ka—Binishi'angoshkabay,* and the woman, laughing so hard she could barely get it out, said, in English, *Stop it, stop it, I'll wet myself.*

The first voice broke in again, but now sharply insistent, even urgent,

They don't want to go with the deal
on Penn Avenue, offer Nicollet. Make them look
bad if they won't pull out. Got it?

What? the man on the other end said.

There followed a dial tone, and the first voice emerged, as if out of a fog, suddenly familiar, cursing in world-class fashion.

I felt *almost* relieved at it: The voice was that of Richard "Skip" King, a candidate for the Minnesota senate. He'd left just after daylight, cut his stay by a week, called down to Minneapolis.

I thought about that floater, and Dick King rushing off the island the way he had—then thought, no. Coincidence. I told myself it was just business, and it would be more of the same on the tape, thought to erase the conversation, but didn't. Instead I pressed *Save,* even as Mardine charged back into the kitchen.

"Out. Now," she said, waving her spatula at me, and I did exactly that.

TWO

In the office at the back of the lodge, I tried to finish some paperwork, doodled nervously at my desk, then lifted the curtain from the window to my right, glanced in the direction of the kitchen.

I was thinking about Charlie and the floater, that boat, and the conversation our answering machine had recorded, Dick King's conversation.

Two boys came out of the kitchen and went up the path to cabin #7, arguing over a coral-red glass insulator they'd found.

I thought to go in and get the tape, but didn't, but couldn't stop thinking about it, either.

I wondered what kind of business Dick King could have with a couple Ottawa, what they'd been talking about. He'd been after something, but then, so what? Dick was always after something, had the phony handshake perfected, gripped your elbow when he did it, your long lost friend and soon to be benefactor.

And the two days he'd been up, he'd used the phone dozens of times, so what was one more call?

The ranger from his cell phone didn't work on the island, he'd explained.

I let the curtain drop, then bent over the yellow invoices on the green desktop blotter, but couldn't keep my mind on them for arguing with myself.

The floater, I told myself, didn't have anything to do with the boat. Every year a number of people drowned on the lake, usually the result of too much fooling around and drinking—all accidents. The rumors Charlie had hinted at were just that, and Dick King, or "Old Skippy," as I thought derisively of him, had squeezed into the desk, and while talking on the phone had done exactly what I'd done. Set his elbow on the machine and started it, though, in his case, recording. Just some real estate deal somewhere in the Twin Cities he'd rushed off to.

No relation to the floater, or the boat.

I might have been able to believe all that, let it go, even the tape, if hadn't been for this:

An investigator had stopped earlier in the week, a smallish, tan-skinned man in green twill pants, black windbreaker, and crepe-soled brogues, who'd asked all kinds of questions about where I'd been the last few days, had asked to see my gun case and guns, and had taken the serial numbers off them, had been so long at it I'd left him there, had Mardine watch him from the kitchen.

This . . . Michaels had stopped at the dock on the way out, stood over me. I was down in one of the boats, repairing an outboard engine.

Already, there was a near chemical disliking between us. "I'll be seeing you around," he'd said, then gone up the dock to his boat.

Just the thought of it now made my breath come short.

I stood, listening through the wall, to the bustle in the kitchen.

I had to go in there. If Gwen erased the message—or a call came in for Gwen, on my line, and the message was taped over—

But I couldn't go in. Gwen and Mardine were talking on the other side of the wall, right in front of the machine. Gwen laughed, the KitchenAid coming on again.

I rummaged through my desk. In the upper-right drawer was a manual for the answering machine. I got out the spare cassette in the box, my hands shaking, and stood, waiting for Gwen and Mardine to leave the kitchen.

Mardine's ululating voice came through the wall now. She sang a bit of a Red Lake 49'er, a song you'd sing after powwow, "Geronimo's Cadillac," a bitingly bitter, but funny song and Gwen, working beside her, caught up the refrain—

Hey, ho, I wanna go
I wanna ride in Geronimo's
Cadillac

It wasn't that I could hear all of it through the wall, I knew the song. All I needed was the thread of it, and it caught me up.

I stood there, that spare tape in my hand. One minute passed after another, ballooned out, timeless.

I cringed at each sound that made me think the phone was ringing, or the answering machine coming on with its characteristic beep.

I put my head near the window. The window was open and the curtains luffed in, but still I felt suffocated and full of shame. Gwen and I'd had this understanding since a bad season two years earlier, when our son had died, and those who'd done it, had come after us.

We would not protect each other by holding things back, we'd promised.

But what could I tell her now, anyway, other than that I was nervous and seeing trouble where there might not be any? What I'd do was, get things straight with Charlie, find out what was on the tape and decide for myself—first. After all, we didn't need any more borderline news or scares, which amounted to nothing so much as runs in the fabric of our now, sometimes, fragile relationship.

Gwen and Mardine's voices trailed off suddenly.

I went into the kitchen, the breakfast rush still on, fifteen, twenty people in the dining room, warm clatter of silverware and conversation, and giving my best show of nonchalance, I faked writing something on the counter while I snapped the old tape out of the machine.

Mardine marched in from the dining room, set her hands on her substantial hips.

"What are you doing?" she said.

"You need groceries? I'm makin' a list," I shot back. She cocked her head at me, confused.

"What for? You just went into Pine Point yesterday. And don't touch that—"

Gwen came in, glanced at Mardine. I was punching at those damn buttons, trying to get the new tape to seat, which it didn't seem to want to.

Gwen's eyes went wide, just a second. There was a hissing, and the machine rewound and came to a stop with a loud snap, even as I feigned reaching for my cigarettes, dropping the old cassette in my shirt pocket.

I was going to say, I guess I erased the messages, hating myself for it, but the look of relief on Gwen's face stopped me. Had there been something on the machine she hadn't wanted me to hear?

"Paul's going into town," Mardine said to Gwen, "need anything?"

Gwen got an almost sly look on her face.

I shook myself at it. But then she smiled. Stunningly white teeth, and those blue, blue eyes. Not a touch of a shadow in it, I told myself, and I smiled back that same smile as best I could.

BUT I WAS not smiling, standing in the boathouse doorway. Hugh, shoulders squared combatively, spun around, the first to see me. They'd been arguing about something, I'd heard it on the path down, Hugh, and my two other guides, Napoleon and Elmer.

"All right," I said, "spill it."

I was in no mood for it, so waited, looked from Hugh, to Elmer, and finally to Napoleon.

Napoleon, seventeen and cocksure, grinned impishly, tossed an artificial worm. It slapped across Hugh's forehead and stuck.

Hugh stood there as if at attention, his eyes, narrowed to angry slits, trained on Napoleon.

"You're pushin' it," Hugh said.

Red gelatin, the worm wriggled there a second, then fell.

But I'd seen it anyway—off to my right, Elmer, beside Napoleon, had swayed suddenly, and Napoleon had taken his arm and held him.

Elmer, my project. Just sixteen, it had been summer work at the lodge, or juvvie down in Bemidji. I'd thought to give him a chance, have him learn the ropes guiding. Now he kept his head down, his complexion ashen; he'd been drinking again, and Hugh and Napoleon were trying to keep him from getting canned, I thought.

"Looks like you had a rough night there, El," I said, "You ready to go out?"

Napoleon let go of Elmer and he nodded, then quickly ran his fingers over his head, his hair spiky and matted, tried to comb it down, put himself in order.

Something was wrong there, but just then I couldn't make out what.

He was wearing the same khaki shirt and pants as always, but instead of being covered with yellow dust, pine pollen, there were flecks of green here and there. And his boots were a dark, oily cordovan color, and I knew he hadn't polished them.

"He's all right," Napoleon said.

For a second I wondered, almost relieved, had it been the boys out in that boat? Elmer and Napoleon?

Napoleon left evenings—Hugh told me he had a girl on the Angle somewhere, though nobody'd seen her—and as often as not he took Elmer with him, returning in the early morning. But they hadn't been out overnight, I'd checked the docks to see if our boats were all docked—and they had been. Every last one.

All that was right in front of me there, and I was dead wrong about all of it.

But it was dark in the boathouse that morning—they hadn't thrown open the windows—and I was distracted by what Charlie'd got me thinking about, and the smell of water rot, and gasoline, rubber, kapok, and old musty magazines and tar from the new roof—

All that said, here was just some squabble, an argument.

Still, I turned to Elmer, to give him one last, closer look, and right at that moment, Hugh crossed the warped floor, decisive.

"Hey!" he said. "See these carburetors?" He grinned proudly, motioning to his right.

It was as if a switch had been thrown, and whatever darkness there had been in that place, flew.

"Take a look," Hugh said.

I stepped over to the engine he'd mounted in a fifty-gallon drum of water.

Hugh had gotten all that from me, tinkering with machines, but this, the outboard engine, was his first baby, and he was bursting with pride over it.

I felt myself smile at that.

"Got 'em off an Italian motorcycle," Hugh boasted. "Got accelerator pumps so you just crank the throttle one time— I mean, watch this—"

He twisted the throttle linkage, then yanked on the rope starter. The engine roared mightily, filling the room with oily blue exhaust, but after a minute or so, no matter what he did with it, the engine died, and all that good feeling died with it.

Napoleon and Elmer moved farther back into the boathouse where it was dark. Hugh kept his eyes on the engine, wouldn't look at me.

I knew what was wrong with it, but wasn't about to tell him. I'd reached the end of it, this complicit little game we were playing. I'd overlook whatever trouble they'd caused themselves, and they'd get to work and take care of it themselves.

"So—" I said to Hugh, "you got everything set to go?"

"Of course," Hugh lied.

Somehow, that put me over. If he meant to manage, as he'd told me he did, I couldn't have him siding with the help. Or lying to me, especially when I was trying to cut him some slack.

We're late, he could have said, and left it at that, but no—he hadn't done that.

Right there I decided to teach Hugh a lesson, all the meanness of my day going wrong behind it.

I lifted my hand, checked my watch, glanced back at Elmer.

"Your first boat's out in twenty minutes. What's the program?" I said.

"Pike," Elmer said, sharp as could be. Which surprised me. He wasn't one bit hungover. "Or walleye. We'll use sliding sinker and split shot. That doesn't work, slow troll—night crawler, leech, minnow."

I pointed with my chin at Napoleon.

"Where?" I said.

Napoleon's eyes narrowed. He knew I was after something.

"You don't know," I said, appealing to his vanity. That got him.

"It's midsummer," he shot back, "so—drop-offs, small islands, reefs. Points of land. That's rocky bottom, so we'll lose a fair amount of tackle. That doesn't do it, weed bottoms, and with the wind blowing the way it is today, mostly shoreline I'd say. Use fireline or spiderwire."

I turned to grin at Hugh. Elmer and Napoleon had spit back what I'd taught them. I thought Hugh would do the same, and I'd catch him there.

"So—you're going to move a lot." It was pure provocation.

Now it was just Hugh and me in that room. I meant to dress him down, the boys, Napoleon and Elmer, both there to make it worse.

"Exactly," Hugh said.

"So, it's all in here." I stepped over to the portable kitchen, glanced down into it; empty. "Since you're going light, you'll be around Snowbank. Scoot in for lunch, right?"

Snowbank was just across the bay, where I could keep an eye on them.

No one fished there, for exactly that reason.

"You got all this squared with Mardine, right? What she needs in the kitchen?"

Hugh cocked his head to one side, a line of muscle tight across his jaw. It was quiet in there, a nasty, heavy quiet. We both knew what was at stake—his job.

I was calling Hugh on his lie—he would either have to lie again now, about Mardine, put her on the spot and hope she liked him enough to go the distance for him, or—

What?

Elmer was poking a screwdriver at the spiderweb he'd tattooed on his left hand with a ballpoint pen and a Bic lighter. Napoleon grinned. Elmer gave it a shot, too—the result a kind of purposeful grimace, so much pain in it I felt my throat swell.

Right there, my self-righteous anger became a kind of grief. I wasn't worried about Hugh or Napoleon, they'd make it somehow, but Elmer?

All that spring, I'd had the kid at my table, had shown him how to tie flies, use the fishing gear, had shaken him out of sleep mornings, had gotten him new clothes.

Gwen had packed lunches for him, talked on the porch with him nights.

"Those scars he's got all over his legs, the burns?" Gwen said one morning. "He didn't get them falling into a campfire."

"I know," I said.

I had a scar on my upper lip, a white line thick as a piece of yarn. Another in my right eyebrow, where the hair didn't grow. I didn't smile, I just turned my face at Gwen, and she got this shocked look; first, a kind of betrayal in it, seeing those scars for what they were.

Then, pity, which I didn't want.

I'd told her I'd gotten those scars catching fireflies, had fallen on my glass jar. It had been an easy lie, since it was almost true.

So the kid and I had those kinds of fathers between us.

And here he was now, poking at his tattoo again, was weighing out the possibilities.

Should he tell, or not?

He was absolutely alone, there in the dark, grinning at me and poking that screwdriver at his tattoo, wanting to do the right thing, but there being two right things now, get out of trouble and not be a fink, and no in-between.

Right there I saw, surely, they were in some kind of trouble of their own. Real trouble. Maybe it did have something to do with that boat after all?

Or was it just Elmer?

Watching him, something in me was urging, come on, it can't be that bad, can it? I was leaning into it, how I'd fix things for him, try to bring Napoleon around, who couldn't but hate Elmer if he ratted, when Hugh said,

"We'll go up to Nestor Falls," and that moment of possibility was gone forever.

Nestor Falls was as far north as we went. The equipment he needed for a shore lunch was already boxed and ready.

"I'll let Mardine know you won't need anything," I said.

Hugh nodded—but wasn't about to say *yes*. By covering for Napoleon and Elmer he'd gotten himself into heavy work and then some, a trip all the way up to our satellite lodge, a fourteen-hour day, at least.

A boat was coming in, and I went up the hillside to watch.

From below, I heard Hugh say,

"Listen, you fuckin' little peckerwoods. Don't *ever* expect me to take shit like that for you again. Got it? You take care of yourselves from now on. I don't care what it is you two've done. You gonna work, or do I gotta get your asses canned?"

On that hillside, waiting for the boat of new guests, hand over my eyes like a visor, I did not feel clever, like I'd won something. I felt I'd failed, at what I could only guess, and to make it sit right, I promised myself to fix it.

But I never got the chance.

Only to square things, finally, but that never brings them back, does it?

THREE

In our cabin, I lay awake most of that night, one moment in a cold sweat at what I imagined might be coming at us, the next almost laughing at myself for getting spooked so easily. Gwen turned on her side, her face moonlit and lovely, and I told myself I would be better off down in the boathouse. There I tied flies, organized tackleboxes, spooled line on reels—but all the while listened for some interruption in the usual night chirrus—crickets (to pass time I gauged the temperature by them: beats per minute and add forty) katydids, a loon.

Now and again, I stood out on the dock, smoking, watching.

I was doing that, just after dawn, when Charlie came in through the narrows, standing at the wheel in his official-looking white boat, a gold star on the side the size of a dinner plate, the top up so I could only see him through the clear vinyl side curtains, nearly opaque now with condensation. The boat veered suddenly, then came to a halt, water sloshing over the stern.

Then Charlie was shouting at someone, and I thought it had to be some kid, and a hope swelled in me, the kid was connected to the boat, or whatever mess it was Napoleon and Elmer were caught up in, all of it nothing more than kid stuff.

I kicked the bow of the boat back when Charlie slid up to the dock, threw a line around the bow cleat.

I couldn't see anybody in the boat but a thumping came from the tiny cabin just in front of the steering wheel.

Charlie tossed the top back, set his thick-fingered hands at his belt, steel watch, chunky class ring, and wedding band—I sometimes wondered why he wore it—waiting for me to bring the stern around, but I froze on the dock a moment, taking him in.

He'd put on some weight in the four weeks since he'd last been out, and his gut, in cop-blue cloth, spilled over his belt like a sack of rice, now larger. His blue uniform was worse than rumpled and the brass bars over his left breast pocket were tarnished, but there was a hard-edged, no-nonsense something there, all business.

"You gonna pull the stern around so I can get out, or just stand there?" he said, angrily.

I brought the boat around, my legs leaden, and Charlie as much stumbled onto the dock as stepped onto it, and there he slapped his thick hands together, as if to get something off them. He smelled of beer and stale cologne.

"Son of a bitch," he said. "When it rains, it pours, right?"

I grinned, but didn't say yes.

"This here's just something I want you to take care of, and then we'll get to it, all right?"

That thumping came from that tiny cabin again, and I felt my stomach knot.

"Gwen isn't allergic to fur or anything, is she?" Charlie said.

I gave Charlie a wary look, waiting for the rest of it.

I knew a stumble pitch when someone threw one at me, and Charlie was doing it now. Someone on the reservation says, Hey, how's it going? And you say—stupid, proud you—Going great. And your new pal says, Business is okay? and you answer, Couldn't be better, and the next thing you know, out of good conscience or whatever, you're handing the guy two crisp hundred dollar bills, and he's saying he'll have it back next week sometime, which you know will be when hell freezes over, or Wovoka rises from the dead, or there's a revival of the Ghost Shirt Society.

"Why?" I asked, finally, and not a little meanly.

Charlie bent down toward the boat.

"You," Charlie shouted. *"Get outta there, goddammit!"*

I was seeing red, was primed to give Charlie a piece of it. What had Charlie done to the damn kid, after all? But then a bulldog, cream and red-brown, poked its head through the little door that separated the cabin from the back of the boat, a bulldog wrapped in a white sheet, what looked like bloody hamburger coming through.

Charlie winced, looking at it.

"Think of it as a trade," Charlie said. "I'll help you with this boat business, and you—you take the dog."

I wanted to laugh, or something. I did. But it wasn't really funny. I hurt for that dog, she was so battered looking.

The dog tried to jump onto the driver's seat, but fell with a loud clatter.

"Somebody up from the Cities must've just turned the damn thing out of the car," Charlie said. "Probably got hit on 525. I found her over by the Inlet trying to eat rotten minnows out of a bait bucket. Damn thing jumped into my boat."

I rubbed my hands over my face, pressed my palms into my eyes. I did not need an injured dog—and ugly!

"Well?" Charlie asked.

I didn't say, Why'd you bring it here? I said, throwing my hands up and shaking my head, "All right, Charlie. All right."

A SHORT WHILE, and a few bites later, the dog was lying on her side behind the kitchen in the shade of the pines. Mardine removed what was left of the sheets from her jaws. I watched from some distance with Charlie, smoking.

Gwen came out with water in a dish, tried to get the dog to drink.

"Breaks your heart, seeing somebody treat an animal like that," Charlie said.

The dog lapped the water up sloppily and settled again under the tree.

I nodded toward the path to the backside of the island and Charlie followed.

"THIS IT?" he said, up the path from the boat. You could see the boat through the trees, where I'd winched it onto the sand.

I went around him, meaning to go on ahead, and he caught my arm.

"What?" I said.

"Want you to see something."

He craned his head around to look behind us, then up and down shore, digging into his breast pocket, then handed me two eight and a half by eleven sheets, both folded in quarters. I knocked them flat on my forearm and looked.

On each sheet was a color photocopy of a Polaroid snapshot. The first was taken from the side of something on a gray background, the second from above.

I lifted the second to look closer, what appeared to be driftwood, whitish gray sticks, with some reddish material wound around them—gave another look at the first, on the right of the driftwood a stump, markings on it, the kind teeth would leave.

Charlie turned the page ninety degrees, and I felt a wave of nausea, before I even understood what I was looking at.

"I'd say he got into some trouble and lost his head."

"Oh, Christ," I said.

Charlie pointed to a black band, around the middle. "The guide who found him never would've even seen it if it hadn't been for this belt here."

"Where'd you get these?"

"Friend, works for the coroner's office. Sons of bitches wouldn't even let me near the damn body, or even in the office for that matter."

I didn't want to hear it, but I had to ask anyway.

"Why."

"Potential conflict of interest," Charlie said.

"You mean me. You coming out for dinner and—"

"Yup. And on account of how you been messin' around in politics up here again."

"I haven't been messin' around in *anything*," I said, which was at least half true.

"Yeah, right," Charlie said.

I bent over the photos, as much to get a closer look as to avoid having to deal with Charlie wanting an answer, could see the gray-green stomach now, under the ribs, swollen, what must have brought the body to the surface.

"They figure it was animals got his head," I asked, "or was it—"

"Like I said," Charlie said, "they've shut me out, so all I got on this is what you got, right in your hands, and I'll tell you, I've enlarged the damn things, looked at 'em through a magnifying glass, the whole nine yards, and I'd have to say something tore his head off the way the neck looks, but then who am I to say? I mean, I do know this. He was banging up against the shore of the Angle who knows how long, and then the coyotes got to him."

"Great," I said, setting the photos against my leg. "Just great."

Charlie looked off in the direction of the boat, and I led him down to it.

The boat, a midsixties Glasstron, with a big Merc 100 on the back, was nothing special to look at, red with a white top. There were fifteen, if not twenty, just like it registered and licensed on Lake of the Woods.

Charlie leaned over the gunnel, carefully stepped into the boat but didn't touch the wheel.

Whoever had leapt from the boat had tied the steering wheel with a bungee cord, so the boat would make a circle of a specific radius, and right out front of the lodge.

With the toe of his black shoe—the laces broken and knotted—Charlie poked at a Nut Goody wrapper by the gas tanks. Opposite, a Mounds, a Butterfinger, and a Sugar Babies, in a banana yellow package, like you'd get at a theater, had slid into the corner by the battery; there also, a bottle of whiskey, and cigarette butts, Old Golds.

And there were other things on the floor of that boat, too, things I'd wanted Charlie to look at: three wooden stakes, about five inches long, with steel ends; a hundred-foot tape measure; and a length of orange plastic band that had been nailed to something, like lath, for a lath and plaster wall.

All that was jumbled together, in that corner, with the candy wrappers, bottle, and cigarette butts.

And the wrappers had been crumpled, then flattened. As if they'd been snatched up, elsewhere, put in a pocket, and thrown into the bottom of the boat, later.

But why would anyone do that?

Charlie tossed his head, and his mouth pursed, glanced up at me.

"I don't see any blood," he said, setting his hands on his belt. "Shit, I don't know, maybe this was just kids. I mean, look at this crap. Who else would drink rotgut and eat Sugar Babies? Probably no connection between that floater and this boat. Hell, probably woke yesterday on some island somewhere lookin' worse than that bejesus dog I brought over."

He'd said *probably* twice; I hadn't missed that. Or that he hadn't mentioned the bungee cord, holding the steering wheel in place. Charlie gave a grunt, lifting himself out of the boat.

"I'll be back out for the boat later tonight, store it around Pine Point. Don't bother calling, I'll come out when I've got something."

I handed him the photocopies and he stuffed them into his

breast pocket.

"Hey," Charlie said, and squeezed my forearm. "Give it a rest. Probably just coincidence, huh?"

"Sure," I said.

"Don't want to hold up the Circus," Charlie said and grinned. "It's all yours. And you get some sleep tonight, huh?"

"Does it show?"

"That dog's got nothin' on you, pal."

We went around shore to the boathouse and dock. In minutes Charlie was out on the bay, headed back out toward Pine Point.

Then the first of the guests threaded down through the birches along shore, laughing; the three boys went out and away with the lot; and I stepped into my day, all the happier for the distraction it afforded.

What, after all, was there to do but get on with it, go back to work as if nothing loomed out there, just waiting to catch us up?

My grandfather, Nita, when I was just a boy, taught me this: Ritual work, like a steady, reassuring heartbeat, would save my life. Put your life into what you love—enh? he'd say, and poke me. *Nisidotam,* understand?

So, I did that.

THAT WEEK, UP before dawn, I'd leave Gwen and Claire in my cabin, then hike the perimeter of the island, a mile long north south, a little over a quarter mile wide, east west, anxious to spot anything out of sorts. From the spine, high over everything, I'd watch the sun splash the lake with red and rose and ocher.

Akange, my grandfather used to say, a red coal.

Morning after morning like that, high on the spine, I waited for Charlie.

If I were with a guest, there were things I'd point out.

See anybody? I'd ask.

No, they'd reply.

Some mornings I'd explain how that didn't mean anything—
you could hide anywhere, if that's what you wanted. There were
more islands on Lake of the Woods than on any other in the North
American continent. To give a real sense of the size of the lake, I'd
say, you have to understand shoreline, or navigable water—the first
cartographers, in the 1700s, working for the Hudson's Bay Company,
found the shoreline so varied and extensive as to be unmappable—
sixty-five thousand miles of it, more than Lake Superior.

It wasn't really one lake at all, but fifteen thousand intercon-
nected smaller lakes.

See? I'd say, and point. Seventy miles of that, all the way to
Kenora. But all that was figures, just proportion.

I'd done something in February, and here, in front of me was
now, was why I'd done it.

Beautiful, granite islands, in sky-blue water, pines and white
birch down on shore, lake after lake, each a jewel, amethyst— opal—
aquamarine, depending on the time of day.

Almost eight thousand Chippewa lived out there. I'd been born
and raised on the lake myself.

Invariably, a guest would say, It all looks sort of . . . the same.

I always had to laugh at that.

How could I tell them, the lake became as familiar as your body?
How you learned to read signs, a rock outcropping with petroglyphs
on it, for example, a sacred place where you'd camped, and dreamed
dreams you'd never forgotten, or had your first kiss, or made love
there, on gray-green moss; how, at another place, rust-red iron scars
on granite, your family had traded with trappers, going back seven
generations.

Smell of gum pine. Taste of fry bread. Kick of shotgun, duck
hunting. Burning leaves. Soft pine needles underfoot, blue-green
lichen on granite.

The land, our blood and bone.

Fought for, hung onto, the barbed wire fences that divided our
land pushed back, time and again, the Private Property signs bullet-

riddled, until legal means returned the land to us, prayed over, and loved like our very lives.

How could you explain that?

Look, I said, the sun rising over the trees, the lake on fire with it. And I'd say, to this new guest, all over again, as if in a song, a gift:

Akange—a red coal, my grandfather called it.

But now, always as much to reassure myself I'd done the right thing, as to pass the time.

FOUR

Friday of that week, I stopped in the kitchen before making my walk around the island.

"What's with the long face?" Mardine said.

She shoved a roll at me, on a blue plate, which I wanted to refuse; I was going to look like Charlie if I didn't watch out, have a damn truck-tire-sized bumper at my waist, but I ate the roll anyway. Cinnamon, cardamom icing, the center still hot and sticky and yeasty. Nervous as I was, it made me feel queasy.

Gwen, in cobalt blue, looking over her shoulder, stepped into the kitchen with Claire.

That roll caught in my throat. I hadn't really seen Gwen all week. Evenings, after dinner, I'd driven north of Pine Point, trying to run into an elder who could listen to the tape for me, or had poked around in town, after what I wasn't sure.

"Hey, beautiful," I said.

"Hey, handsome," she said in return.

Gwen tossed her head, that lovely Irish blue-black hair over her shoulders. Claire looked like one of those cherubs in a Renoir painting, red-haired and beautiful, only she wanted to get down and into things now. My eyes got all glassy at it.

"*Manesiwin,*" I said, what do you want, and she smiled.

She pointed to one of the rolls, her finger crooked almost double. "*Zaasakokwan!*" Fry bread, but she knew the difference.

I washed my hands at the sink, then set her on my lap. With Gwen laughing, and Mardine nudging her, their backs to me while they put together what would be, that evening, dinner—steaks marinated in red wine and peppercorns, and some fancy cake—I fed Claire.

Claire got that icing all over my shirt and pants, but I felt like I'd been marked by love itself.

Just then, I thought I was crazy. I was just being paranoid, I thought, complicating my life over nothing.

The phone rang and Mardine picked it up, told me it was Charlie. I heard a typewriter clacking in the background, Darilyn, a girl he'd hired that summer, his first ever, saying something I couldn't quite hear.

"You're sure?" Charlie said, and then there was the sound of something held over the receiver, a muffled hollow, and silence.

I smiled at Gwen, then down at Claire, who had her hands on the chain around my neck.

"I thought you were coming out," I said.

"You know old Eugene Morreaseau?" Charlie said, something hard in his voice.

My heart gave a kick. It was Eugene I'd tried to hook up with, get him to listen to the tape if I could.

"Well?" Charlie said.

I wasn't about to step into it. *Everybody* knew Eugene Morreaseau. He was a kind of legend, a Waubunowin, a reservation boogeyman.

"What about him."

"It's his boat," Charlie said.

"So why haven't you gone out there?"

Charlie didn't answer. There was a mulling over silence on the line.

"He say something to you?" I said.

"Yeah, he did," Charlie said. "The last time I was out to see Eugene he told me to take my white Irish ass off his property."

"When did that ever—"

"You know that bullet hole in my cruiser?" Charlie said, "That I told you some wiseacre kids put there?"

"The vandals—"

I squeezed Claire, then set her on the floor; she ran for Gwen, who swept her up and carried her into the lodge dining room.

"Well, it wasn't any vandals."

"You mean he shot at you," I said.

"Way to go, Einstein! All your ducks are quackin' today, let me tell you. That top-notch noodle of yours is just astounding."

"You want me to go out there with you," I said.

I could hear a gurgle on the other end, Charlie drinking something. I hoped it wasn't what I thought it was.

"Ten points for the home team," Charlie said. "We aughta get you on that show, what's it called . . . Jeopardy, with that—"

"What's gotten into you," I said. I really wanted to know.

"Meet me at ten."

"Tomorrow," I said. We were that busy.

"You can dig your own grave," Charlie said. "Doesn't matter to me. You were out to Eugene's yourself, what, how many times? Maybe we can skip going altogether and you can just tell me what he had to say, huh?"

When I didn't leap to it, he said,

"Cat got your tongue?"

"Hardly."

"I'll see you in an hour," Charlie said. "You can tell me all about it then."

IN THE LAUNCH, headed for the government docks and Pine Point,

I lit a cigarette, trying to come up with a simple explanation of what I'd done for Charlie. I was so agitated I could barely keep myself behind the wheel.

I cursed myself for being drawn into another of George Stronghold's messes.

Why had I done it? Just then I was furious with myself.

NIKAN, GEORGE ALWAYS said after knocking at my door, brother, let me in. Always unannounced, out of nowhere, and near midnight or after. He'd done it that snowy night in January, down in St. Paul.

So I'd let him in.

"It's nothing," he said, over our table in the kitchen. Even sitting he was huge, the bridge of his nose thick where it had been broken, his hair in braids. He always smelled of patchouli.

Gwen had been polite, and then our daughter, Claire, had cried, and Gwen went into the bedroom.

"Look, it's another boondoggle, that's all it is," George said as soon as she was gone. "It's not like that deal with—" And there he caught himself up short. But he didn't have to say it—that deal with Al. Al Eagle, my old friend, and I had opposed an earlier development scheme. Al had been murdered, and then they'd come after me, all leading to the boat accident.

George had helped save our lives that night.

All that was part of the reason I let him in, night after night, if it were one, or three—or even after five and he'd been drinking and needed a place to crash. I was beholden, and then some. (Which was why I'd hired Napoleon, Al's little brother, too.)

So I listened, did that night.

"You're *not* signing on with anything, or *doing* anything," George said. "The State's gonna call and ask for a right-of-way through your acres on the Angle, and all you gotta do is say, Let's wait and see. Just hold 'em off, okay? That simple enough? You do it, and other people'll go along, buy us some time."

I asked what they needed the right-of-way for.

George explained that the State was offering to build a road in from Highway 525 to put up a second dock south of Pine Point. The road would pass through reserve property, some of it mine. Some of it other Red Lake Band members'.

"So what do they really want from us?" I asked.

"I'll be honest with you," George said. "I haven't got a clue what's behind it, but it just *smells* bad."

At the door, we'd shaken hands. He had started out, and had at the last second turned, looked at me over his shoulder, as if he'd just then remembered something.

"Don't tell anyone," he said. "That road deal is only speculation right now, a come-on. That they're gonna build it and all. Just the higher-ups know. You tell people and it's gonna make for a whole lot of bad feeling, no matter what comes out of it."

"You don't think the development side'll be a bit short with me for holding things up?"

George had grinned. "By spring there won't be so much as a word about it. We'll shoot the proposal down and it'll end right there."

AND IT HAD. Didn't hear a word all winter.

We opened, late May, and I forgot about all that with George. We'd expanded, on a shoestring, in the two years since we'd nearly lost it all, and this summer now—good weather holding—had the potential to sink an arrow right into the black by August.

That's what I'd put my mind to.

I was working sixteen-hour days, but the future looked bright: now the lodge would seat sixty, twenty-foot-high ceiling on the fireplace end, the fireplace masonry rechinked and set, new skylights, new slab-pine tables and chairs, and where we'd had phony beadings on the walls, I now had the real thing, donated by people who'd wanted the moccasins, cradle boards, and knee bands for fancy dancing, all quill work, and trade beads of crow blue, corn yellow, and blood red, where people could appreciate them.

On loan, for favors—afternoon guiding jobs for sons, or husbands, kitchen work for wives. Josette was one of them.

And we'd gotten a new refrigerator, deep freeze, kitchen gear, new linoleum counters, new desk in my office—new to us, really a nearly two-hundred-year-old Hudson's Bay desk, solid butcher-block oak, worth its weight in gold, but given to me by a banker in his will. New generator and boathouse, and three new cabins to replace those that had burned in the fire two years earlier.

Right then, we had it all, it seemed.

Gwen just wanted a piano, to keep her hands limber over the summer, and sometimes in the fall, when we stayed up for duck and deer hunting.

The only thing we couldn't count on was the weather and time, I'd thought.

JUST PAST EIGHT, I came through the door of the Western Cafe. It was crowded, Hank Williams on the juke, scent of bacon, pancakes, and smoke; at the tables, the usual mix of Indians dressed in plaid and khaki, and tough-looking farmers in worn overalls and denim shirts. In back, the Red Lake council, in beaded vests, jewel-tone shirts and dresses, and some applique work, turned in my direction, looking at me with what I took to be a certain almost amused hostility.

Two white guys in navy-blue suits sat with them, and Truman Wheeler, a dirty cream Stetson jammed on his coffeepot head.

Walter Davis, the acting tribal chairman, grinned, then gave me a big, clownish wink.

I stepped in his direction, intending to ask him what the hell he thought the big joke was between us, when Charlie slipped out of a booth to the right.

"Siddown," he said, and I did that.

"What are those lawyers doing here?"

"Fucking everybody over, what else?" Charlie said. "Now it's some threat of imminent domain bullshit. They can't get people to say yes, Truman'll try lawyers."

I set my elbows on the table, rubbed my forehead in my palms. That road mess had come back to life, and I didn't like it one bit.

"So what did you hear?"

"Truman told me you got people behind you thinking you'll bring in AIM, make a big media mess out of it if they try to push that road through."

"Gimme one of those," I said, and fished a cigarette from Charlie's pack. I sucked that cigarette down, a meanness in it, blew a plume of smoke over the table. "You believe that? From Truman?"

"It isn't just Truman, it's all kinds of people. I mean, I talked to 'em myself. Some of them would just as soon hang you as look at you."

I leaned into the table. "Do you think for one second I'd do something so stupid as all that? Blow my mouth off like that?"

"So I'm not to take this complaint somebody filed against you seriously."

"When'd that happen?"

"Just this morning."

I held my hands out, grinned for Charlie. "I've hardly been off the island in weeks, when would I even do something like that, huh?

"So you didn't threaten to 'blow the government docks up'?" Charlie said. "I mean, you did buy dynamite, didn't you?"

"I had to build a containment tank, on the island. Remember? You *don't dig* through solid granite."

"If you haven't done anything," he said, "why's there all this talk about you?"

"George—"

"Oh, good. George. I should've known he'd be in this somewhere."

I told Charlie about how a few of us had stalled on that right-of-way. Charlie tapped his cigarette over the ashtray, gave me a sharp look.

"So why were you out there at Eugene's, if you didn't want to blow the balls off those development hotshots, make a big mess? You think about that?"

So, we'd finally gotten to it. Eugene, and how it looked, my having gone out there a few times.

Out the front windows, a car went by in the street, the sun flashing off it.

"It's just business as usual," I said, trying to shake Charlie out of it. I had no intention of telling him about the tape. It would just complicate things. So I said,

"I loaned Eugene one of our outboards, and I went over to get it back. Okay?"

Charlie grimaced. "Really. And what are people gonna think if Eugene's dead?"

"You think that floater's Eugene?"

"I'm just sayin' 'what if.'"

"I didn't talk to him."

"You're gonna tell me he wasn't there, right?"

"No. Not at first."

"What do you mean, 'Not at first.'"

"I mean," I looked over my shoulder at the council members, "I drove in there all right, but he wasn't in. Twice. The third time his car was parked on the side, but he still wasn't home. So he had to have been alive then, see?"

"You think the car showing up there means he was alive those first two times, is that what you think?"

The thought that somebody would mess around like that shocked me.

"Hell, I don't know," I said.

Charlie caught my arm, squeezed, an ugly look on his face. "Either you're givin' me a load of shit, or you're not gettin' straight with me here. *Are you,* or are you *not* caught up in it?"

"Caught up in *what?*"

"We're talking murder one here," Charlie said, gripping my arm harder.

"Don't," I warned, a sudden rage jacking fistfuls of blood into my chest.

Charlie sensed what I did right then—something in me that wouldn't stop at hurt—threw his hands up, fingers outstretched.

"Hey," Charlie said. "You're all pissed off because somebody's messing with you, but it *isn't* me, got it?"

And there he stopped himself from saying what he'd always said years ago, when he'd picked me up for stealing a boat, or somebody's car for a night of joyriding and took me here, to the Western, instead of down to Bemidji, and juvvie lockup. He didn't say, no whining or moaning about how tough life's been, how life isn't fair, or how your old man's beatin' you up made you do it.

"Somebody's tryin' to put your tit in a wringer, big time," he said. "You want my help, you're gonna get straight with me this time, deal?"

I barely managed to nod.

"I mean, shit," Charlie said, "You don't think I'm doin' this for my fuckin' health, do ya?"

FIVE

Still, headed up the rutted gravel road to Eugene's, I gripped the door handle of Charlie's cruiser. The old Chrysler slammed down hard, then rocketed forward, the pines going by in a blur, then the road rising, and the car humping up, and flying down the backside of yet another hill.

"Any reason you gotta go sixty on a piece of road like this?" I said.

"Ducks," Charlie said.

"Ducks?"

Charlie turned to me and grinned. "Gotta get there soon as we can."

Before we'd left the Western, he'd gone into the men's and hadn't come out for ten minutes. Out again, he'd bent down by me, drank his glass of orange juice, top to bottom, swishing it in his mouth, almost as if gargling. He'd winked at me, and we'd both gone out to his car. Now, in the car I could smell the tonic he'd put in his hair. A powerful, oily smell.

"Yeah, ducks," he said again, chuckling. "I gotta get a better recipe—maybe like Peking duck? I mean, mine—Jesus, even after all these years, it comes out like . . . sawdust, you know?"

I was tempted to make a crude joke of it, relieved to have him with me now, but resisted.

I knew it hadn't been any ducks he'd eaten that had kept him in the men's so long; Charlie was three sheets to the wind. Vodka didn't smell, and the hair tonic masked what you might otherwise suspect.

Right there, I felt a little thirsty myself, swallowed hard at it, turned to look out the window, the pines outside flashing by.

Going to talk to Eugene was enough, I thought.

Eugene was one of those rare people you had to look at askance: he was a direct descendant of a famous chief, Conquering Bird. They all had enormous-eyed, long faces, hatchet blade cheekbones. In the 1930s Eugene's father, Ishtakubig, had been featured on a postcard of the Mesabi Iron Range, with the caption, *World's Biggest Indian, World's Biggest Open Pit Mine, Hibbing, Minnesota.* Eugene wasn't as big as his father had been, but was close to it.

In the late forties and early fifties, he'd been in a couple westerns out in Hollywood. One I'd even seen on TV. The legend was he'd been in Nevada, out in the desert on a shoot, and had some kind of vision.

That's when he'd come back to Red Lake, adamant against outside involvement in Red Lake life, especially so developers, and had gotten hooked up with the Waubunowin, the dark side of tribal medicine. Some were said to be shape shifters, Bear Walkers, who killed their enemies at night.

I didn't exactly believe all that, but it spooked me just the same.

Now the car humped up one last, steep rise and skidded to a stop out front of Eugene's cabin, under the shade of two enormous, craggy cottonwoods. Charlie, glancing over at me, mouthed, *Honey, I'm home!*

I turned to look through the windshield, a cold sweat on my scalp. The cabin was a humpbacked log place, squatting there in perpetual shade.

Eugene's army-green '53 Biscayne, brown cancer around the fenders, was parked off to the left.

"Listen," Charlie said. "I come in, I'll just blow the whole thing."

I got out of the car, and as I moved off toward the front door, gravel crunching under my feet, Charlie said, from the cruiser, trying to take the edge off it,

"Hey! Maybe he can get you a job out there in L.A.? You two geniuses can turn tinsel town on its head. I can just see it. Big marquee, in lights, *Dances with Canoes,* or, maybe, *Last of the Chippewas.* They can bring in Jay Silverheels, or—"

I glared over my shoulder. "Tonto's dead."

"Shit," Charlie said, and with a grunt was out of the car, too.

"What are you doing?"

He'd sobered up suddenly. "I didn't *mean* anything—I mean. . . . He hasn't come out yet. By this time, when I was here last, he'd already taken a shot at me."

Charlie unsnapped the top of his holster.

"What's *wrong* with you?" I said. "Get the hell back in the car."

I knocked at the front door, the door at head level, scratched down to yellow pine in a rough circle, and stained in a halo of thin, red featherings. I waited what seemed forever, then turned the knob—the door was unlocked—and went inside.

It was cool inside, smelled of sweetgrass and sage and cedar. The floor was yellow pine, hand polished to a deep satin smoothness.

Off on one end of the cabin, herbs hung upside down from the rough-hewn rafters; a sink and green Formica countertop, and a small stove, butted the wall. Opposite was a length of windows overlooking the lake, and a desk, on it a red Prince Albert tobacco tin, yellow #2 pencils in it, beside the desk, a bookshelf, seventy-five or eighty books, all in alphabetical order.

A one-room cabin, the bed back of the door, army surplus blankets tucked in military sharp, which I knew was Eugene's work, two galvanized pails at the foot of the bed, red cloth over them.

One of the windows facing the lake was held open with a

butcher knife, but, still, something smelled in there. I stopped, over the threshhold, recognizing the smell, something rotting.

It occurred to me what might be in one of the buckets, and so, I put that off.

I looked at the books, surprised at what he'd been reading. Histories, on plains settlement. Books on alchemy, the cabala, the mystics Saint John of the Cross and Hildegard von Bingen. There were dog-eared copies of the *Minnesota Law Review*. I felt the hair stand up on the back of my neck. A few of the books were out of order, the titles and authors confused. Alphabetical, but for the wrong reason.

Someone had pulled them out, and in a rush had replaced them. And it hadn't been Eugene.

I made a quick circuit of the cabin and found what I was looking for.

It had to have been bad, what he'd been going to do, or something he feared, because, near the east wall, back of the stove, outlined in artemisia, a purifying herb, were the faintest outlines of feet, enormous bare feet.

Eugene's.

He'd prayed there, purified himself, before.

And just then, I knew, looking at things, Eugene had left something, for the right person to see. In case he didn't make it back, and they'd come looking for it, after—I didn't think more specifically than that.

After—

I rifled through his desk now, in a rush pulled the drawers out and looked at the bottom and back of each. Nothing. I was looking for something and didn't know what. Pried at a tin patch on the floor, dug under his sink through the old iron skillets and Malmac plates, slammed his cupboards open, went through his flour, sugar, made a circuit of the room, lifted a rug, my hands shaking.

He'd left to do something, and hadn't returned. But there was something in the room, something they'd wanted, and badly.

I strode to the pails near the bed—just had to see now.

—pulled the red cloth back from the left. Inside the pail were herbs wrapped in colored cloth, in human shapes, the heads twisted oddly. Fetishes.

Stood, heart pounding over the right, snatched the cloth back, and my breath caught short, a kind of doom bursting in me. Not that floater's head, but to my thinking, maybe worse.

In the other pail were the remains of an owl, the eyes shriveled, the claws bent around a piece of barbed wire. The bird had had its foot tangled in the wire, had first torn the flesh off its leg, and then had died, hanging upside down. Over Eugene's door. That's what I'd seen on the door coming in, where the owl had clawed at it, trying to right itself.

If anywhere, I thought, it would be here, and I knew why.

You didn't touch gookooko'oo.

I got a cigarette from my pack, shredded it, my hands shaking, dusted the bird, and humming to myself, reached down and turned the bird on its side.

I reached into the breast feathers, a powerful stink making me avert my head.

There was a sachet of salt and cedar in the bird, just as I thought there would be, Eugene putting it there in an attempt to reverse the medicine, and jammed up behind it, a piece of paper, folded thick.

My fingers clumsy, I unfolded the sheet.

Vincent Chemical was stamped in bold black across the top of the page, a four-color band above it, beginning with a mauve band, going to brown, the last band black.

There was a list of metals under all that, with percentages following each: aluminum, zinc, manganese, iron, and then compounds, SiO_2, phosphate, hydroxyl, alkali, aluminum silicate.

All worthless. Kneeling, I rocked back, balanced on my heels.

I knew SiO_2 was just granite, or quartz crystal, sand—you could make glass out of it, but not much more. The things listed there I thought, correctly, and oh, so *in*correctly, common as dirt.

But where had the core sample come from?

Or had Eugene just happened to use this sheet of paper to protect the charm he'd put in the owl? And why had he scrawled, at the
bottom of the page, *Bakade,* hungry? I recognized his handwriting,
an oversized, sharp cursive.

"Hey," Charlie said.

I bolted back from the owl, nearly knocking the pail over.

"Jesus, Charlie," I said. "Don't ever do that, come up behind me
like that, got it?"

UNDER THE TREES outside, we leaned against the car, the dappled
sunlight shifting at our feet, the cottonwood leaves rustling like running water over us.

Charlie got his cigarettes out of his pocket, shook one from the
pack. He cocked his head to the side when he lit up.

"So," Charlie said, "you say that owl was—what—some kinda
death threat. Medicine, I mean."

I nodded, kicking at a stone in the drive, glanced up to look
across the lake.

"Know who'd do something like that," he said, "—with the owl,
I mean?"

Neither of us was willing to say what seemed pretty clear by
then. "Could be anybody," I said, and added, "and who knows,
maybe he's run off."

Charlie crushed his cigarette under his heel, swung the door of
his cruiser open.

"Sure," he said, nastily. "I buy that."

SIX

In the cabin that night, I sat in bed beside Gwen, trying to read, but was only turning pages for all that with the floater, Eugene's boat, and what we'd found in his cabin spinning in my head.

Gwen reached for my book, set it on the nightstand.

"What?" I said.

She turned her back to me, and I pulled the pins from her hair, and her hair fell down, ebony, silken, heavy, a curtain, parted. I took her brush, and slowly, carefully, began at the bottom. Long, slow strokes.

"Remember, when we first came up? You'd just cut out, and let Frank run things, and we'd take the boat, and not even let Frank know we'd gone."

"We can do that," I said.

"But, see? *Can.* Everything's the future—even down in St. Paul now. It's business."

I didn't know what to say. I was too tired and distracted to rise to it.

"You could give Hugh more responsibilities—free up some time that way."

I pulled Gwen close, talcum and rose scent.

"I mean a weekend—we could drive into Winnipeg, stay at a B & B, catch our breath. Something like that."

It was impossible, I thought, even if this mess hadn't come up, but I wasn't about to say that. So we lay there, saying nothing, and the curtain luffed in, and I tried to think of something to say, but only managed,

"What do you really want, Gwen. What is it? It's the piano," I said, tugging her closer. "I'm sorry, I forgot."

Gwen dropped back on the bed, her eyes set on something distant.

"I want—" she said. "I want flowers, in pots, red roses, and geraniums, and impatiens, all over the island, and a garden, with sunflowers and things we could eat, and—and a horse, on shore, so I can ride, and to just have evenings to ourselves, and put my hair up, and go into the Angle, see Mardine's family, I promised I'd bring Claire, and I want—"

But she didn't say it. Because to say it would bring up Bobby, our son who'd died. And Claire *was* our child, after all, and it wasn't right to speak it.

But I asked her, anyway. "What, Gwen, what do you want, really?"

She shook herself, then smiled, something else entirely now. A sidestep.

"I want to bring my parents out. They want to visit, I mean," she said.

It occurred to me that *that's* what it had been on the answering machine that morning. On the other tape, what she hadn't wanted me to hear.

All I could say was, "Why?" though I was relieved to be off what she'd been onto.

"Could you be civil if they came up?" she said.

"How haven't I before?"

"Paul," she said, "the last time you spoke Ojibwemowin with Hugh the whole time they were here. Or with Mardine or whoever."

"I did not."

"You did, and you know it. You even did around me. When do you ever—"

"I don't speak it around you because—"

"*Onji*—" she said, because why?

Her pronunciation was so good it sent a chill up my back; she had this ear that amazed me. But it was even better now.

"Mardine hasn't been talking adopting you into her band again, has she?"

"Don't change the subject."

I looked away, not wanting to tell her what I was really thinking. On more than a number of occasions I'd warned her to keep some distance. Still, I'd never explained: if I were the only one connected up here, by blood and association, if push came to shove, and I was killed, they wouldn't come after her.

"You don't have to hide," she said.

"Oh, good," I said, sitting up and turning my back to her. "You bring something up and I ask about it, and that means I'm hiding, does it?"

I knew that hurt her. Still, I couldn't bring myself to tell her that what I was really feeling was an almost irrational, protective choler.

I didn't want to get into it.

Even after all her years away, Gwen's parents hurt her, over and again, by implying, subtly or not so subtly, that her stepping out of their life of social climbing was tantamount to failure. But what they didn't understand, was that Gwen was about re-creating herself, we both were, and in a place of almost infinite horizons, she was free. And what of her old life she still wanted?

She had that down in St. Paul.

So it was time we were circling around, and time in Gwen's way of thinking was freedom, all over again—really, it was for both of us.

"Why not toward the end of the season," Gwen said.

"Why not not-at-all?" I replied.

Gwen had her hand on me. I should have just turned away.

"You're taking it too seriously," she said, stroking me.

"You're manipulating me," I said, laughing.

"You're funny," she said.

I found her spot, and then we were moving slowly, achingly.

"Maybe funny *looking*—" I said.

"Oh, contraire, mon cher," she said, and rolled me over and drew her nightgown over her head.

"REALLY, WHAT COULD happen?" she said.

I had to laugh at that. Gwen's calm, but certain persistence. I thought, just then, to use this thing with the boat, and Eugene, and what it was coming to, as an excuse to keep her parents from visiting.

But didn't. It was too good here, finally, and so I said nothing.

"So I'll call them," Gwen said.

"All right," I said, and we rolled over in the dark, spoons, and Gwen said,

"You!"

But Claire let out a cry, and that was that.

SEVEN

Two weeks passed. We filled the cabins, got through the Fourth down in Warroad, and on the island survived the guests' kids' bottle rockets, smoke bombs, firewheels, Black Cat firecrackers, puncs, Roman candles, any and all of which could have sent the whole island up in a blaze—it hadn't rained in nearly three weeks, and between runs into Pine Point for supplies and to pick up new guests, I nosed around to see if anybody had dirt on Eugene.

Now, late morning, I'd already tried the hardware store, the Ben Franklin, the Woolworths, so turned in the direction of the Rambler's, and short of it, climbed a steep hill where I could watch from above, hidden by a thick stand of pine, got out of the truck and, cupping my hands around a match, lit a cigarette.

Out front of the Rambler's, Truman Wheeler leaned up against his car, all five foot six of him, one hundred ninety pounds, in his cordovan leather vest and denim shirt and pointed-toe boots, his radio playing so it carried tinnily up to me.

Truman shifted his boots, jabbed a toothpick into his mouth, the radio carrying in the breeze—

I go out walkin'
after mid-night

Every now and again, Truman craned his head around to glance at the Rambler's behind him.

The Rambler's wasn't much to look at, a yellow, ramshackle building, two bicycle frames tied together on the roof and festooned with what looked, in daylight, like a rat's nest of wires and colored lights, that were at night a star. All over the Rambler's there were green and blue and red Christmas lights, neon signs in the windows, reading, *P st, ain elt, oors.* On the far end was a roller rink, and between the rink and bar, the grocery, where, a few days a week, I got supplies.

A tan Pontiac with government plates pulled into the lot, just up from the bar, and Truman, hooking his thumbs in his belt, went out to it. The driver and Truman talked briefly. Then the driver handed Truman a manila envelope, Truman ducked down, bent into the car, his hand darting through the window, and the driver turned, gave Truman a mock salute, and I recognized him—even as he went out of the lot, in a spinning of tires and dust.

Michaels, that cop who'd been by the lodge earlier.

I wondered why Michaels wouldn't have the usual equipment, a black and white, or a highway patrol car? And what kind of business could he have with Truman? It made my stomach knot, thinking about it.

Now, nearly lunchtime, first one truck, and then others slid into the lot, loggers, and resort help, and DNR workers laughing, high school kids, the door into the bar slamming, then opening, and slamming again.

Truman, though, didn't go in.

A convertible, an old Catalina, canary yellow, without a muffler, *Free Leonard Peltier* stickers pasted all over it, skidded into the lot.

I knew some people by their cars, and did this one. The Catalina belonged to Napoleon, my kid, who was supposed to be out on the lake guiding.

He strode by Truman, and they didn't so much as exchange glances, Elmer coming around the north end of the Rambler's, rangy as a coyote, both Elmer and Napoleon going around the stoop and ducking inside.

Truman marched right to the door and went inside after.

I cupped my hand over my eyes, a visor, waited there in the sun, the cicadas chirring in the pines.

A short while later, Napoleon came around from back of the roller rink with a couple big kids. They were right on top of each other, somebody behind that knot of broad shoulders and long legs, short, stout, with braids. They scrambled into the Catalina, Elmer off to a station wagon that had been parked in the trees, and then they drove away in a wash of yellow dust, Elmer toward the Angle Inlet, Napoleon toward the government docks.

But it was Napoleon I watched:

The sun cut through the plastic window in that Catalina's convertible top, and I saw, between the two boys in back, the man they'd whisked out, magenta cloth in his braids.

But thought then, only a *woman* would wear that.

A moment later, Truman thumped back outside through the front door, into the light, sniffed, as if at something he might want to eat. He dug into his breast pocket, and turning his face to the sun, bent the temples of his sun glasses over one ear, then the other, fixing those dark lenses right over his eyes, and his belly preceding him, pearl buttoned, and looking the picture of one rapacious appetite, he skipped down the steps to his car, and was gone.

I sat up in my truck, stunned, as if I'd seen a snake swallow a mouse.

It upset me so, I forgot why I'd gone to the Rambler's in the first place, and didn't remember until I was in the launch, and halfway back to the island, so had to turn around.

Always groceries.

I DIDN'T GET back to the island until early evening, went right to the bunkhouse. In Elmer's corner, the bed had been stripped, but his pictures were still there on the wall: eagles and hawks of all kinds, he'd been crazy about them; and pictures that spoke of a yearning, a dreaming—a card of a white buffalo on a background of star-studded sky, and a picture of a Thunderbird spitting lightning.

I looked under the bed. In his dresser.

All of his things were gone, clothes, his duffel bag, shaving kit.

IN THE LODGE, the guests were having dinner. I nodded Hugh over, determined to get out of him what Napoleon and Elmer had gotten into. At a table with a girl prettier than pretty, Hugh grimaced, as if he'd been waiting for me, then smiled, his whole face lighting up for her, and, on the balls of his feet, carried his plate to the kitchen.

Mardine was at the sink, washing. I sent her away, then brought her a plate at the table she'd taken, there with Gwen and an older couple, both gray haired, but colorful, poppy red and teal, like exotic birds, at the lakeside windows.

Back in the kitchen, Hugh was already washing. I dried, he scrubbed.

"So, how'd it go today?"

"Great," Hugh said, dipping into the soapy water.

He was braced for it, the way you wait for someone to throw a punch your direction. Feet wide, his shoulders squared, the lies he thought necessary now waiting to come uncoiled in his mouth.

I wanted to see how far this went; I didn't feel good doing it.

"You're getting along all right?"

"Comin' along."

That's what I had always said to him, especially when we were in trouble. Why did he say it? He knew I'd recognize it for the dodge it was.

"Coming along *how?*"

I could see he was trying to bear up under it. Surely, with Elmer gone, he and Napoleon had run the whole show, all afternoon, but there was something much worse in it. I admired him for trying. Hugh lifted a plate out of the water; he scrubbed at it so forcefully it popped out of his hands—like a watermelon seed—onto the counter and shattered.

"Shit!" he said.

Lunging for it, he cut himself. I got the first aid kit, put on some Betadine and a patch, and we switched positions. I washed.

But Hugh didn't say word one.

BY THE TIME I got down to the cabin, Gwen was in bed, wrapped in a blanket, reading, Claire asleep in the far room. I sat on the edge of the bed.

"How you doin', sweetheart?" I leaned over and kissed her.

"Good," she replied, and kissed me back.

"Anything new?"

"Walter Davis called," she said.

"Did he say what he had in mind?"

"No," she said. Setting the book down, and looking at me, she laughed.

"You're so transparent!"

She could see I'd expected something from her, and hadn't gotten it.

"All right. So what about Elmer. Do you know why he just *ran off* like—"

Gwen's mouth pursed; her china blue eyes seemed to go one shade darker.

"Ran off? What do you mean? Didn't Hugh tell you about it?"

I shook my head, surprised.

"They got into it right in front of the lodge; Elmer really asked for it. It was so bad I had to pull them apart."

"Elmer and Napoleon—"

"No. Elmer and Hugh. Elmer started it."

That didn't make sense. Elmer was half Hugh's size, and Hugh was tough. "Are you sure?"

Gwen said she was.

"Oh, well," I said. I thought, then, maybe the trouble Elmer and Napoleon were into wasn't that bad, if Elmer hadn't run. Just private.

"I want you to go and find El tomorrow morning, can you do that?" Gwen said.

My policy was, those who left on bad terms, for fighting with the other help, or the guests, or for one too many shows of bottle flu— didn't come back. But I was already prepared to let Elmer.

It hurt me a little that she thought she had to ask me to do it.

"Come here," Gwen said.

We faced each other on our sides. I got that thrill looking at her.

"Hey," I said.

"You," she said, and the book clunked to the floor, but neither of us paid it any attention.

EIGHT

The sun bright, just over the trees, I sat outside the Tribal Office the following morning, on the bench there, nursing a cup of coffee and dreading going inside. I would get this thing with Walter over, then look for Elmer.

So I waited.

I felt like a school kid, watching the council through the office windows. The office was a small, red brick building; in front, a picture window, a desk behind it; on the opposite end more windows, a conference room with four or five tables there, a meeting in progress, those lawyers I'd seen earlier in back.

Walter Davis at the front of the room looked somber. Now and then he'd jot something on a tablet, glance out the window at me.

He was a handsome, compact man, a metis, a French Chippewa, dark and businesslike, which, when he worked for you, as he had for me, doing carpentry after the fire two years earlier, was reassuring and then some.

But now? I felt more than a little threatened. I knew Walter had leapt on that road bandwagon. And surely, he'd heard that nonsense about me, that I'd threatened to blow up the government docks and bring in AIM.

All that we'd have to set straight.

Waiting, I worried over it, so I tried to read the *Tribune* I'd picked up at Oshogay's Gas. But it was impossible, and I crossed the street, leaned against the fender of my truck and smoked.

I smelled at the air, rain in it.

Two dead Cadillacs with broken glass sat angled across the parking lot. From the flagpole in front hung a Minnesota state flag, and, in tatters under it, the old red, white, and blue. There wasn't so much as a hint of a breeze, but to the northwest, on the horizon, was a dark line of a front moving in, heavy as an anvil.

Walter flashed me another of his inimitable glances, heavy lidded, but right on target.

I shuddered at it, looked away; just low, one-story buildings on this end of Pine Point, the youngest of the Kingbird girls, in a T-shirt and cutoffs, pedaling by on her creaky Schwinn, the bike so old now it was stylish again, high-rise handlebars, banana seat, and chrome sissy bar, candy apple green.

"Hey, Loreen," I said.

"Hi, TP," she shot back, giggling, pedaling up the block.

THE COUNCIL MEMBERS came out of the office, colorful as songbirds, those jewel tones and reds they ran to, Roy Waseya, yawning, slapping Bill Neyadi on the back; Edna Frobisher and Irma Kobeckaneck still talking animatedly; and those two lawyers, the only dull ones, in navy and gray, Samuel Running tying up the rear.

I got out of my truck, where I'd fitfully slept with my forehead against the wheel, and called out,

"Walter!"

He turned to smile, hooked his arm around "Hey, Youngblood," he said, *"Ambe!"* Come on! and I marched right into it, a big grin on my face.

At the back of the Western, I took a seat beside Walter at a large round table he'd had them put up, barely squeezed in.

But I didn't want to fit in there, wanted to keep my distance, and, too, now, the ten or so of us hunkered down over greasy menus reminded me of nothing so much as that scene early in those westerns, almost obligatory, where the wagon train formed a circle, and those inside it fought to the death with the savages outside.

There was an irony in my thinking it that wasn't lost on me.

"Don't look so glum," Walter joked, and threw his arm over my shoulders. "Revolutionaries, no matter how serious they get, gotta eat, too, right?"

I thought to make a joke about easy crucifixions, or how there just happened to be twelve of us there, I'd counted, and me—not a good sign either way—the thirteenth.

I bent over my menu, mimeographed purple print, the prices penned in alongside the specials.

Why did I feel like a damned kid here?

I ran a business as big or bigger than any of the council members.

But, too, it was awkward because I'd bad-mouthed them, the council, all their soft solutions, their bartering with the state BIA.

But really, it came down to this:

The council still had a legal interest in the lodge—the continuation of my lease was contingent on certain improvements, upkeep, environmental considerations, or, in other words, the council's approval. So they had me by the shorthairs, and I liked to be reminded of that about the way somebody with, say, heart disease in the family wants to be reminded of it.

And, I was just waiting for the left hook now. Crooked or not.

I ordered, on my own ticket. We ate, clatter of flatware on white Buffalo china. Hot coffee. Wild rice, venison. Eggs with a dash of salt and pepper.

They were talking a mile a minute there, most of it in the old language, or dialect.

I could only understand part of it, and was too embarrassed to ask what people meant when I didn't, and so sometimes I was nodding my head like an idiot, and agreeing, *Enh, enh,* yes, yes, that's right—when I had no idea what they were saying.

In the middle of all that—legislation over mechanical rice harvesters, a deficit in the fisheries budget, and gossip, personal and political, Walter turned to me and said,

"What would it take to get you to move your lodge to your Angle acres?"

I choked on my coffee, spilled it on my shirt, held the mug out over the table, tried to brush the coffee from my shirt, but just made it worse.

"Are you *crazy!*" I said. *"What* would I do that for? I can't do that!"

Walter put on an especially serious face; like throwing a switch, he smiled, china white teeth, laughing, and the others laughed, too.

"I'm *not* gonna move."

"We can't make you."

"You're goddamn right you can't," I said, setting my mug down and looking at the lot of them. But they *could* revoke my lease, and what then?

"I was just trying to make a point," Walter said.

One of the attorneys leaned into the table. "Bill Watson," he said, extending his hand.

I didn't shake it. I turned to Irma, who, even though she was the darkest of all of us, blushed awfully.

"You want to make me out to look like an asshole, well, fine. *I'm an asshole.* It's about that goddamn road, isn't it, and that land of mine on the Angle."

The council members looked abashed, a few disgusted with me. The attorney, Bill, opened a briefcase, got out a folder thick with paper.

"It has long been believed—"

"Since when?" I said.

I knew he'd been about to say the central corridor acres, where they wanted to put the road through, were uninhabitable. Worthless.

"By who?" I said.

"I'll get to that if you'll allow me to, Mr. Na'joi'se."

No one used that name—I didn't. My father didn't.

I felt something harden in me. Someone had been doing research on me, and on the Angle. I thought of all kinds of nasty things to say, but stood, nodded politely, and excused myself from the table.

In the lot out front of the Western, I set myself behind the wheel of my truck, trying to calm myself enough to think what I needed to do. Walter came out, set his hand on my door.

"People are just trying to make a living, Paul," he said. "But it gets away from us. The others that want that road can't change the fact it crosses your land, see?"

I shook my head, wouldn't look at him.

"There's some . . . pretty sorry stuff goin' around about you," he said. "You'd give right-of-way across those acres, it'd clear up a lot of it. Isn't even givin' it up—just a lease."

I thought to say, Truman put you up to this? but there was a sorry tone in Walter's voice, as if he'd been trying to help me.

"There's something *wrong* with all this, Walter, don't you see that?"

"Is there?" he said.

"You watch me prove it," I said, and making a motion as if tipping a hat, I started the truck.

I DROVE IN a near rage out of Pine Point, then, gritting my teeth, hammered up a rutted drive, turned on a sandy offshoot, shade again, the sun flashing in the pines, and still driving hard, thinking I was just driving to drive, passed a green canvas icehouse, rotting in the shade of red pine and ferns, *Olson* printed in black letters on the side, and only then, admitted to myself where I was going.

It was a place I didn't like to go.

The land rose and fell, the truck whining, then foot harder yet on the gas, I rushed forward, until I could make out the allotment my mother had left me, and that I'd let go to my old man, and coming up alongside it, the garage nearly collapsed, the house a faded blue, the chimney held up by ratty-looking green nylon ropes tethered to the four corners of the roof, I skidded to a hard stop.

I looked out the window, and what I saw didn't make me any happier.

The junk was still there in the yard, but now even more of it. A washer and dryer, eye-scalding chalk white, the lids up, as if they were waiting for another load; an old, industrial green furnace, the ducts having rusted and fallen off to the sides; a Ford Fairlane, battered, and on tires so bald the cords were showing through, and beside it now, in the drive—

my eyes narrowed at seeing it

—a Jaguar sedan, the windshield cracked, a makeshift wooden rack on the roof, the sides of the car so heavily mudcaked the car was more brown than red.

Jesus, I swore to myself. This was why I never came out to the house.

Now, behind the wheel of my truck, I didn't know whether I felt more shock at my father's using the car, or indignation. I'd had it up on blocks, under three tarps, in the garage, a blue cocoon, since the boat accident. For a time, I almost wished someone would steal it and take it off my hands.

That Jaguar was all kinds of things, an accusation, a memory of pain too deep to let surface, a marker of time passing, an intimation of death, and, of a miracle, a gift I'd gotten that, maybe, I hadn't deserved.

It was Clark's, my old redheaded friend's, car.

After Clark had been killed, that night of the boat accident, his then estranged widow, Jackie, had asked if I could store the car—just for a few months, since Baudette, where he'd left it, was a short drive from Pine Point.

So I'd done that, put the car in my father's garage. And when I'd discovered antifreeze in a pool under the engine the following spring—after it'd gotten down to forty below, and that without wind-chill—I'd let Jackie know, and she'd had an adjuster come out.

The adjuster had done her a favor and written the car off as totaled. Block's cracked, he'd said. A rebuild would cost more than the car's worth. Jackie told me just to keep it, she'd send up the title, which she hadn't, and like that, it became mine. Sort of.

It wasn't totaled, I discovered, but needed a radiator, among other things.

I'd told myself I'd repair the car for the past two years, sell it and give the money to some kid in Pine Point who wanted to go to trade school or college. But I hadn't been able to so much as look at what was left under the tarp—much less mess with it.

A 1973 Jaguar XJ 12 L. With six Webber carburetors—six grand, Clark had told me he'd paid for the modification, a mechanic's dream; an owner's nightmare. It'll do an honest one sixty now, he'd boasted. My old pal, boyish Clark.

I'd tried just to forget it, like everything that had gone wrong that summer, but here it was, like some nightmare come to life.

"Enh?!" my father shouted from the stoop. What is it?

I'd been so stunned, behind the wheel of my truck, I hadn't seen him come out.

"Pizza Man!" I said. "Anchovies and pineapple, heavy on the marinated artichokes."

"Like hell," my old man grumbled and held the door open for me.

LARISSA, MY SISTER, had moved out, and now the place had all the charm of a three-car wreck. The kitchen smelled of fried food. The green sofa, in the living room, where he thumped down, had wads of yellow foam rubber coming out of it.

I held out my cigarettes, and Zozed took one. I lit mine, gave him the matches.

All my mother's loving touches here were tainted with time and use now. Smoke grime, along the ceiling, obscured the floral patterns she'd put there to brighten the room. Larissa's beadings had fallen off the walls, and Zozed hadn't put them back up. The hardwood floor was dark and scarred.

It occurred to me what I was going to do: I'd get Zozed to come out to the lodge for a week, and while he was away, pay some kids to haul off the junk and paint the house and clean up.

That was the only way I could sit there. Make more promises to myself. (Oh, I was full of promises that summer, am full of them now.)

"All I know is this," Zozed told me, giving me a sidelong glance, then took a hard tug on the cigarette, his face lighting, orange.

"The road deal's been in the works for over three years. Five if you want to go the full distance back. The Red Lake Band's been crying for their own docks on the Angle, but got no shoreline to build on. Enh? See? So the State's been pitchin' some kind of land swap, and the Red Lake council, all this time's refused."

"Land swap." Now I got the full import of Walter's come-on at the Western.

"That's it," my father said. "Get those with land on the right-of-way to lease, and the BIA'll exchange a piece of shoreline. And as a show of goodwill to us Native Minnesotans," he chuckled, "they're gonna give us a cash settlement, since we'd be givin' up the use of about a thousand acres to their—I don't know—how many acres is eight blocks by six?"

I figured it my head.

"A couple hundred," I said. "Well, I think . . . one seventy-six."

"They're offering twelve hundred fifty an acre for the difference."

I knew the going rate on the Angle wasn't much more than eight hundred.

"So, a million bucks," I said.

It was less than a drop in a bucket if they doled it out to all eight thousand enrolled band members. One hundred twenty-five a head. My salutation about the pizza became a kind of black joke there. That's about all you could buy with the State's offer.

"They want rights with the lease?"

"They're gonna build a road, right? So they want mining in it, so they can excavate, fill, all that."

My father pinched the cigarette, back of the ember, hit it hard again.

"It's one hell of an offer. That's what they're writin' in the *Tribune.*"

"Yeah, sure," I said.

He was testing me. He knew something, but didn't quite trust me with it.

"Well, I guess that's it," my father said, when I didn't press him for more, a note of bitterness in his voice.

He crushed his cigarette, just a hot nub, out on his shoe, his way of ending our conversation.

I WAS STARTING the truck when he came out, kicked through knee-high grass to set his hand on the cab.

"Call George," he said, peering in at me. "He's down there in St. Paul snoopin' around. Maybe he can tell you something."

"It's that bad," I said.

"It's worse, and you know it."

He waved his hand over his head, and glancing over his shoulder, called out,

"They're doin' the survey out of Warroad. Look around down there, why don't you?" and went in.

BACK IN PINE Point, I tried to find Elmer. I went from the Rambler's, to the government docks, to Elmer's old man's place—Franklin

McCloud's—where I was cursed in three different dialects of Ojib-wemowin, and run out of the driveway.

"You tell those SRS people to shove it up their asses, you hear me?" Franklin shouted. "Fuck you and your brother and sister and mother, Two Persons," he shouted.

I fought an impulse to flip him the bird, then gave in to it, but wasn't one bit gratified. Here was just more ugliness, buried under it the shame I felt at my own failure with Elmer.

So, even though it was late afternoon, and I'd been gone too long already, I tried one last place. Our Lady of the Pines, where Elmer and his mother, Edna, had attended mass for years. There I suf-fered the scalding looks of Father Charles. I hadn't seen Father Charles since my wedding, not at Our Lady, anyway.

His mouth puckered, his eyes positively hot, Father Charles told me Edna attended mass down south now, maybe I could find her there.

"You might be a little more specific," I said.

And when he didn't answer, I added, "It's a family emergency."

"Warroad," he said, "St. John's," which sent me on down the highway, to hell with being late.

I TURNED OFF the highway, motored up Main. Warroad slid by out-side, a rough, clapboard shack of a town trying to pull itself up by its bootstraps. To do it, they'd catered to the construction business in the area, and government jobs—both the northern arm of the Depart-ment of Transportation, and the BIA.

St. John's was closed, and there was no listing for an Edna Mc-Cloud in the local directory.

So I asked after Edna at an Embers, a knickknack place selling northwoods kitsch, and a Cum and Go gas station (that was a con-cept), then thought to try the grocery, but caught some nasty looks in the parking lot—rusted Ford 4 × 4s, gun racks, snarling dogs in the back, and turned instead toward the DOT office across the street.

If I couldn't find Edna, I'd poke around, see if I could get something on the road.

There was construction going on, and I ducked under the scaffolding through the front door. Inside carpenters ran saws, plaster dust fell from the new Sheetrock. Masons hammered at a brick wall.

I asked if there were any DOT people in.

"You the guy up coming up from St. Paul?" one of the men there asked.

It occurred to me my khakis could look like a uniform, with my pad in my pocket and pens. I said I was.

"The surveys are over at the library," the man replied. "A Don just called here, said he was running late. He'd meet you there."

AT THE LIBRARY desk, a stout woman in navy polyester glanced up from her polishing, gave me a more than wary look. I smiled a friendly, but concerned smile, hiding my near elation. The surveys weren't open to the public, but I had a shot at them now, though only if I got it right, and in what time I had. So I said,

"Don sent me over."

Which was a mistake, I realized the moment it came out of my mouth.

"Nope," the librarian said.

She grimaced, sprayed something that smelled of lemon on the counter. The spray was to have forced me back, and she gave the counter a few more shots, higher this time, so sure to carry square into my chest and face. My eyes burned and I stifled a sneeze.

I felt some kind of meltdown going on in my head, the easy-in I'd thought I had going critical. Dislike wasn't even in the range of this woman's feelings for Don.

"You mean he's late again," I said, improvising, fumbling at the pens in my pocket, engineer chic, glanced back at her.

"Waltzes in here whenever he wants to."

"He didn't call?"

"Not that I know of," the librarian said. She'd stopped her polishing. "And you're—"

"From the tribal council, playin' watchdog over the DOT's affairs here."

"Ah," the librarian said. She liked that, that Don could just like that, get sucked up into something as messy as tribal politics.

"I'm gonna get his ass canned," I said. "I've had it." I looked at my watch. "You mind if I just get to it? I'll be out of here in minutes and Don can find his own ride back down to the Cities."

I think that woman smiled just then the first time she had in years.

"Be happy to help," she said.

SHE DIRECTED ME to a shelf of enormous books in the rear, set a hand on her hip. I yanked one of the books from the shelf, about two and a half feet long, bound in cloth-covered cardboard. The survey dates were written in a cribbed longhand on the bindings. I opened the book to the Angle, whipped back the pages.

"Do you have a breakdown of this here?" I said, pointing to the central corridor acres.

The librarian pulled out another book, opened it, and poked her crimson, glued-on fingernail into the page.

"It's all yours," she said, and with a toss of her head, she went back to the front desk.

I tried to find our bay out of all the bays and inlets on that roughly made survey, here and there jottings in pencil, transit stations, line-of-site readings, and elevations. I couldn't get oriented, then realized the engineers had used outdated Canadian names north of Longworth. So, here, our bay was *Binishinuk Bay.* I wondered what that was all about.

Binishinuk were powerful spirits that had the appearance of eagles, thunderbirds to most people, and, in the dialect I spoke, were called *Pinesiwak.*

Pawaganak, for which our bay was named, were dream visitors, only thunderbirds in *kind, not* appearance, and anyone sharp enough to understand the names at all, would also know not to confuse the two.

Only outsiders would do that.

Yet, when I searched the whole map, I saw a number of older, incorrect names, all of them on the Angle, and I wondered if it weren't just some fudged collaboration with Canada's DIAND (we called it, Dead Indians Ain't No Danger), the Department of Indians and Northern Development, or some old and pissed-off bureaucrat still putting it to us.

And, it wasn't unlike the BIA to try to save a few dollars by using old maps. Or an informant who was out of touch.

The front door shut with a bang, and I nearly leapt out of my boots.

A man dressed in green work twill went up the dirtied track to the desk, where my library lady was on the phone now, grinning and nodding.

Broad shouldered, the man waited there, glowering.

I got right down over that survey, forced myself to keep looking. I could see someone had already run centerline across the Angle, worked out the road grade so as to get around one feature in particular. The deal wasn't even done yet, and they'd engineered the whole length of road. But just *one* proposed site?

But when I looked closely, I could see a page—no, a few pages— I counted them, *six*—had been cut out, right down at the binding, with something sharp, like a razor.

I heard the clatter of the librarian setting the phone down, and when she came at me with this Don, I slipped the surveys back on the shelf and aimed for the front door.

But couldn't go out. I'd rolled two boxcars there, just had to go for a third.

So strode to the desk, Don all the while going through those surveys behind me. That librarian had her back to me, her rear end stuffed into her polyester pants like potatoes in a blue sack.

"Excuse me," I said.

The librarian spun around, surprised to see me.

"It's my job to keep tabs on these guys," I said. "Is it just Don you've been having trouble with?"

The librarian glared in Don's direction. *"Everybody* was up here," she said, sniffing. "NSP, the BIA, some horse's ass of a congressman, the DNR, bunch of . . . Chippewa, a mining outfit, McKennet Mining, and some . . . *research company* or another—always parked their car in my spot, so I'd have to ask them to move before I came in."

I craned my head over my shoulder. Someone was pulling into the parking lot, the man from St. Paul for all I knew.

"But I'll bet you didn't go to the top, did you?" I said. "To someone in management."

"Didn't I?" the librarian said, her chest swelling with indignation. "I'll tell you, I got so *tired* of it, their parking in my spot every morning I called the police and had their car towed. The officer in town told me who it was. Had to have some leverage. Guy turned green when I told him I'd talk to his supervisor if he didn't stop parking in my spot. I've just had it. See? I mean *look* at what they've done to my carpet."

I gave the mud-stained carpet a sympathetic once-over. "Terrible," I said.

"This . . . *company* down in St. Paul said they'd replace it. I've called twenty times if I've called them once—"

I glanced behind me again; Don was putting the books back on the shelf.

"Gimme a shot at it," I said. "I'll see what I can do for you."

The librarian grinned—Don coming at the desk behind me—was going to keep her mouth shut, but at the last second, said, in a near whisper,

"Ryder—Geologic."

I nodded, turning, passed this Don, my back to him, gave a smile to the man coming through the front door, probably the man from St. Paul, and outside, gunned my truck out of the lot.

AT THE LOCAL bank, Warroad First Security, I got Edna's address out of a teller in twenty seconds flat. Landlord, I told her, Edna'd written me a rubber check.

We looked into all that.

ﬠINE

I tried the back door of Edna's tiny, robin's egg blue ranch. The door was closed, but not locked, and I went in. Edna had rifled through her desk and dresser, had taken all her identification, letters, anything that would connect her to someone, or someplace else.

There was junk all over the floor, a veritable blizzard of paper.

A car pulled up outside, quiet, tires crackling on gravel, then a second car up the alley, blocking it.

I froze a second, staring around the kitchen. There was a note on the fridge, in a peculiar, cribbed hand. I snatched that, went out the bedroom window on the north end, even as they burst through the back door, shouting for me to stop—firing, when I didn't, leaped backyard fences, like I'd run hurdles in school, out east, set a record right there in Edna's backyard, and I didn't stop until I got to my truck.

LATER, I DROVE by the house, hunkered down in my truck. Different shirt I'd got at the IGA, a green seed corn cap, on the crown of it, a yellow corncob with red wings, and in black letters, *PHISER-DEKALB,* farm garb. Three officers were in the house, a car there in front. Now, I realized, a car I'd seen before. Tan Pontiac sedan, government plates.

The officer in it glanced up as I went by but didn't see me.

It was Michaels.

TEN

"Is one of the horses sick or something?" George shouted into the phone to make himself heard.

I was calling him from the lodge kitchen, still a bundle of nerves. As always, it was noisy in there. Rattle of KitchenAid, the refrigerator kicking on. A fan whirred over the grill. Clatter of china, and Mardine marshaling the new girl, Josette, in and out, four plates at a time balanced on her forearms.

Gwen was greeting our guests in the adjacent foyer.

"No, it's not the horses," I said, nearly shouting into the phone.

I was still, by proxy, running George's stable, on the Angle, but I'd turned it over to a girl who was horse crazy and she hadn't let me down.

"Listen," I said, "I need you to check something out for me. Could you call around to see if a Ryder Geologic made a bid on that construction this spring?"

"Take five minutes," George said, "call you right back."

It was pandemonium in that kitchen. I had the note that had been on Edna's refrigerator, turned it over, yet again. It wasn't a note at all, but a line drawing, of the sort done on Midewiwin scrolls, continuous from left to right, containing a warning.

In it, a woman of one of the bird clans, from the jagged tuft on her head, turned right at what appeared to be a door, behind it, two men with guns waiting, held at opposite sides, left and right, each gun a line with a circle at the bottom.

I thought the left and right of it then was just some artistic flourish, to balance the drawing, but I was wrong about that.

A woman, long-haired and wearing a uniform of some sort, stood behind the two men, all three in a posture indicating a readiness to attack.

I tried to make something of it, then it occurred to me what it was. I chuckled grimly to myself. The woman of the bird clan, I figured, was Edna; the door, that of the refrigerator; those waiting behind it, guilt.

I folded the note and put it in my pocket. Just some dieting nonsense.

My sister, Larissa, had once put a sign on the fridge that read, *Once past your lips, forever on your hips.* She'd been so damn skinny already it made me sad.

The phone rang and I picked it up. *"Gidub'ena?"* I said, You there?

"Nin ota," George replied, I'm here. There was a tired resignation in his voice. "The answer's, No. So what of it?"

"I was trying to find Elmer's mother, down in Warroad, to see if she knew where he'd run off to," I said. "Somebody tried to seriously mess me up. Or it had to do with my looking at the DOT surveys over at the library, that road."

"Shit," George said. "I don't believe it. It isn't about that stupid road. They're not gonna build it."

"Why not?"

"Too expensive."

"But I just saw the surveys."

"Yeah, right," George said. "They been doin' that for years. *Geng-*

inawishkis—" Quacking like ducks, stupid bunch of assholes! "You think they'll give up what they're makin' at the Angle Inlet? Much less dump all kinds of cash to put a road through south of there?"

I said I wasn't sure.

"It's just another bait and switch," George said. "They figure you're holding cold *doonoo—*" excrement "—in your hand you'll take rhinestones for it and smile. I mean, you ever wonder why Frank didn't do something with that acreage on the Angle?" George snorted. "Have you ever so much as gone out there?"

"No," I said. "I've been too—*nin ondomita,"* I said, I've been too busy.

"Kitchi amo—" All that just buzzes by, huh?

"Can't pay attention to everything," I said.

"Nibashkiwin, Nawaji—" You're sleeping too much, Nawaji.

I was tempted to tell him where to put that.

"You'll look into it anyway, see if this Geologic company's been poking around up here before?"

"Hell, yes," George shot back. "But I'm tellin' you, nobody, but nobody, wants to build on that land. You get out there and take a look."

I told him I would.

I FUMBLED AROUND the lodge, then in the dining room, tried to have a conversation with a doctor and his wife up from Chicago, both sharp as pins, navy dinner jacket for the doctor with a gold crest over the pocket, his wife lovely in green gaberdine.

I embarrassed myself, I was so distracted, so, with an excuse about a troublesome outboard, grabbed a sandwich in the kitchen and went down to the boathouse. There I could easily waste a few hours or two, and maybe avoid doing, for today, what George suggested I might.

And like that, distracted, I strode over the threshold into the dark, and something lunged at me, and I was punching at nothing and everything, my heart hammering in my neck, until I connected, hair and dogflesh, dodged back outside, and that bulldog came with me.

I'd forgotten all about the dog, had been training her to guard the boathouse—and she saw who it was now, and with that big, wrinkled face, stood beside me, her sad eyes watching.

God, but that dog was ugly. Still, just then, I felt all the more for her because of it.

My heart was still pounding, and I couldn't sit, so walked a circuit upshore, the dog following me, and then came back.

How could I not fall for her?

She cocked her head to one side and snuffled. I knew bulldogs had sinus trouble; sometimes it killed them, and here was this dog, bred near to death. Unconscionable, I thought—she'd gotten sick, and they'd just gone ahead and dumped her.

She was so ugly, the scars on her back like lines of wrinkled pink rubber, which, I laughed to realize were a lot like those on my head, so that I couldn't help doing what I did—gave her my sandwich, then sat on the stoop, and she came and sat beside me. Hugh and Napoleon were off somewhere. The guests were having dinner. No one would be going out. It was quiet there, the lake like something right off a postcard. Mirror smooth, blue-black water, white birch reflected in it.

Company that liked me made it even better. I watched the dog eat. I patted her back, and she growled a bit.

"That's right," I said, "don't let the jokers take the food off your plate."

I scratched behind her ears, and she lay against me, my bosom buddy, my tagalong, my pal, whether I wanted her to be or not.

"All right," I said, and a name popped into my head for her.

Gwanatch, beautiful. Somehow, that stuck.

SHE SAT UP in the bow, sniffing at the lake while I ran the motor at the stern, my Remington twelve set across my feet, five deer slugs loaded up, dome of blue sky overhead so blue as to make your heart ache. The air was cool and a breeze was blowing from the northwest. But I was anxious, all that with what had happened when I'd poked into Edna's house riding me now.

And why had Michaels been there?

We motored east, then turned south, went down the shore of the Angle, mile after mile of dense forest, here and there a sheltered bay, the water glass smooth. In one, a boat of bass fishermen tossed lures on gossamer lines into water lilies, butter yellow and ivory white. Even from a distance, you could make out the jeweled flash of dragonflies down low.

I was looking for a landmark, a river that emptied into Big Traverse Bay.

The land to the west rose up from the water, and the sun was behind it, so the ground, covered with red pine needles, was the color of coals, and the pines and tamarack and cedar lush blue-green.

But no river. I moved at trolling speed, barely faster than walking, blocks offshore.

I was happy to have the dog with, if for no other reason than that this land in evening sun, high, and lovely, when I'd shrugged off my fears, made me almost unbearably sad. There were reasons I never came down here.

Had never so much as looked at my land.

My mother was buried here on the Angle, on a hillside with hundreds of others, their resting places marked with spirit houses, remnants of charms hung from them, eagle feathers, beaded love charms, shadow catchers. My grandfather, Nita, was buried here, too, and—that trouble with Larissa, my sister, was buried here—but I wouldn't think about that.

Which just got me thinking about all the rest of it, the floater, Eugene's boat, Elmer running off the way he had after meeting Napoleon at the Rambler's, maybe somebody else, like me, trying to locate Elmer through his mother. Which could only mean he and

Napoleon had done something after all.

And so I hummed, to get my mind off it.

It was a cheery little Bobby Darrin tune, and I gave it embellishments, and warbled there like an idiot, until it struck me what the title was, taken by Darrin from a Bertolt Brecht play.

Shocked at myself, I tried something else. "The Girl from Impanema."

"So, dog," I said, and ruffled Gawan's fur, and gave the boat another scoot along shore. "Just another shitty day in paradise, huh?"

CLIMBING THE SHORELINE, the boat tethered, the dog out front sniffing, and bolting, and doubling back, I was hardly breathing my chest was so tight. I told myself it was just being out here this time of night, near gravesites.

But they were miles to the north, and it was just a way to fool myself all over again.

It wasn't the dead I feared now.

I had my compass out, and from the hard, flat dome of DeVerendrye's Bluff, which I'd picked out in the map in that Warroad survey, I paced into the woods with the Remington thrown over my shoulder.

It was all second-growth white pine of extraordinary height, one hundred, one hundred fifty feet tall, some trees with bald eagle nests at the top. I had my notepad, and ticked off every hundred paces. I had a mile to get in through the wildlife preserve, and from there, another half mile to my acres. The dog, after a time, didn't bolt, but stayed just fifty or a hundred feet ahead. The path closed behind me as I elbowed my way through ragweed, nettles, sumac, bitterberry, raspberry, chokecherry.

Here and there were oaks or maple, then an open area, grassy fields. A doe and fawn fed in one.

When we came to my land, I tied a checkered towel I'd taken from the kitchen to a basswood, walked in a circle around the tree, looking for what I wasn't sure.

And found it.

A circle of orange paint, on a rise of granite. When I looked to the east, a faint line of orange strip hung in the softwoods, marking the proposed right-of-way.

I walked up the line. At one point, halfway to the lake, I found a spike set in the ground, the steel end rusted. I walked in circles around it and found nothing. So, that was all there was to it, I thought. This one right-of-way down to the lake, just as they'd said.

From where I stood now, I could follow the remaining orange markers nearly to the water.

I paced into the center of my five thousand acres.

Here the trees were all scrub. My land was in a valley, so it was damp and the mosquitoes were biting, and just so much basswood, nettle, and sumac grew on it. There was the smell of damp, decaying vegetable matter.

But what had George meant, really?

If they did put the road through, it would be some monumental difficulty to drain this land. They'd have to truck in . . . I couldn't imagine how much fill, just to make grade, which, I knew, had to be around level, and at the worst, six percent, or—a rise or fall of six feet per one hundred feet of road. So how did they think they'd get around DeVerendrye's Bluff?

No one in their right mind would build a road here—unless they intended to excavate, and use the fill for roadtop—but George hadn't said that, he'd wanted me to see it for myself.

Still, it made no sense. The road they'd surveyed ran smack down the marshline.

"Go on," I said to the bulldog, which had become a kind of joke. A play on her name.

I swatted at the mosquitoes. There were clouds of them. Beautiful sat on her haunches, big glassy eyes studying me.

"What a . . . godforsaken lot of lowland, huh?"

We hiked north, and the sky turned orange overhead, the stars cutting through.

There was a high point of land, about a half mile distant, to the north, and I meant to make it there, then cut back along the shore to the boat.

THE GROUND HEAVED up under me, now all granite, soft pine needles, moss. Lovely again.

At the top of the hill, I could see for miles in all directions. There was a twisted cedar there, and I reminded myself, now that we were near gravesites, not to whistle. Which I had been, "The Girl from Impanema," to calm myself, but now that song tittered maddeningly in my head.

I tried to ignore it. Lit a cigarette, and watched the night come on.

Nothing. There was nothing here at all.

It was like being at the end of the world, the sun, all ablaze, sinking under the western horizon, a depthless royal blue replacing the orange.

The dog had gone off somewhere, and I thought, now I'd have to find her.

I shouted, "Beautiful!" The dog did not bark, but that didn't surprise me.

It would take a while for her to respond to the name I'd given her. But just then the dog did bark, but wouldn't come back.

Stupid dog, I thought—no, stupid me, for bringing her along.

I HAD TO be careful now. Here, where the glacier had receded, were sinkholes.

A sinkhole is formed when a stone, in some declivity, is spun by strong flowing water, under ice, and so the stone becomes a kind of drill. Sinkholes could be up to thirty or forty feet deep, two or three feet, to thirty feet, in diameter. Most of them were filled with water.

Sometimes you'd find the stone that did the drilling in the bottom.

Coming down the path, I brushed sumac from my face, swatted at mosquitoes.

I skirted one sinkhole, then another, not even taking the time to look down them. As a kid, we'd pretend there were treasures in them.

Now and then, someone would fall down one.

I was thinking that when I came on the dog. She was ghost white in moonlight. I shouted at her, and when she wouldn't come, I got her by the skin of her neck and pulled. She wasn't going anywhere.

We stood looking at each other, and when I stopped tugging at her, she went off to the side of the path, and I followed, the vegetation heavier yet.

A lichen-covered rock outcropping rose out of the sumac, on it, buffle marks, to one side a sinkhole, a big one. I got down on my knees at the rim of it and sniffed a few times.

Jesus H. Christ. But so what? Deer fell down these things, too. Raccoon, beaver.

I took my matches from my pocket, and holding the sleeve of my arm over my nose, lit half the pack and held it over the hole. What I saw down there wasn't a deer, squeezed my heart like a fist, and dizzy, retching from the smell, I slid away on my backside, afraid to so much as stand.

ELEVEN

"So, what was he doin' down there that's so strange—the crawl?" Charlie said.

Climbing the path to the sinkhole the following morning, just before daylight, Charlie was doing that irritating thing he always did when he was nervous, making off-color jokes.

I'd mentioned maggots. Lots of them.

Still, I wouldn't say more. I wanted him to see for himself, as he'd done with me and that floater. I didn't want to prejudice his first impressions.

Whoever had fallen, or been pushed down that sinkhole, had had a rough time of it, had managed to wedge a branch between the walls of the sinkhole and climb out of the water onto it, who knows how long he'd lasted, but had then collapsed, his head going into the drink.

I had a fair idea why.

Now we were both breathing hard, climbing to that high spot, moving as fast as we could. I'd called Charlie when I'd gotten back to the lodge, and he in turn had called the BCA, and we were doing our best to beat them to the site, at the least a two-hour drive from Warroad, or four from Beltrami County.

Ahead of us, the bulldog wasn't having an easy time of it either. I'd brought the dog along, just to make sure we could find the place.

I stopped on the path, leaning against a huge pine, waiting for the burning in my hip to subside.

"Gotta cut out those fuckin' donuts," Charlie said, setting his hands on his knees. "Or get down to a couple packs a day."

I lit a cigarette.

"Gimme one of those," Charlie said.

I don't think he was quite sober; but he was trying. He was sweating, and he didn't look so good, was a little ashen.

I wanted to ask him what his excuse was for being half blotto at five in the morning, what was eating at him, but I didn't want what might come with it.

My father once told me after I'd started working for Frank at the lodge, A white man cries on you, watch out. You're his best buddy then, especially if it's night; but the morning following, in daylight, because there's this built-in class thing, he's gonna hate you. He might just even try to get you fired, so his vacation place isn't ruined. You aren't gonna be closer, you're gonna be worlds apart, he'd told me.

And he'd been right so far, pretty much, though a few men, and one woman, had proven him wrong.

But Charlie? I'd get the story from Gwen, I decided.

"How tough are you, Charlie?" I said, going by him up the hill.

And he said into my back, "I humped a fuckin' M 60 up hills three times as steep as this," he said, "got it?" then passed me, pumping his legs with his hands.

WE STOPPED ON the path, the light coming on; voices carried to us through the trees and heavy scrub.

"Now what the—" Charlie said, frowning.

Just up ahead, where I'd hiked in the night before, a black and white helicopter sat in a grassy swale, its Plexiglas canopy catching the morning sun.

"Two's company—three's the Bureau of Criminal Apprehension," I said.

"I wouldn't be making jokes around these people," Charlie said. "Why don't you just zip it, keep your eyes open, and I'll take care of it. All right?"

And before I could tell him what I thought of that, he marched off.

BACK OF THE sinkhole, though, we were both persona non grata. The BCA had sent three men, in green twill pants and black wind-breakers. Two were at the sinkhole, hard-set angular faces, one fitting a lens to a camera, the larger checking the winch they'd erected, what's commonly called a cherry picker.

A shudder ran up my back, the second reminded me of the man I'd seen at the library—but that couldn't be. It was just the green twill, I told myself.

The third had his back to us, crew cut, a plastic bag in his hand.

"I'm Charlie, Pine Point station," Charlie said, and that third man turned from the brush he was poking through, and Charlie froze. A kind of shock—like being caught in a bright light—registered on Charlie's face. Then he threw on the best expression he could.

I was no less shocked myself. At Charlie, and at the policeman—Michaels. There was some bad blood between Charlie and Michaels, something Charlie hadn't shared with me.

"I was the one called in last night." Charlie pointed to me with his thumb. "Paul—"

"Found him," Michaels said.

"Right," Charlie said.

Beautiful came up behind us, sniffing. Michaels turned to me, his eyes going wide. *"Get that dog out of here,"* he nearly shouted, *"tie it up,"* he ordered, pointing to a stand of trees.

I looked over at Charlie—he was surprised at Michaels now, too, but only gave me a somber nod. I was back in a minute.

"You move anything?" Michaels said.

"Yeah, sure," I said. "I had dinner right there beside the hole, didn't want to litter, so I tossed in my paper plate and cup."

Charlie pinched the back of my arm so hard I grit my teeth at it. I jerked my arm away, wasn't about to take much more.

"What were you doing out here?"

"There's been some pressure for me to give right-of-way across my acres," I said. "Just wanted to see what it amounted to."

"You have any idea *why* he would have been out here?"

"How should I know?" I said. "I don't even know who it is."

"I thought you said you looked?"

I turned to Charlie, gave him a what-the-hell-is-this stare.

The smaller man at the sinkhole lowered a wide hose down, attached it to a portable gadget, then started it. The engine whined.

"Ventilator," Charlie said.

When they'd finished with that, Michaels sent the larger man down on a cable, pulled him up, then with the second spool, raised the body.

Even from a distance it made me gag, but Michaels got right in there, wrestled the body off the cable and lay it on the grass. He bent over it, as if checking for something, his fingers in surgical gloves, the smell something fierce.

I lit a cigarette, gave one to Charlie, shoved a stick of gum in on top of that, chewed, shoved in a second, gave Charlie one, too, when he put out his hand. The man who brought up the body marched off to the helicopter, leaving the other to take pictures, which he did, ducking and bobbing with his camera.

Michaels nodded us over. The body was badly decomposed; the portion that had been above water was crawling with maggots. The back of the body was alive with them.

Michaels pulled a blue mask from his pocket, squirted something on it from a bottle—something smelling powerfully of mint, and somewhere, patchouli—then slipped the mask over his nose and mouth, and bent closer. The body was on its stomach now—but hadn't it been on its back? The decomposition was such that when Michaels turned it over, the head lolled off to the side, and I drew in a tight breath.

Flash and rattle of that camera opposite us, I bent down closer.

The brow, a greasy curve of bone; lips eaten away from the teeth. The eyes opaque, bloated big as hard-boiled eggs, distended. Bruises, on his neck, what was left of it.

On his forearm, which was relatively intact since it had been under water, was an elaborate tattoo, a bald eagle with a rattlesnake in its claws.

A parachute, over it, 477th.

That did it. I knew that tattoo. Wasn't altogether surprised—that would come later.

"Can you identify him?" Michaels said.

"It's Eugene Morreaseau," I said.

Already, the officer who'd gone off to the helicopter was back with scuba gear, a full bodysuit, which he tugged on. They lowered him down the sinkhole, the hand that gripped the cable, his right, missing the middle digits, all three, a kind of black claw. I wouldn't have noticed it, but he'd taped the middle fingers of the glove down over his palm so they wouldn't get in the way.

The dog was whining, and Michaels asked me to do something about him. Charlie took the dog for a spin, which drove Michaels near mad: he kept telling Charlie he shouldn't be going anywhere, he didn't want the crime scene contaminated.

Charlie ducked and bobbed his head, nodded agreement, but all the while moved farther away.

I was wise to Charlie. Charlie was taking guff like I'd never seen him do before. Was acting like a—*gegibadisid,* I thought.

A fool, a bumpkin. Or, like Trickster, who could be up to anything.

Michaels had a small tape recorder out and was speaking into it. He cut away Eugene's plaid flannel shirt.

"Ventral stab wounds, three, about two inches apart, a fair amount of bleeding evident. What looks to be a . . ."

He pried apart one of the puckered knife wounds, an ellipse of silver there.

". . . the blade appears to have broken off between the ribs."

Michaels turned the body over, onto its stomach, nodding to himself.

"Dorsal rupture, the result of gunshot, small caliber, at close range to the chest, specifically in the area of the heart. I'd say, just missed the heart. Do we have a depth?"

The smaller man nodded. "Twenty to the water, another fifteen feet to the bottom." The cable gave two sharp tugs. "He wants up."

Michaels nodded. "Where's Groten at?"

Groten? "About one ninety-five," I said.

"Two fifteen," Michaels shot back, one upping me. He just had to do it.

He'd said it without the slightest hesitation. Maybe he had that kind of memory. I doubted it. But my suspicions about Michaels now were not just about his memory.

The whole thing had the feel of calculation, I was thinking.

Then the diver was up, and he had something in his hand. My heart gave a big, ugly squeeze in my chest, and my breath caught short.

I recognized it before I even knew it:

It was a bone handle from a fillet knife, a name machined onto one side. I didn't need to be closer to see the etched scrawl on the side opposite, as well. Or make them out.

Either of them.

THE HELICOPTER LIFTED the body out in a sling tied to the landing gear. High over the trees, its nose dropped, and it slid quickly away with that characteristic chopping sound. The body would go down to the Beltrami County morgue, Michaels would take the boat with us into Pine Point, to do what we didn't know.

Now Charlie shuffled down the hillside behind us, the dog tugging him along on its leash.

"You go off with that dog again," Michaels said, "I'm gonna make a note of it in the report I'm sending down to the BCA office, that you tampered with this crime scene—got it?"

It was a threat that had some history behind it; I didn't miss that.

Charlie grinned, as much for me as Michaels. Now he was positively clownish, but under it was a fury that was almost white hot.

"Come here dog," he said, and yanked Beautiful on her leash so hard she almost came off the ground.

Cicadas were whining in the trees, dull, insistent, a kind of drilling noise. Michaels made a circle of the site, then with his hands on his hips, said,

"Well, I think that does it."

CHARLIE DROPPED MICHAELS off at the Inlet, tethered his boat there, then drove me to the government docks. I jumped out of his cruiser, and holding the door open, bent inside.

"What was it you found?"

Charlie reached inside his jacket, held out two wooden stakes, both steel-capped.

"Familiar?"

I nodded. They were duplicates of those we'd found in the bottom of Eugene's boat.

"They're called guineas," Charlie said. "After I brought Eugene's boat in, I asked around about 'em, but—hell, wherever there's roadwork they use these things. So, so what, you know?"

I asked what they were for.

"You set a calibrated pole on top of it—the guinea's supposed to be stationary, see, and then somebody using—hell, an eyepiece with a level in it would even work—and you get your road grade. Cut or fill, for a rough estimate of whether or not a site's even possible."

He paused a second for effect, then let it go:

"Somebody's done that *all over* the fuckin' place out there."

"They've only proposed one site," I said.

"Yeah, that's what bothers me," he said, and nodding, added, "If Michaels gets out to your place tomorrow morning before I do," he said, "—and he shouldn't—don't say anything about that boat, not word one. Only how's the weather and all that. Like you do with your guests, right?"

Just then, Charlie had no idea exactly how little I intended to say. I thought to ask him what Michaels had meant about tampering with crime scenes.

Charlie tossed the guineas into the back, leaned out his window. He bent the middle fingers on his right hand to his palm, pinched his little finger and thumb at me.

"What'd you think of the guy who did the diving? Our dryland lobster? That guy give you the creeps, or what?"

I said he had.

WHEN I GOT back to the lodge that evening, thirty some guests still in for coffee, and cake, Gwen went by, a blood-red dress with black poppies printed in the fabric. I wanted to hold her but had other things on my mind.

It had been a busy, relentless day, guiding, and I intended to find out what those boys had been up to, and not a second later.

"Where's Hugh?" I said.

At the new cabin, Gwen told me, and I turned on my heel and went out.

CHARGING UP THE spine to the last of our cabins, I had to stop.

Hugh wasn't here either, I could see by the cabin's dark windows. A kind of desperation leapt in my chest. I felt unable to stop moving, and at the same time felt I might collapse. I took a deep breath and tried a smile. My eyelid had begun to tick.

There on the ridge, the gloaming coming on, I tried to stuff it all back in, paced, hands clenched into fists at my sides.

I'd been singled out, but had no idea by whom, or for what.

I was alternately furious—with Michaels, with myself, with Dr. Piper, who otherwise had been a godsend, but most of all, just then, with Father Prideaux—and was as quickly in despair.

I told myself, the worst, the impossible had happened after all these years.

Michaels knew. He had to. He'd set the whole thing up at the sinkhole, witnesses, photographs, murder weapon. And Eugene's boat, which had just happened to show up, turning circles in the bay, the night Eugene was killed? And me just happening to find it?

I wouldn't buy a story like that.

But if somebody wanted to set me up for Eugene's murder, ruin me that way, why complicate it with what had happened with Father Prideaux?

I told myself I'd gotten caught—or had I?

No matter how I studied it there on the ridge, it all came down to that knife, and whether or not Michaels knew what he had in it. Father Prideaux's knife.

LARISSA HAD BEEN ten, I was thirteen, when Father Prideaux threatened to kill her if she told how he had violated her, and countless times. Our mother was dead, our father sunk in drink, so she came to me.

That was when I truly began another life.

AT MASS THAT Sunday after, I'd watched him.

All Father Prideaux's phony good cheer, his condemnation, his anger. After the service, he'd taken me aside and asked if I wanted to go out on the lake some evening, fishing.

He didn't want to leave from the government docks, but from the shore closer to Our Lady. A few of the other parishioners would be coming with, it'd be more convenient.

It was that last part that made me do the easy thing, say yes.

Those others.

But when I got there, having walked miles, it was just Father Prideaux, and someone hovering around inside Our Lady, white and bright in the early evening sun. Down by the dock, there was a door set flat on sawhorses; a wire net of bone-white fillets sat on one end; on the other, fishheads tossed into a bucket, flies swarming over them.

There were two boats tethered to the dock. I took note of that.

"Come on," Father Prideaux said, his voice all good cheer.

I remember, like some sleepwalker, I went up the dock and got into the boat.

Even as we left shore, whoever it was who'd been in the church, had been cleaning the fish, came out, and Father Prideaux turned and they waved.

Far out on the lake, Father Prideaux'd lit a cigarette. He was someone else now, in his gray shirt and lavender pants and Red-wing boots.

He had those rings on his fingers, a thick class ring, from St. Thomas Seminary. A big topaz, that made me think of nothing so much as a cougar's eye; and a pinkie ring, which on his thick, hairy hand looked—I would say, now—brutal.

But the thing I acted on was this:

We caught a netful of bass, with casting lures, and then he wanted to troll. So he steered his boat into Nagadisiwin Bay, which was one of the deepest up there. Two, three hundred feet deep.

And cut the engine, the boat rocking.

That wooden hull under my feet felt paper thin, that water underneath, an abyss.

You didn't fish Nagadisiwin Bay. We all knew that. Kennebeck, underwater panthers, were rumored to inhabit its depths. Lightning struck more often here.

Father Prideaux pulled the live net into the boat, and with a blade sharpened to a razor fine edge, began to gut one fish, then another, those we'd caught earlier, tossing the offal over the side.

He was bent forward, doing it, his thick, hairy hand adroitly ruttling the knife from orange anus to pink frilled gill, the clean white bellies peeling open and the gray-green intestines and red heart spilling out.

I was sitting just feet from him, in the bow, my breath caught in my chest.

On shore, on top of the butte there, in the trees, just a hundred or so feet to our right, I could have sworn something was moving. A breeze was blowing, and the sound carried—

There was a rattle of stones overturned; a flash of something in the last of the sun, but Father Prideaux didn't take notice.

Right there, I realized I couldn't just jump out of the boat and swim into shore.

He had someone waiting there, I thought, the man who'd been hovering around Our Lady. Or was it just deer, coming down to drink? something naive in me said. And like that, I sat paralyzed, watching myself as if from some great distance.

There was the boy on the seat, giving the appearance of calm, and there was someone else, too, aware of the large, cinder-block anchor, the green rope that was, I noticed then, not tied to the bow, but the stern, a breakaway knot securing it. Was that a coincidence, or by design, that inner person thought. Here were Father Prideaux's thick, hairy hands, working that knife, and here Father's face, which had something—*bishagishka,* dark, in it.

"You and your sister are close, aren't you," he said. "She tells you things, doesn't she."

I didn't answer. I was watching his hands work that knife.

"She's a very, very pretty girl," he said.

There was nothing I could say to that.

"Little pitchers have big mouths," he said. "You ever hear that one?"

I thought, it was "little pitchers have big ears," but wasn't going to say that, and anyway, I understood him well enough.

"You're a very clever boy, Paul. You don't mess up, you'll go places," he said.

With that sharp knife he gutted yet another fish; I could feel myself staring. It was uncoiling there, right in front of me, my death.

"So what do you have to say?"

I felt as if I'd turned to stone.

"Stand up, Paul," Father Prideaux said.

I did that, and he stood up, too. You don't stand up in a boat like that, not ever. He took all those bass fillets, held them out to me in the bucket, asked me to rinse them off. I knew not to take the bucket.

"Take them," he hissed.

My hands at my sides leapt to it, obeyed, but something stronger brought them back down, at my sides. And a voice, that younger voice, was all the while saying, This isn't happening, not happening, none of it. Which got in the way, the moment ballooning, like all of life itself, a war going on inside me: I was terrified. He was a priest. I couldn't defend myself.

The boat shifted and I caught my balance.

Did he lunge at me then? And miss?

That younger self, wanting *not* to believe, told me he stumbled, the knife in his hand.

But the other Paul, deep inside, that Paul knocked Father's arm back, slipped around him, tripping him, so that he fell facedown in the bow, and even as he was scrambling to turn himself around, I snatched up the anchor rope, undoing the breakaway knot, looped the rope around Father's foot in a clove hitch, and when he came at me again, the knife in his hand—

(even then, the naive one in me said, he was just trying to catch his balance)

—I tackled him at the knees, so that he fell over the gunwale with a great splash, and when he tried to climb back in, tried to come over the gunwale, clutching that knife, saying, as if I'd gotten it wrong, *You don't have to do this, you can just go on as if it never happened, can't you?* I brought the cinder block down on his hands, the knife clattering into the bottom of the boat, and even then, he lunged for me, caught my shirt, nearly pulled me over the side into the lake with him, and I kicked free from his grip, and with all that was in me,

—tossed the cinder block over the side.

Father Prideaux, eyes staring, was yanked under, bubbles streaming out of his mouth, carried down, hands tearing at the surface, until he was gone, and the boat swung in a hush, liquid circle, with me kneeling in the bottom, trying to catch my breath, and someone, far off it seemed, crying. Me.

When I got back in, whoever had been at Our Lady earlier was gone.

And so was that boat.

Had whoever it had been there followed us out, docked south, and gone up the shoreline to watch? Or catch me, if I'd leaped out of the boat?

Had he seen what had happened?

I lay awake all night in our cabin, that knife held over my heart, the only thing that seemed to prove what Father Prideaux had intended for me. The rest of it, already, was just—*memory,* and I couldn't touch it, and it seemed to shift on me, slippery, as if my mind wouldn't accept it, couldn't, and I had to tell myself—

This is what happened. Over and over, until I couldn't think anything else.

It got so bad, I was going to tell someone, had to, anyone, but the following morning, I discovered Father Prideaux had told people he was going to be up in Kenora for a day or two.

No one had missed him at all.

And he'd never told anyone he was going fishing, not at Naga-disiwin Bay, and certainly not with me. And like that, one day went by, in which I said nothing, and now it had been twenty some years.

And the knife?

Dr. Piper, who, at the hospital, had looked after me when I'd tried to take my own life, for not being able to live with it, and later, saved me again, by sending me off to that fancy school out east, told me to keep it. Lock it up somewhere, he said, and when the bad dreams come, or you can't think straight, or you feel all that darkness coming on, take it out, hold it—

remember, *exactly,* how you came to have it.

FROM THE RIDGE, I studied the island now, our cabins, warm yellow lights coming on in the windows, a mother calling her boy in from the lake, where he was splashing with four others, a loon calling. Pines whooshing in the breeze coming off the lake, woodsmoke, scent of tobacco, a muted laughter, Mardine talking to that dog in the old language behind the lodge kitchen. Gwen stepped out back with Claire. A quiet settled over it all, and I felt something hard, even cold, rise up in me.

Here was what I called my life, I thought.

Our life.

And if hanging on to it meant gunning against them all out there, whoever they were—well, then that was exactly what I'd do. I wouldn't give it up to anybody.

Not for any reason.

STILL, A SHORT while later, in the cabin, I lay on the bed, worried the mess I might make would endanger Gwen, and Claire, or Mardine, the boys, Josette. Even Charlie. And even then, another voice argued, I wasn't in any mess. So that morass of nonconnections, near connections, and just plain fear, ground like badly machined gears in my head.

When I couldn't stand it, I picked up a book I read when I was at my lowest, something by St. Augustine.

I loved the simplicity of Augustine's formulations, his directness. All questions, I read, could be reduced to variants of three basic questions:

Who is God? Who am I? and *What is the world?*

I set the book down, grimly amused, stared out the window, something Henry Selkirk, my old teacher, had taught me going around in my head as insistent as a heartbeat.

Wase' nitabinos. Light around you, light in you, light below you—

A prayer, an invocation, a conjuring chant.

It occurred to me I should go see Henry about the tape, but I dismissed that. Bad history there.

Gwen swung into the cabin, almost dancing, had Claire in her arms, who reached for me, and said,

"Hold! I want hold!"

Gwen obliged. I had Claire in my arms, red-haired and smelling of girl and talcum. With her pudgy hand, she tried to get into my shirt pocket.

Before I could say anything, Gwen was in the bathroom and came out in a hat, and a blouse that was—well, it was for me, that's how I'll put it.

"What do you think?" she said.

I held Claire out, to see, but she pressed her head against my neck.

"You look like life itself," I said, trying to hide the glassiness in my eyes. "Absolutely lovely."

After all, what else was there to say just then?

TWELVE

The following morning, breakfast over, and the guests out, though Napoleon and Mardine guiding, and Hugh drinking coffee with me in the lodge dining room, both of us shifting nervously and pretending to read the *Tribune,* Gwen caught on.

I'd told her after I'd put Claire to bed that I had some "things to do" in the morning. That had been my solution. "Things to do" always meant some minor unpleasantness, was just another of the expressions we used around guests to say what we needed to when we couldn't.

That had been the half-lie; that this "thing to do" was of the order of irritation.

But she was wise to it now at the front desk, getting our calendar up-to-date, making a list of supplies we needed. Now and then she glanced over, pen in hand.

I'd figured she'd be out earlier, but it hadn't worked that way.

Finally, it was Charlie striding up the path to the lodge, Michaels in that black jacket and green pants, stoop-shouldered, behind him, eyes hard as stones, that got her to give me an unwavering stare.

"Somebody got killed over on the Angle, on my acres," I said. "It isn't anything. Got nothing to do with us. Really—"

Hugh, dressed in newly pressed khaki, was drumming his fingers on the table; the silverware on his plate rattled. I pressed my hand over his, stopped it.

"What do you have to be nervous about?" I said.

"Nothin'," he said.

The screen door in the back of the kitchen slapped shut and our new girl, Josette, called out,

"Gwen!"

Gwen composed herself. She smiled for me, knotted that blue-black hair behind her head. I'd asked Josette to get the launch ready, call Gwen out, take her into Pine Point. As always, Josette was late, but now even more so than usual. Gwen went out the back. The screen door slapped again, this time harder. Promises, with her, were sacred, and I'd broken mine.

Now Charlie, Michaels behind him, was coming up the last of the hill.

Hugh's eyes slid off to the lake, his mouth bunched tight as a fist. I'd asked him first thing that morning if he'd seen my knife, and to my surprise, he'd said he had.

"Last chance to change your story," I said.

"All I did was see Elmer with that fucking knife," Hugh said, "I *didn't* give it to him. Okay?"

"So how *did* Elmer get it? I already asked Mardine, and she didn't, and you're the only other one with a key to the case and the compartment under it."

"I didn't—" he was going to say, touch that thing, but caught himself there. "What about when that cop was here, gettin' serial numbers off the guns?"

"Mardine didn't give him a key to the lower compartment."

"Well, don't blame it on me," Hugh said.

Charlie, his voice all jocular bluster, knocked at the front door.

"Welcoming Committee!"

At our table, he pulled out chairs, legs grating on the floor, and he and Michaels sat.

I had Hugh stay put, got mugs of coffee for all four of us, returned with a plate of Mardine's morning bake off. Michaels declined. Charlie devoured a sticky bun, his moustache getting bits of caramel in it.

Michaels asked us if we wanted some representation present. I told him I didn't need an attorney, but I worried about the boys.

"I'm fine," Hugh said.

"He didn't ask you *how you were,*" Charlie said, "he asked you—"

"I *know,*" Hugh said.

Michaels hefted a black briefcase onto the table. He reached into the case, tugged out a plastic bag, the knife handle in it, lay it on the table.

"It's been examined for prints. You think those we found might be a match for yours?" Michaels said.

"Yup," Hugh said. "Could be."

Michaels' eyes wrinkled the slightest in the corners. He was enjoying himself.

"And *why* would that be?"

"Filleted fish with it."

"Any *other* reason your prints might be there?"

I pressed my boot down on Hugh's. It would be just like Hugh to make some snide remark. Sure, jammed the sucker into some fat guy's chest.

"Not that I could think of."

"When did you last have the knife in your possession?"

"Didn't—not ever."

"How did you come to use it then?"

"Elmer, our new kid, had it, and I needed a knife and he was standing there, that knife on his belt."

"When was that?"

"Week before last."

"And *who* had the knife?"

Michaels had his notebook out, flipped back a few pages. There was something not right in it all, a kind of confidence Michaels had which wasn't so much a movement toward entrapment as it was game playing. He knew something.

"Napoleon," Michaels said.

Hugh shook his head, "Elmer."

Michaels nodded. "He's Crane clan, right?"

That surprised me. Michaels seemed all too familiar with what that implied: the Crane clan had been against development since the timber rip-offs at the turn of the century. Had been against the road, too.

"Yeah," Hugh said. "All those Streaked Clouds are."

"So, where's Elmer now?"

Hugh shrugged, looked across the table at me. Michaels' eyes followed. I pursed my mouth, shook my head, thought, he just *disappeared*—like . . . *so much smoke.* The idea struck me oddly. Was Michaels implying, now, that Elmer might have used the knife on Eugene?

"You don't know then," Michaels said.

I explained to him how things worked on the island, the schedule, early hours, how kids who worked for me, often, just like that, would up and quit. They didn't give notice, they just didn't show up.

"But you don't think he was in some sort of trouble," Michaels said.

"Well," I said, "if you're implying his running off could only have come from a specific kind of trouble, I'd have to say no."

As I said it, I was watching Hugh, whose face had gone almost plastic smooth, pure congenial agreement written there. What had those two kids been into, Napoleon and Elmer?

"And these markings on the handle," Michaels said.

"They're mine," I said.

"Can you tell me what they mean?"

I was sure he knew exactly what they meant. *Najoise.* Two persons. I'd scratched them into the handle with a nail.

"It's my family name."

Michaels turned the knife over, on the handle, opposite, finely machined into the bone-white horn, *Prideaux.* My eyelid threatened to give me away, tick the way it did sometimes. My breath caught, and then I said, as evenly as possible,

"Manufacturer, an old one."

Michaels considered that, turned to look out the lakeside windows. A cold sweat came up on my back. Then, Michaels's eyes slid around to me again, and he put on a face I couldn't read.

"Well," he said, and lifted the blade out of the briefcase, nudged it, eight inches of Swedish steel in a Ziploc bag, over to the handle.

He turned back a page in his notebook, snapped his pen, pointed it at Hugh.

"So, the 'New Kid' had the knife until he—"

"El told me he lost it."

"He 'lost it'," Michaels wrote in his notebook. "And when was that?"

Hugh stared into his coffee mug, scratched the back of his head.

"Last week."

"Last week—"

"Friday, I guess. Yeah, that's it."

"And how are you so sure it was lost? Did Elmer tell you he'd 'lost' it?"

"No, wait. *You* were up then, and—"

I remembered, with a start, Gwen had told me Michaels had stopped by, looking for me that morning.

"Would you *answer the question,*" Michaels said. *"How* are you—"

"He *told* me," Hugh said, "real upset and everything, how he couldn't figure—because it was the second knife he'd lost, and he didn't have money to buy another. Paul gets pissed when we lose stuff like that, see?"

"But you don't know then *how* he lost it?"

"Why, should I?"

"See," Michaels said, "it's possible that anybody—let's say, even Paul—could have gotten the knife from Elmer, isn't it? Taken it?"

I nearly jumped at that. Charlie frowned, gave me a warning look.

"But you *didn't* see it after last Friday?" Michaels said.

"Christ!" Hugh blurted. "I already told you. Elmer *lost it.* I mean, why should I have cared what he did with that damn knife."

Michaels bent his head to one side, weighing something, then said, to me,

"Do you know *why* someone's who's been shot would be stabbed in the abdomen?"

There was a world of nastiness in that question. Charlie rapped his knuckles on the table.

"Don't answer that," he said. "You're outta line here, Michaels."

Michaels put the blade and handle back into his case, locked the hasps. "So you don't know where we could find this . . . *Elmer.*" He said it as if I might have sent him away, or done something to him.

"No idea whatsoever," I said.

"You're not concerned?"

I tried to look cheerful, but I was worried sick about that kid.

"Should I be?" I said.

MICHAELS AND CHARLIE went down the path to the boathouse. Midway, Charlie stopped, turned toward the lodge. He made a pumping motion with his fist. Obscene. Then shook his head. He waited until Michaels had disappeared over the ridge.

"Don't you go out on the lake screwin' around now, making things worse," he said. "I'll find your kid, and I'll dig up exactly what this prick Michaels is up to, all right? It'll take a couple days. So *stay put,* or god so help me, I can't promise you anything."

THIRTEEN

A late July afternoon, in the nineties, and the Kleinmeyers had gotten fussy—they were both in their seventies and were bickering in that benign way they did sometimes.

"What, does your head grow in the ground like an onion?" Bill Kleinmeyer said. "You *pull,* and reel—*pull,* and reel, *not* the reverse!"

He looked at me for confirmation. He was right, but I didn't want to say so. They hadn't caught anything and were bickering because of it.

At the back of the boat I wasn't paying attention. I was thinking about my knife, and I was wondering how long I'd have to wait for Charlie.

I'd asked Mardine to ring the bell on the island if Charlie called.

But the bell never rang, and at the back of the boat, I was wound tight as wire now.

"Hey, you there?" Bill said. "What's wrong with your eye?"

My eye had begun to twitch again. I was a veritable study of ticks and twitches in that boat.

"Doris," I said, unable to take sitting still one second longer. "Here."

I told her I'd put on a different bait. I bent over the stern, and while Bill and Doris tossed a few more barbs at each other, I fixed things.

I had a bucket on the back and an oversize live net. I reached into the live net and got my hand around the gills of the muskie I'd caught before breakfast. I'd left the lure and leader in his mouth, and, now, snapped Doris's line to it. I knew her line was too light for a fish as big this one, so happily steered that fish to the mouth of the live net, just in that second, my hands not my own, and something in me saying, *watch*—and that fish bolted.

I gave that fish seventy-five feet of free line, the rod caught between my knees, tossed a stone out, and faked casting.

There was that splash of the stone, and the Kleinmeyers turned, and I handed Doris the rig. The fish gave a terrific tug, and the line whirred out of Doris's reel, fifty, then a hundred feet more. I got around her, put my hands over hers on the rig.

"Hang on," I said, "just keep the rod up. Keep it up."

Doris was thrilled, and grinned, not a little vindictively, at Bill— "That's *Bill's job*," she said, "but I'll just have to do it, since *he hasn't lately*."

Bill glared, as much at me as Doris.

The line came to a stop, and Doris yanked back on her rig, and the fish leaped out of the water, the length of a canoe paddle, tossing, silver-green sided, mouth as big as a coffee can.

Beautiful. Hit the water with a bright slap.

"God almighty," Bill said.

Then the fish came right at the boat. I shouted at Bill to get the net. Doris stood.

"Sit down!" I shouted and caught her arm.

She was cranking that reel for all it was worth. You could see the ridge of water as the fish came for the boat. Bill got the net in the water. Doris yanked back on the rod—she just couldn't reel in fast enough. Bill swung the net into the water, the fish had its head in the net, and then gave a terrific kick away from the boat, all will to live and power, and the aluminum handle of the net hit the gunnel of the boat, Bill grunted, almost went over the side, and I caught him by his belt, and Doris heaved the rod up, sliding off her seat to fall in the bottom with a clunk! still cranking and banging her elbow against the bottom of the boat.

There was that characteristic high, then higher pitched stretching of line, and then—an airy snapping, and the fish was gone.

Doris glared at Bill; Bill at Doris. Then, they both laughed.

"You looked like an idiot!" Bill said.

"What do you think *you* looked like, Captain Ahab there with that net?!"

I laughed too, a tight, anxious laugh, didn't even sound like myself.

"What?" Bill said, but it was about my laugh.

"Muskelunge," I shot back.

In the lodge that night, I heard them talking about it at their table. Doris had wrapped her elbow in an Ace bandage, proudly brandished it. I felt worse than a little guilty about that. But then, they'd had an adventure, and every last bit of it real. If you wanted to look at it that way.

Waiting at my corner table for Hugh, drinking cup after cup of coffee, I thought about what I'd done, the Kleinmeyers laughing behind me.

And right there, what I'd sensed, hooking the fish on to Doris's line, struck me.

I kicked back from the table, stunned: saw Michaels handing Truman that envelope in the parking lot of the Rambler's, Truman leaning into the car. Could Truman have gotten the knife, and given it to Michaels, taken money for it in that envelope?

But even thinking it made me feel crazy. Anybody could have taken the knife if I got to thinking like that. No, most likely, Elmer had jimmied the case, had taken the knife himself. It would be just like Elmer not to tell me he needed something, and to work it out that way.

He "borrows" things, his caseworker had told me.

And the rest of it? I'd try not to get tied up in knots, told myself I'd wait to see what Charlie came up with.

I said good night to our guests and went down to the cabin. I sat on the bed, Claire in her crib in the other room, Gwen nervously fingering strands of her hair.

"I'm sorry," I said, when I couldn't take the silence any longer. "I should have told you."

So I did—all of it, but for how I'd come to have that knife myself.

A breeze came off the lake, billowing the curtains in the window, carrying with it the sad, faraway sound of the Burlington Northern, headed south.

I shifted, meaning to stand, and Gwen reached for me, pressed herself to me from behind.

"Come back," she said, in her touch a forgiveness that nearly broke me.

THEN THE WEEKEND arrived and still Charlie hadn't returned my calls, and the waiting went on.

Weekends we reserved for families, and always there's that lame duck I'm drawn to, and we had one that weekend, this time a girl with terrible scoliosis. A twelve-year-old girl, pretty, and shy and with that bent back.

She was terrified of the water. Her parents were, too. Of course she can't swim, they told me.

By Saturday afternoon it was in the midnineties, and that girl was looking at the water, where the other kids were laughing and splashing each other in truck inner tubes and colorful inflatable dragons, with such longing, that I asked if she had ever *tried* to swim.

"I sink," she said.

Somehow, her terror of the water calmed me just then. I was drawn to that.

"What's to be afraid of?" I asked.

"You have to breathe," she said; she couldn't bear to be face-down in the water.

"You ever try sidestroke?"

She told me she hadn't tried anything. Her mother wouldn't let her. So while her parents were out fishing, I put her in a life jacket, and with a rope tied to it, ran her up the dock, and back to shore again. So she could pull herself through the water with her arms.

"Aren't you tired?" she asked.

My hip, that I'd injured in the boat accident, was making me limp, it burned so badly.

"No, are you?" I said.

"No," she shot back, a kind of excited fever in her eyes.

"You can ride a bike, can't you?" I asked. I was going to say, Let's get rid of these training wheels, kiddo, but she said,

"It's too busy where we live in Chicago."

"Tell you what I'm going to do then," I said.

I removed the floatation pads from the life jacket, got my fist so hard around the back of it her arms bulged where the jacket ended. I told her she could trust I'd lift her up if I had to. She didn't believe me, so I did that, lifted her right off her feet.

Then, I walked her between the two docks, thigh-deep water, me lifting her in the vest, just enough so she could feel it, and shouting commands at her: *Stretch* the *right arm!* There you go! Now *kick!* Stretch, pull, and kick! Don't forget that left arm!

I gradually moved her deeper, until I was in water up to my ribs.

There came that moment when I let go of her, and I shouted, and she stretched, pulled, kicked, glided through the water, and then re-alizing I wasn't holding her any more, she panicked. But I was be-hind her and lifted her squarely up in the water.

"You did it," I said, soberly. "You didn't know I'd let go and you did it. Try it again," I said. She couldn't.

And here I played that old trick.

"Why are you in the water at all?" I asked.

She was terrified, now that she was going to do it herself.

"You start to sink, I'll grab you," I said.

She pushed off, did that thing that all first timers do—she tensed up, so badly, squeezing the air out of her lungs, she really could sink, and when I lifted her by the jacket, just enough so she could feel it, she took a deep breath, and I said,

"You can do it now, come on."

We got to the far dock, and I spun her around, then began walking her toward the dock opposite, about seventy-five feet. Between the two, I let go of the vest, and she slapped at the water, reached for all she was worth, kicked, then again. Swam.

I stood there, staring, just then, saw, in that girl's rudimentary swimming, who'd jumped from the boat that night so long ago, who had *not* had on polished boots the morning after, but ones that were *wet,* and duck grass on him. Not pine pollen. The girl reached the other dock and came out of the water, crying.

I gave her a big squeeze.

"See?" I said, as elated as she was. "See?!"

HER PARENTS WERE furious. The girl's father harangued me about a lawsuit, child endangerment. So, sue me, I said. But it was Sunday, they were leaving, and the girl was fine.

They wouldn't be coming up again, the girl's mother told me.

All right, I said.

Napoleon, going by me to the launch to take them into the government docks, rolled his eyes. He was a study of ticks recently, and the look I gave him just then didn't help.

I *knew* now, and I wanted him to see it.

"What a couple assholes," he said, under his breath, glaring at the girl's parents. He jumped down into the launch and started it.

The big inboard burbled. I tossed the bow and stern lines free.

That girl jumped out, ran up the dock. Threw her arms around me and I got all choked up.

"Just remember," I said, "*anything* you want is like that. You have to get in the water, see?"

BUT THE GIRL gone, *I* was drowning.

Monday, Tuesday, went by. I made trips into Pine Point for supplies, ten kinds of cereal, flour, steaks, soda, cigarettes, steered myself to the Pine Point station, where Charlie's girl, Darilyn, who I instinctively didn't trust—he'd never been able to get anyone to work for him, all those years—told me he was out, not to stop by again, he'd call.

Pressed Napoleon about the boat, and he said he'd quit if I didn't let up. Wasn't his problem.

Thursday and Friday went by, then another weekend, an overnight with a church group on Snowbank, which is always work, packing the canvas tents, grills, and the kitchens I'd made, heavy plywood things that could be dropped as often as they were on solid granite and not break.

To make it all the harder, we had a priest along, one with a surprisingly large repertoire of dirty jokes—some that nearly made me blush.

SUNDAY NIGHT, I dropped my shoes on the floor and stretched out beside Gwen, who was holding Claire.

"What does, *nin jagaski* mean?" Gwen said.

"Going through a low door—or narrow, something hard to get through. Why?"

Gwen tossed her hair out of her eyes. "Mardine said that, about what was going on."

"I've done what I can," I said, and Gwen moved in alongside me.

"I'm just worried," she said.

"We'll get through it," I said. "I promise."

I kissed her, and she kissed me back, some great sigh in me, oh, god, *please,* I thought, just let this all pass from us.

There was a knock on the cabin door, and we both sat up, so abruptly Claire woke, crying.

"You there?" Mardine said.

"Come on in," I said.

"No, I won't do that," Mardine replied. "But you better come. Charlie's on the phone, says he's got to talk to you."

FOURTEEN

In the launch, motoring out onto the lake and through the buoys in the channel, I studied the stars overhead, a leaden gloom in my stomach; whatever it was Charlie had found on the east side of the lake, it wasn't going to be good.

Up ahead, the moon stepped hugely silver out of the trees now. Trickster light.

It put me in mind of Nita's, my grandfather's, cautionary tale about Nanabozo, what he'd called the Shut-Eye Dance. Going out to meet Charlie, it rankled me to be reminded of it.

It meant I was being blind to things, things right in front of my face.

Just like Trickster had been, in that old story.

So I thought about that, headed east, the moon rising over me.

THE MOON RISES, and in water, its reflection dances. So said Nita, but as always, he meant more by it than simple observation.

There, in that reflection, is Trickster, grandson of the moon, he said.

We were in a boat that night, after ricing, a deep chill down on the water. I'd quit school again, one of the nuns there, Seraphim, who liked to hit, and hard, after me. Nita, unlike my father, who'd given me more of the same, had asked if I'd like to go out on the lake with him. He'd rucked up my hair, and what could I say?

But out on the water, after a time, joking, Nita rolled a cigarette in his big brown hands, lit it, sprinkled what remained of the tobacco on the water.

An offering.

NANABOZO, NITA SAID, was out on a lake just like this one, right about this time of year, and while he was traveling to the north, he got hungry, and so came on shore and built a fire and started dancing around it, to see what he could bring around. He's singing and carrying on as if he's having the best time ever, and pretty soon six ducks come quacking up to shore, want to know what old backwards forwards is up to in his buckskin and bells. Come and dance, Nanabozo says, and pretty soon, those six ducks are half-stepping around the fire having a grand time—you know what *babapanisid,* what a bunch of jesters, those ducks are, clowns of the bird world, and here they are dancing, and Nanabozo says, close your eyes, it'll help you get into the spirit of it, and what do those stupid ducks do? Nita closed his eyes and made a happy quacking, bobbing his shoulders.

I'd laughed at him, out in that boat.

Ah, he said, but not so fast. *Geget,* of course, Nanabozo has other plans for those ducks than a good time, so while they're dancing, their eyes shut, he kills them, one at a time, only the last hears something, opens his eyes, and seeing what's happening, goes flying out of there, but after has red eyes, for all that blood—that's how loons got red eyes, see?

But by then, old backwards forwards has got those other ducks headfirst in the firepit to roast. He's tired from all that dancing, so he lies down with his back to the fire, and up and tells his anus to keep watch for anyone who'd steal his dinner.

Like that, Nanabozo falls fast asleep, and three foxes come through the woods, smelling the roasting ducks, and the boldest darts out and snatches one of those ducks, and Nanabozo's anus sounds the alarm.

Nita imitated the alarm, and we both laughed, so hard our eyes glassed up.

But even as the anus is crying out, Nita said, the foxes dart back into the woods, so Nanabozo doesn't see them, and the anus and Nanabozo begin to argue. The anus says, They were here, count the ducks, but Nanabozo won't do that. Why should he listen to someone so stupid as an anus? Huh? And with only one eye to see with in the dark?

Three times those foxes dart out, and each time the anus sounds the alarm, though now, each time Nanabozo barely lifts his head to take a look.

Finally, the anus gives up. Nanabozo wakes, and where are the ducks?

It's the same thing, all over again, Nanabozo arguing with his anus. They get so caught up in it, Nanabozo is furious, figures to punish that stupid anus.

I'll put out your eye, he says, and like that he takes a flaming stick from the fire and jabs it, for all he's worth, into the offending party's eye.

Nanabozo let out a howl you wouldn't believe, Nita said. So loud it carried across the lake and back to him, and like that, he got into a shouting match with his own echo, crying his lungs out and dragging his burned hindquarters all over.

NITA GRINNED AT me; I'd settled uncomfortably in the back of the boat. The moon rose higher, brighter. I could smell parched grain, and Nita's tobacco. He held out his thermos.

"Makate?" he said. Coffee?

We came into shore, and I leaped onto the sand there, pulled the boat up, the hull making a rough rasp, and anchored it.

Nita got out, stood over me. He hadn't once mentioned Sister Seraphim, or my father, or the school.

Nita rucked up my hair, smiled that enigmatic smile of his.

"*Bimaadiziwin, Nawaji,*" he said, Live well, Nawaji, and climbed the hill to his old Studebaker, and getting in, winked at me and drove away.

I stood there on the beach, wondering what he'd been trying to tell me.

Who did he want me to take myself for in his story?

The clownish ducks? The man who wouldn't listen to himself, because the part that spoke was too low? Or was it something about self-injury?

There was a whole world in that story, as rude and base as it appeared on the surface.

I knew, even then, though I couldn't have told anyone, that it was a story about being out of balance, that Trickster suffered not only because he'd cut himself off from his body, but even worse yet, when it had given alarm, he hadn't listened.

Out on the lake now, going to meet Charlie, I had a veritable chorus of recollected, and powerful, sensations coming at me: the owl stink in the bucket, flash of sunlight on the windshield of Eugene's car. Magenta cloth in the braids of whoever it was who'd come out of the Rambler's with Napoleon that afternoon.

And at the sinkhole, the man missing the fingers bringing Eugene's body up, but in a controlled way, as if it were important he brought the body up with its back to us; Michaels right on top of it from the first.

That mint smell, but under it, patchouli, but who at the sinkhole had been wearing it?

My thinking about Trickster, and that story, brought that all up.

Those voices on the tape. How Skip King had changed his plans the night the boat had come in. Had rushed off the following morning. How Michaels had shown up days after, poking around.

Still, in the boat, examine things as I did, nothing came clear out of it but this:

The owl, decayed as it was in Eugene's cabin, meant push had come to shove long before my kids, Elmer and Napoleon, stumbled into it. Even if they had. And Eugene's car, appearing beside his cabin? A cover-up, to buy time. I thought it was just more of that road mess, getting ugly, and all that with my knife, and Eugene, and Michaels at the sinkhole? Just a way of twisting things that didn't directly have to do with me, to keep me out of it, I told myself.

What Charlie found changed all that.

CHARLIE WAS ON the dock, a hooded figure in black, smoking, when I motored up to Painted Rock Island shortly after midnight.

"So, what's it about?" I asked.

"I'd rather you see for yourself," Charlie said.

I'd been to the cabin here only once, years ago. It was a steep hike, the path sandy underfoot. Charlie was breathing hard, but there was something angry in it. He pointed,

"Up ahead."

It was a big place, and in the moonlight, you could still see remnants of a fur camp that had been built here in the mid-1840s. Iron bars drilled into boulders, at head height, for tanning hides, a firepit, the ribs of an old Hastings boat. And up from that, the cabin, the windows too small, to conserve energy. Glazed tile chimney, the logs creosote soaked, so that coming on the cabin you could smell it, a resinous, tar smell. DIAND stored things here, for winter use. Canned goods, spare snowmobile parts, gasoline, canvas tarps. It was a stopping place and no more.

Charlie went through the back door, away from the lake.

"It was broken open when I found it," he said, and then, blocking me, so I bumped into him, he added, "I don't have to tell you not to touch anything—not *anything*, right?"

Already, through the open door, I could smell it.

Charlie gave me a look that made my heart lurch, a big, sad, ruined face.

"You're not gonna like this," he said, and snapped on his lantern.

HE WAS AT the table, poor kid, in what was a kind of dining area.

A sleeping bag was stretched out against the far wall, jeans rolled up at the top of it, a pillow. There was a pack, and he'd opened a couple cans of soup at the table and eaten the contents with a spoon, not even bothering to warm them. His forearms, I noticed, were bony. He hadn't eaten well since he'd run. My throat swelled, and I couldn't talk.

Charlie didn't say anything.

Then, he put his flashlight full on what, it would seem, had killed him. A plastic bag, and in it, a white rag. The gasoline-soaked rag had melted the bag, and there was a circle of residue on the wooden tabletop. From the placement of his hands, it appeared he'd held the bag over his nose and mouth, had passed out, and, the bag and gasoline still secured to his face, that had been that.

Even the way his face had settled around the plastic bag, a fold of skin bunched up, proved he'd lost consciousness like that—the bag couldn't have been put there after.

"Did you know Elmer was a huffer?" Charlie said.

I shook my head. It was all wrong, though. Every last bit of it.

There were things that were just too clean about it all. The pack, the sleeping bag, the makeshift pillow, rolled, not wadded, into the corner. Elmer hadn't been like that.

"Why were you out here?"

Charlie worried his mouth around. "Tip from somebody; phone call, wouldn't say who."

I leaned closer, and Charlie held me back with his gloved hand.

"Look at everything," he said. "Don't touch."

I did exactly that. Later, down at the dock, I thought, for a second, Charlie was going to embrace me, but then stuck out his hand, said,

"I know what this means to you."

"No, you don't," I said.

I PULLED THE door of our cabin shut behind me, sat at the chair by the window. The night spilled in from outside, the last of the moonlight on my legs, my hands pressed over my knees.

I felt very calm, and very tired, and then was choking, and trying not to make noise.

"Paul?" Gwen said. "What is it, Paul?"

I coughed, for Gwen, and she threw the covers back.

"No, don't," I said.

And when that passed, I felt a rage come on, pure, and focused, and cold.

"Sons of bitches killed Elmer," I said, and Gwen reached for the lamp beside the bed and hurled it against the far wall, the glass bell shattering.

"BUT NEITHER NAPOLEON or Elmer would say what happened out there," I said, not liking the almost pleading note in my voice.

Gwen tossed her hair back in the dark, knotted it behind her head. There was static electricity in it, green sparks. We were standing, an arm's length apart, Gwen crying one moment, and the next, pointing an accusing finger in my direction.

"You're sure it was Elmer who brought in the boat?"

I said I was. I told her coercion with people like Hugh, or Napoleon, only made them get harder, more determined not to give in.

"I tried, Gwen," I said.

She took a deep breath, drew herself up, tall there in the dark.

"Will you do something now?" she said. "Whether you like it or not?"

"What, Gwen?" I said.

THAT AFTERNOON, I sent Napoleon into Pine Point for supplies, then took a bunch of Kiwanis out on the pontoon boat. I left Hugh at the dock, perplexed at what I was doing. All of it Gwen's maneuvering.

"You sure you don't want me to take them out?" he said, even as we throttled away from the dock.

"Give Mardine a hand," I told him.

Passing the big, phosphorus white buoys in the channel, I kicked open the cooler nearest me. Terry, a big guy in a lime-green Munsingwear golf shirt, with the alligator on it, tossed beers out to the others.

There was a general cheer. Sure, why wait till we were out in the middle of bum-fuck nowhere? Start the party now. I was watching Hugh climb the steep path no one used to the lodge, his shoulders set in that insolent way of his, and I could bet he was talking to himself, was giving his boss a good beating. But the last laugh was mine.

Gwen had told Mardine he was coming. Tough as Hugh was, he was no match for Mardine. By dinner, that lodge would be shining in ways he couldn't imagine, and we'd have dinner, invite Hugh to the table, and we could, while he ate, fuming—

pretend.

We could pretend that he knew nothing, and when Napoleon came in from Pine Point, Gwen wanted to see how Hugh took the news.

Take him apart right there.

ONLY, IT DIDN'T work like that.

I asked Hugh if he would join Gwen and me at our table, so we could discuss some business, and we ate, discussing nothing, Gwen seated beside Hugh, and the cold in her was even a little frightening to me. Our phony conversation was enough to make your palms sweat. I checked my watch, time and again, complained about Napoleon, late as always.

We had pie, then coffee. Still no Napoleon. Already I knew what he'd done.

Finally, Hugh stood and excused himself.

"Business, remember?" I said. "Sit down."

He did that, now a positive cloud over him.

"What are we waiting for?" he said.

"It's *who*—not what."

Gwen looked at her watch. It was a little after eight.

"Any reason Napoleon would have just disappeared?" she said. "I mean, he's an hour and a half late."

"I have no idea," Hugh said, and shrugged.

"He hasn't run off then?"

"Not that I know of."

"Did Napoleon say *anything* to you?" Gwen said.

Hugh frowned. It just killed him to lie to her, he couldn't look at her and do it, so he turned in his chair, looking back into the kitchen.

"I've got things to do," he said, taking his plate.

As he was moving away from the table, I said,

"Pick up the launch in Pine Point—let me know when you come in."

Hugh nodded, and Gwen gave me a sober look from across the table.

I stood and pushed my chair back, watched him go.

WE HAVE A saying up there, The tightest ball of sinew unwinds. That's what I thought as Hugh came down the path to the boathouse, hours later.

He stopped, then came on again in the dark, stopped again and went off somewhere.

I fed the dog. Broke down one of the Merc 20's, box end wrenches, torque wrench, Allen wrenches, finely machined parts, all fitting into this simple, but complex design, a water-cooled two cylinder two-stroke, no valve gear, but ports, and removed the pistons and crankpins in one piece, from the bottom. The compression ring on the right piston was burned into the ring groove, so the engine would still run, but with no compression, no power.

I finished that, then repaired Hugh's engine, jammed it into the fifty-gallon drum of water, was about to tighten it down, when Beautiful growled.

I glanced over my shoulder, at the clock first, two hours had gone by, and then at Hugh, in the doorway.

"What's up?" I said.

He shrugged. I didn't mean to make it hard for him, but it was. "What?"

He went down the bench from me; the dog, in her crippled way, hobbled over to him, licked the back of his hand.

"Hey," Hugh said, a kind of utter melancholy in it.

He sat on the blue milkcrate there. He was putting everything he had into holding it in. It was eating him up something awful.

"I shoulda told you, about Napoleon and Elmer," he said. He pressed his eyes shut, the muscles around his mouth going tight.

I felt sorry for him, standing there, wrench in my hand, sorry for him, and angry.

"You knew about Elmer, all day," Hugh said, "didn't you?"

I told him I had.

"You were just . . . *watching* me. I mean," and then his voice caught, and he was shouting, "DO YOU KNOW HOW *FUCKING IN-SULTING THAT IS,* THAT YOU'D EVEN THINK I HAD SOME-THING TO DO WITH IT, YOU FUCKING APPLE! HE CAME HERE BECAUSE OF ME!" Hugh said, jabbing at his chest.

"Did he," I said.

"HE SURE AS FUCK DID. I GOT HIM THIS GODDAMNED JOB AND NOW HE'S DEAD!"

He lifted his fist, in frustration, and hurt, and the dog there began to growl, confused, and when Hugh shouted, "Stupid dog!" the dog lunged, and there was this pitiful little circus, me pulling the dog away on her collar, the dog in a frenzy, teeth barred and slobbering, Hugh backed into a corner.

It took some time for things to quiet down; I gave the dog the rest of the sandwich I'd brought with me. While Beautiful was eating, Hugh paced.

"It was Napoleon's idea to go out there," Hugh said, finally, glancing over at me.

"Where?"

"Over to the Angle. They took one of the Lunds, big enough to carry stuff. It was Napoleon, he wanted to see what they were doing. See if there was something to steal."

I asked who was out there.

"Hell—I don't know who all. Neither Napoleon or Elmer'd say."

"What were those people out there doing?"

"They wouldn't tell me that either, told me it was none of my business. But I know this, they were all the way north, I don't know why. Miles north of where they say they're gonna build that road and new dock."

I didn't say, That's my land.

"So why'd they take Eugene's boat back here?"

"It was Elmer. Elmer took Eugene's boat, it was the fastest. They came after them, and Napoleon went down the Angle shoreline with our boat, got whoever it was to follow and lost them out there." Hugh leaned against the bench, set his head in his hands. "They thought you'd look into it, the way Elmer'd left the boat running out in the bay like that and everything. Napoleon thought they wouldn't have to tell you, and then Elmer just lost it. He just ran."

"You weren't really fighting with Elmer, were you?"

Hugh said he hadn't been. Elmer hadn't wanted to explain leaving, so had picked a fight. I was looking out the window, just darkness and stars. But why wouldn't Napoleon and Elmer make up another lie, if it was just over stealing?

And then it struck me, my eyes going wide there:

The two boys, out fooling around, had stumbled onto what had happened to Eugene Morreaseau. No, it was worse than that. They'd seen it all. Eugene murdered, and then those men had come after them.

The two boys.

Whoever had done it had already tied things up with Elmer, and maybe his mother, Edna, who, surely, the boys'd gone to after.

Now they just had to find Napoleon.

LYING BESIDE GWEN, I tried to sleep. Every noise made me start, so that, finally, I slid the Remington out from under the bed and sat in the rocker on our porch. I had a shell pumped up, not shot, but a deer slug in it.

A deer slug is about the size of the base of your thumb, solid lead. I'd cross-cut mine.

The shell was a full load, as many grains as you could put in a shell and not worry it'd blow the barrel of your gun apart.

Just a movement of my thumb and I'd have the safety off.

I sat staring into the dark, all that turning in my head, sharp glass.

FIRST LIGHT, I had George Stronghold on the line.

"Yeah, what it is?" he said, his voice heavy with sleep.

I told him about Elmer. I had to find Napoleon now. Maybe somebody'd give him up if they knew it was for his own good. They'd give him up if George asked.

"When has givin' somebody up like that *ever* been for *anybody's* good?" George said. "You know how the courts work. And anything you know right now, Napoleon knows and a shitload more. You think he'd be stupid enough to come out, the way things are?"

It had to be something to do with that road, I said, but on the north end of the Angle.

"Like hell," George said. "It's just another BIA boondoggle. *Nobody's* gonna build any road—it's a dodge. Like that time they sent us up those combines, as if we were ever farmers.

"I'll tell you what I think it is," George said, "it's an election year, and somebody was trying to look good, but now that things have gone to hell, he's not gonna stand up and take credit. Somebody like that sack of shit Skip King, who used to show up at those Hang the Timber Nigger rallies who's trying to run the democratic ticket and look PC now.

"You know how it is down in the Twin Cities. As if *we* don't know who he is—Minnesota's own David Duke. But all those voters? Fucking clueless."

I had no idea what he was talking about, so kept my mouth shut.

I'd meant to ask him to listen to the tape, but just then couldn't.

While George ranted on, I felt consumed in a kind of inky self-loathing. My scalp crawled. I felt myself almost bodily falling into it.

(Out east once, I'd imitated a birdcall and had been asked to do more, not realizing the calls weren't making people laugh, it was *me*. And even when it did occur to me what was so funny, I'd gone on warbling anyway, hot with shame and fully aware of the clown I was making myself out to be. *Why* had I done it?

Now, though, I caught myself, kept my mouth shut, until I could make sense of things.)

"All I want from you, you son of a bitch," I said, "is some help. I don't need a goddamn lecture. Okay?"

"It's dirty politics, Paul," George said. "I'm not just pissing on your shoes here."

I told him I wasn't so sure about that, and he told me I should try arm wrestling with the dickbrains myself—should attend ses-

sions of the BIA as a council member, then I wouldn't be the igno-
ramus that I was, I'd see what people were up to.

"We've got to do something, and now," I said.

"You say the most insulting things," he said, and hung up.

THAT EVENING, IN the lodge dining room, at a table, I had my pad
of paper out, doodled. I'd left a message for Charlie, *Call immedi-
ately, No excuses,* and was waiting for him to get back to me. I nodded, smiled for our guests. The place was a rush of familiar faces,
now our August crowd, contractors, businessmen, doctors, the Gold-
steins, Fitzpatricks, Denmans, only two kids, both kicking at their
chairs, anxious to get outside.

I lit a cigarette, knowing Gwen would tell me to put it out if she
saw me.

I was at my wit's end.

How do you find a seventeen-year-old kid, on a lake of fifteen
thousand lakes? A kid who, if he built a fire, was smart enough to
smother it, so it wouldn't smoke, to use the coals, for cooking later?
A kid who, since he was twelve, had been living on his own, pretty
much, and knew all the tricks, and then some. A kid who could
evade cops, the SRS, and even his older brother, Al, who'd been one
sharp punch and a connected reservation boogeyman?

A kid who didn't want to be found, who was running for his life.

No tracks to follow on water.

No signs on shore, even if you did get lucky enough to pass by
the island he was on.

No smoke, floating debris, no color—he'd be wearing summer
camo gear.

How?

Just motoring out, and looking, would be a complete waste of
time. And I'd be tipping my hand.

And why should I assume Napoleon had gone back out onto the
lake anyway? The kid could be anywhere. Winnipeg, Toronto, or

even Chicago by now. But that wasn't right. After all, he hadn't run before.

He'd even gone into town, had been at the Rambler's, risked being seen there sometime after. Why would Napoleon have risked coming into Pine Point like that, after what had happened?

And what had Michaels been doing there?

And Truman?

I drank a cup of coffee. Smoked a cigarette. Then another. Music of small talk, a lull around me. People came and went. Mardine was in the kitchen doing the dishes, clatter of china.

In that warm dining room, the night coming on, I realized, part of me didn't want to go looking for Napoleon for fear of what it would come to.

I thought of Elmer at that DIAND cabin table. Of Eugene, in the sinkhole, and what I'd found in his cabin. Of Michaels, with his murder weapon.

Father Prideaux's knife.

If I was going to do this right, it was going to cost me.

Before I jumped in feet first, I had one person I wanted to ask about the bill.

FIFTEEN

I said as much to Gwen, my back to her, getting undressed, and pulling the quilt on our bed up.

"You're drunk," she said.

"No," I told her. I'd gone into the office, taken a belt from the bottle I kept in the drawer, and had spit it in the wastebasket. "Just flirted with it. I haven't been so sober in months."

I took a deep, long breath. Told her what I was going to do. It meant getting connected to some people she might not want to meet.

We sat there, side by side, all that dark outside rushing in.

"You might find out some things about me you don't like," I warned.

Gwen reared back suddenly, the headboard banging against the wall. She went into the other room and got Claire, and cradling her in her arms, slipped under the covers, stared off into the dark.

"You *get every goddamn last one of them,*" she said, and hugged Claire to her breast. "I don't care what you have to do."

Right there I got out of bed.

I WENT INTO Pine Point, to the Rambler's, to see if I could unravel a bit more of that ball of sinew, get a line on Napoleon. And I wanted to talk to Charlie.

I pulled the truck into the lot and sat in the dark, watching.

Friday, near midnight, there was one mess of rodeo belt buckles, pointed-toe boots, braids bound in bright red cloth, denim shirts, and people up from Chicago, Detroit, the Twin Cities, and as far away as New York, drinking in the lot.

The outsiders were just this side of wary, though some were drunk, and friends of the Indians now, imagining themselves in the Wild West, a woman too far gone and looking for trouble, a lascivious look on her face, draped over Simon Stronghold.

Seeing Simon in the lot, ragged denim, the knees worn through, still in his logging corks, put me in mind to call George back. The door thumped open, Vince Gill on the juke, something new, which was a relief, and a disappointment. For the longest time it had only been Patsy Cline, Bob Wills, and old Mr. Mournful himself, Johnny Cash, who could make a bad drunk feel good, that gravelly voice burrowing into you, until you had to laugh.

I thought to just drive back to the docks, because it was all there in me still, just walk through the front door, order that boilermaker. Ice-cold mug, and that shot of Walker dropped in, and the whole works frothing over, and tossing my head back, throat shucking like a pump, that cold, cold liquid, shooting out into my body, a door swinging open and a twisted, mean sunshine in it.

I set my forehead on the steering wheel.

Then I shook all that off and got out of the truck, headed for the front door. Simon tossed his braids over his shoulder, two hundred pounds of yard dog, which would have been impressive, but George dwarfed Simon.

"You hear they identified that floater?"

I'd made it to the stoop. There was more to it—I could see that in the way he was grinning at me, amused at something that would soon cause me extreme discomfort—but he wasn't going to say what.

The door swung back and I caught it, hot, smoky air, thump of bass, roll of laughter from inside.

"You don't watch TV?"

I shrugged. "Don't have the time."

"Check it out," he said, winking and lifting his bottle.

INSIDE, THE RAMBLER'S was so packed I had to nudge through people to get to the bar. A guy in L.L. Bean gear, all fresh khaki, got up to go to the men's and I slipped into his seat.

The TV was on in the corner. As always baseball, the Twins, now, after their wonder years, back to the usual, embarrassing themselves in the American League. I watched Pucket tap his shoes with his bat, square himself over the plate. Why he didn't leave the Twins was a mystery to me.

But who cared? I looked behind me, dance floor, fifteen or so couples there, jitterbugging or making a pass at it; those Christmas lights, red, blue, and green, spiraling from the ceiling, that big, jolly-looking, life-sized Santa in one corner; overhead, the ceiling green with crumpled bills, all signed, and waiting for the night they'd come down in a raffle, and there'd be free beer all around, the winner stuck with playing bartender; turned to the bar, set my elbows on the counter, the bar, large, mahogany, like a shrine, a mirror set in it, over the mirror, a pen, six feet long, with a sign tacked to it that read—

If you can sign your check with this pen, we'll take it.

Years ago, when my friend Al had run the place, I'd given him the idea. Now, under it, was another sign, in cheery red script:

Please don't tell others about the Rambler's.

It's your seat.

At the bar, polishing glasses and tilting taps, was Dexter Skinaway. Gaunt as ever, glancing into the mirror now and then, deep-set dark eyes, taking it all in.

He nodded tome—he'd be over in a minute.

Dexter, once town drunk, and now my informant. He'd moved from one side of the bar, the receiving side, to the serving side, and we had a thing going. He had a jackelope, a rabbit with stag horns, over the register, and if he hung his blue and red Twins cap there, he had something for me and I'd shove a ten spot, or a twenty, at him, and he'd dish out some dirt.

The hat, for the first time since Eugene's boat had showed up in our bay, was there now. I lay my hand flat on the bar, the bill under it, and when he came over, he threw his white bar towel across the counter, spun it back, dipped down to pull a cool one from the ice.

"What'll it be?"

"7UP," I said.

He set that green bottle in front of me; I poured it into the glass, tossed some back. *"Ondjita,"* thanks, I said.

Dexter kept his hands moving, polishing, taking a five and passing two brown bottles over the counter, dropping a tip in his jar, which read—

Collection for Geronimo's Cadillac. There was an irony in it. We all knew Dexter had had his license permanently revoked. And, after all, it was a drinking song.

"What's new?" I said.

"Inakamigad—babamadjimo masinaigan," lots of news, Dexter said.

I slipped him another bill.

He told me about a rumor that had been circulating.

The BCA was looking into suspects—in that floater killing—in Pine Point and on the lake. Coroner down at the Beltrami morgue figured out what had killed the guy was drowning, but drowning brought on by blood loss due to a gunshot wound.

I told him I knew all that, to keep him talking.

"Bet you don't know this," he said, so quietly I had to lean closer to hear. "He died a lot later than they thought—in fact, just hours before they found him, they're sayin' now."

"Like, *when?*" I asked.

I'd been out that night, picking up a replacement Mercury from a marine company. I hadn't gotten back to the lodge until after midnight.

"Sometime around ten," Dexter said, and shrugged. "Since they've pinned the time down, they're looking for the shooter. Guy got popped out in his boat they're sayin', went over the side. Floated right into the rocks, and the waves busted him all up. So bad it took all this time to identify him."

I wasn't about to say how bad.

"A cop," Dexter said.

"The guy was a *cop?*"

Dexter laughed. "Why are you always the last to know? No, don't tell me," he said, and nodded to the big guy behind me, whose gut was bumping against my back. "You were out on the lake, right?"

Dexter took a ten, made change, passed two bottles over my shoulder, then stooped, his face in mine.

"You'd listen to how Truman tells it, they as much as have you trussed and gagged."

A shudder ran up my back, then a swell of blood.

"So why hasn't anyone come out and served me with a warrant?"

"They know where you are," Dexter said.

"And this guy that floated up?"

"You listen to what the BCA is telling the news, he was a super straight-arrow. Wife, kids, veteran."

Dexter stepped back from the counter, tossed that towel over his arm. He took another order, but out of the corner of his eye gave me a look that spoke louder than anything in there.

They needed somebody to hang it on.

Everybody knew now, I was it.

CHARLIE'S HOUSE STUNK. Something had burned on the stove, tendrils of smoke curling out the kitchen windows. On the stoop, I knocked at the back door again.

Lightly, though, thinking maybe I should just slink off to my truck and drive away. But that might look worse. He was arguing with some woman, and I couldn't hear what it was all about, an odd timber to her voice, and giving him a mouthful, and I cringed at it, there at the door. They couldn't have heard me, but I was sure that they had now, because their argument had that feel of something interrupted, so cut short.

I kicked my feet against the stoop. Moths batted against the night-light. Charlie's cruiser sat angled across the driveway.

Still, no one came. A door inside the house slammed.

"I'm comin', dammit!" Charlie shouted.

I went back to my truck, leaned against the driver's door, giving it some distance.

The house was a split-level, green shake siding, blue asphalt roof, white shutters and aluminum screen door. The lawn was dotted with clumps of sand, and the elm tree in front was going brown.

"Yeah, yeah," Charlie said, and he came to the door finally, looked out, gut swelling under his T-shirt, a hole on the right side, white skin, his pants hanging low, but his arms as big as ever, and now, tattoos—an anchor, with USMC under it, on his right bicep.

"Jesus, what are you doin' here," he said.

He was embarrassed, had been drinking.

"I have to ask you something," I said. I was trying not to be angry.

He turned to look behind him, at the kitchen clock.

"It's half past one."

"I just came from the Rambler's."

"Oh, great," Charlie said.

"Dexter tells me they identified that floater, he was some kind of cop."

Now Charlie looked doubly embarrassed. I wondered what

could have caused him to not so much as call, to let me know—then saw it wasn't that at all. Charlie ran his hand through his hair.

"You want to go inside?" I said.

"No," Charlie said, too sharply. And then he blushed something awful, came out onto the drive.

"It's not that, goddammit—" he said.

Some people up there wouldn't let Indians in their homes.

That other voice called from inside the house. Was it a woman's voice? Charlie and I looked at each other in the drive, sand under foot, the moon riding high in the clouds. Something ugly in it.

"They're trying to pin that floater on me," I said. "That's what Dexter says."

Charlie was nervous. Who was in the house? He glanced over his shoulder again.

"It's standard procedure. You finger everybody who could've done it, look into their backgrounds, the BCA has a heyday over everything, and then they get serious down the road."

Look into my background, I thought.

"Sure, you're a suspect. You been one for a few weeks. Truman Wheeler, who steered 'em your direction, he's a suspect. I didn't tell you 'cause I knew it would all blow over. Now with Eugene, that's something else. But why put you out for nothing—after all, it's *me* they're out to hang, not you."

"What do you mean?"

"Michaels is IA."

I didn't get it.

"Internal Affairs." Charlie's eyes narrowed, he let go a short, sharp breath. "They're sniffin' around for dirt—cop dirt."

Someone came clumping through the kitchen, a long-haired teenager, went through the back door, letting it slap shut, came across the patchy lawn.

"Who the fuck are you?" the kid said, in that voice I'd heard inside.

He had a gold nose ring, a bunch of jewelry on his left ear. A boy, maybe sixteen.

"You always just drop by and bug people in the middle of the night?"

I wanted to tell him, he wanted to talk to me, he had to at least give the appearance of civility, but I was giving him a surprised once-over instead.

Freckles, thick arms, short legs, squarish face, and reddish blond hair.

Charlie sniffed, nodded in the kid's direction.

"This is my son, Jimmy," he said, and I put my hand out.

"This the fuckin' Indian guy's supposed to be some big friend of yours? Gonna help get those BCA guys off your back?"

I smiled in the kid's face.

"No," I said, and then stepping closer, added, "I'm some murderer he's been trying to track down, just decided to turn myself in. But—hey, what's another if you've already done one? I mean, we got time here."

"You can shove that," the kid said, and went stomping back into the house.

The kid slammed the back door, but there came the clatch of the dead bolt.

"Jeez, what a charmer," I said.

We stood there under the light, neither of us saying anything. The crickets droned. Far off, in town, from the direction of the Rambler's, there was the roar of an engine, the screech of tires. A race. The car picked up speed, then hit 525 and really let go. They had to be pushing a hundred or more.

"Speeders," I said. What else was there to say? We were both in it now, and then some.

Charlie turned his back to me, looking up at the stars. "I'll see you in the morning, first thing," he said, and pulling his shoulders back, strode, as best he could, up the lawn and into the house.

BACK AT OUR cabin, in bed, I asked Gwen if she knew what was going on with Charlie.

"It's a Catholic divorce," Gwen said.

I told her she wasn't making sense, I didn't get it. She explained there were a lot of things I didn't know about Charlie.

"You mean he's still married?"

Gwen nodded. Sitting alongside Gwen on the bed, I didn't want to get too close to it. Claire was having some kind of nightmare, making short, whimpering cries, and I got her out of her crib, paced with her, Gwen glancing up at me.

Claire clutched at my shirt, lay her head on my shoulder; I felt a protective impulse so strong, I had to push it aside.

"So why? Why's the kid up here now?"

Gwen considered this. Would it be a breach of trust to tell me? What did I need to hear? Or would she be a better friend, to Charlie, if she told me what he could never tell me himself, but should have?

"He remortgaged his house down in St. Paul, a year or two back. He's had to send his son to a private school, Kate's had some . . . health problems."

"He lost her house, didn't he?" I said.

Gwen studied her hands, turned them over, her fingers lovely, slender, glanced up at me.

"Someone's making a case against Charlie, claiming he's falsified case records to protect himself," Gwen said. "You should think, Paul, what that would mean to us, before he comes out tomorrow."

Lying there in the dark I did just that:

All Charlie had suspected about the boat accident, he hadn't put in his report. Or about any of it that night. All, or any of that, would ruin us, easy as anything coming at us now.

SIXTEEN

He was there, at the docks, a little after first light. Hugh was out with two parties, for bass. I thought to tease Charlie, say, You look like a three-week-old pizza, don't hold the mushrooms, which would have been true, but it wouldn't have helped anything.

He was wearing his black quilted vest over his blue-black uniform, which he'd pressed; but there was a swatch of ketchup on the forearm, a fleck of yellow mustard on the collar.

"How about a cigarette?" he said. His hands shook when he lit up. "You won't believe this—"

Waves shlopped against the floats, rhythmic. I poured him a cup of coffee from my thermos. He spilled it, and I just went ahead and poured more.

"I called the BCA this morning," Charlie said. "Talked to that asshole, Michaels."

"What'd he say?"

"They want me to stay put in Pine Point, until their investigation is over, steer clear of you, since you might be caught up in what's behind all this . . . *unrest* he called it."

Charlie sipped at his coffee, shook his head, followed the movement of a boat across the lake.

"But here's the strange part," Charlie said. "Like I said, I called Michaels. Seems they've worked up this whole story. Old Morreaseau and this cop were fighting over something, who knows what. The cop was out investigating something, more IA.

"Your kid Elmer's been out a few times already to steal anything that isn't bolted down, right? But this time they're waitin' for him. He's a proven rotten apple, Crane clan, you know, they got that reputation for fuckin' with development, and they got Eugene there to talk to him, only Eugene and this cop get to fightin' before he shows, and the cop, not one to just stand there getting clobbered, is giving it back—all that on the bodies, contusions, Michaels said, proves Eugene and the cop were fighting—and just then the kid wanders in there, with a 30.06 no less, the cop tries to go after him, but seeing how Eugene's tryin' to hold him back, Elmer panics and shoots. Only, he *hits Eugene.*

"The cop comes on after Elmer and the kid puts one through him, too, but the kid still gets down to shore and takes Eugene's boat. The cop takes the other boat after him, capsizes, and tries to swim to shore."

"What about the stab wounds in Eugene?"

Charlie nodded, chuckled to himself. "Yeah, that's what I said."

"So?" But even as I said it, I knew.

"Kid made sure the cop didn't get into shore, then went back, and—hell, that kid wasn't about to drag that body anywhere. So what does he do?"

"Gives it a couple jabs with his knife," I said, "so it won't float, and pushes it down the sinkhole."

Charlie chuckled again, more grim than ever.

"Yeah, knife and all—national brain trust that kid, right? So they got the bodies, the knife Elmer used, the shots match, on the cop and Eugene—a 30.06, most common rifle around—Michaels figures the kid just dumped the gun in the lake when he took off. They're calling it second-degree manslaughter.

"Your boy goes back to work like nothing happened, but can't hack it, so runs off to the Canadian side of the lake, just until it blows over. He's a huffer, hasn't eaten well in days, and getting high on the gasoline there, he passes out. Dead."

Charlie smiled and clapped his hands together.

"Voilà! One nice, clear picture! They got the whole thing wrapped up. End story."

I was holding my breath.

"Did you tell him about Eugene's boat?"

"I told him I got an anonymous tip. Hadn't gotten around to finding out who it'd belonged to." Charlie pinched a bit of tobacco from his lip, spit. "Far as he's concerned, that's the truth."

Out on the lake, ducks lifted off the water, flew low to the west.

"You, my friend," Charlie said, "aren't telling me something." He chuckled, "Gossip in a town like Pine Point travels faster than fire, Paul."

"What?"

Charlie set his elbow on one of the posts holding the dock up.

"Enough horseshit," he said, "we gotta help each other on this one, the whole way this time. Right to the fuckin' rotten end, whatever this thing is."

I had to shake my head at it; Charlie mistook it for something else—a refusal.

"That you've been so calm about all this had me fooled," Charlie said. "It's just that you've kinda known what you were gonna do all along. Haven't you?"

There was a breeze off the lake, and the sun coming up, and that homey noise, clatter of pans, and smell of bacon, coming down from the lodge.

"Somebody—somebody with a lot of pull—and I mean the whole nine yards," Charlie said, "means to shut us up, make us back off, or take us out. You go it alone, you just might get by. But what you did in that boat two years ago was one thing. This would be *premeditated* now, and I would be accomplice to it. Do you understand? I can't have that. You have to let me in on this one. You can trust me." He put his hand out. "You got my word on it."

I looked at his hand. That ruined face, badly kept uniform. Shoelaces all messed up and tangled.

I thought about my knife, then Elmer, felt sick all over again, a calm and certain rage in it.

I reached across there, miles, and miles, thick hand, callouses.

"Napoleon Eagle," I said, looking out across the lake. "It was Al's fucked-up little brother—he brought Elmer along. They saw the whole thing. That's what they're not saying. What's got them tying things up." I made a sweep with my arm, taking in the lake "Napoleon saw the whole thing, and he's out there, and god so help me, I'm gonna find him."

"Jesus," Charlie said, and blessed himself.

IN THE LODGE, Charlie and I had what appeared to our guests to be a cheerful breakfast. Charlie cracked jokes with the Meyers and Jaklesons, two couples who always came up the same week. We had twenty or so in the lodge dining room, Mardine frying pancakes and sun coming in through the skylights, Gwen waltzing in with Claire, and Claire rubbing her eyes and running to me, and clinging to my leg, in such a way that I had to grit my teeth, even as I swung her up.

I could almost believe everything was fine.

"Hey, sweetie," I said, and she bumped her head against mine.

Then Charlie was gone. I went into the kitchen, steam, and Mardine glaring at me again—I was always too caught up in things, and I knew what she was thinking. I wasn't treating Gwen or Claire right.

The phone rang and rang down in St. Paul. George answered on the seventh ring.

"I'm not home," he said. "Leave your name and number and I'll call you back."

For a second I was confused. There was no windup noise, like our machine had—some people had complained it sounded like a helicopter in the background—no clicks or beeps.

I thought to leave a message, so waited for a tone, and when I didn't get one, said,

"Just gimme a ring—it's Paul."

There was a sigh on the other end.

"Why didn't you say so, you son of a bitch. You got me sweatin' here. Every *oppwam* up there is callin' and askin' how it'll affect the Angle. It's like a damn shitstorm hit."

I had no idea what he was talking about, had called about Napoleon, but it didn't sound good; still, I didn't want to be just another fat ass.

"You know," I said, "one of the advantages of having an answering machine, George, is you can screen calls."

"What made you think I'd have a goddamn answering machine?"

"Ah," I said. But I had to ask now. An image struck me—a hand reaching into a fire. "So what's your take on it?"

George was only too happy to oblige.

MY FATHER, AFTER Calmenson Paper had done him in, had a saying about state politics and our people: If you're out to beat a dog, you're sure to find a stick. He never explained that to me, but it became clear enough over time, and even more so after I'd taken on the lodge.

Now George was putting the latest specifics to it. Either he was enjoying shaming me; or he was upset himself, and I worried it was the latter.

"Don't you get a paper?" he said.

"Of course. The paperboy trolls by every morning in a boat. Tosses a paper at the dock. It went into the lake today, though."

There was that phone line hum.

"Just read the goddamn thing," I said.

"*Record State Allocation Earmarked for Northern Development,*" George read.

I felt something sink like a hot stone in my stomach. "That's it?"

"No. Here's the kicker," George said,

The Minnesota Senate on Monday in a surprise overturn of earlier fiscal policy voted to fund development on five reservations. Red Lake, the state's poorest, will receive the bulk of funds for improvement of roads, community services, and public housing.

"If you didn't get that," George said, "that's you, and everybody else and his brother's parakeet up there."

"Great."

George rattled the paper; I imagined he was folding it square.

"You must've been around when it came in," I said, "so why didn't you call?"

George was never one to apologize, but, just then, he came as close as I'd ever known him to.

"Votes changed. A hell of a lot of them, and most of them republican. I tried to find out why."

"What about the road?"

"It's comin' at you, about a hundred miles an hour, I'd say. Somebody in the Senate's got a real hard-on for that project, god knows why, even with everybody screamin' handout down here."

I told him why I'd called.

"I'll twist some arms down here, ring you the minute I get something," he said.

I set the phone down. Gwen strode into the kitchen, wearing a green shirt with frogs in top hats on it, Claire, in a lemon yellow jumper, on her hip.

"What now?" she said.

"I was just talking to George," I said. Then added, "I'll tell you tonight. I promise. Okay?"

BUT I WAS out that night. And the night after, and the night after that. I was gambling. Weeknights in the Rambler's it was slow. Now, Wednesday, it was especially so. Twins on the tube, the illuminated Santa behind me, the Christmas lights a whirl of colored stars, I nursed a 7UP. Dexter, grinning at me, smoked a cigarette, served the four fishermen in the corner.

"Well, I hope the overpass doesn't pass me over," he said, joking, pointing to my glass.

I nodded and he set out another 7UP. Right then, something startled me and I craned my head over my shoulder, behind me, warped floor, black-topped tables, chairs bent every which way, the stuffing coming out of the seat cushions.

But again, nothing.

I'd sat there nearly every evening that week, a dull fear eating at me, hour after excruciating hour, knowing it would get around, and if Napoleon were in any way near, he'd contact me. I just knew it.

It wasn't the first night I'd sensed something, but each time, nothing had come of it.

I turned back to the tube, put my elbows on the bar, my chin in my hand. Herbek at the plate knocked the bat against his shoes. But now I got that jolt again. I clutched the cold, sweaty glass in my hand.

In the mirror at the back of the bar, I could see the west window, in it a silhouette behind the curtains. I ordered two beers, and Dexter set them in front of me, not quite sure what I was doing.

"Smile," I said, "make a joke."

"I'm lookin' at you, aren't I?" he said.

"I'm going out the back door."

"It's locked," Dexter said, "double bolt, gotta use a key to get out. Guys working for me were going out the back with anything that wasn't nailed down."

"Give me the key," I said.

He made to reach into his pocket, and I punched him, as if in fun, on the shoulder.

"What the fuck is wrong with you?" he said.

"Put it in the bar towel, slide it across."

He wasn't going to budge, so I dipped into my pocket, lay a twenty on the bar; he swept it up, passed the key across under the towel.

"That's the right stuff," I said.

"Shove it, Paul," he said.

SIXTEEN

The Rambler's back door caught on the door frame, made a rough brushing sound on the concrete stoop.

But it was enough. Even as I went out the door, I heard footsteps crunching in gravel, the whir of a starter, and coming down the steps I caught the rail there, flung myself out into the lot, a battered bronze truck tossing gravel and heading up the road in the dark, and where the road Y'd, to go around a marsh area, he took one side, I couldn't tell which.

I got in my truck, hit the starter, and burst up the road behind him, my foot heavy on the accelerator, the trees winding up outside, fifty, sixty miles per hour on that gravel, and coming to that Y, thought—

left— right.

The truck up ahead was still moving north. The roads on each side branched off in different directions—the right to the east, the left to the west.

Left.

At the Y I pulled hard, swung over, so sharply I slid on the truck's bench seat. The marsh was about five miles long. If I were to get anything out of this, I had to at least come abreast of him. If I were on the wrong side of the road, then at least I could see who it was.

I thumped the gas to the floor. He hadn't planned on that. I buried the needle, doing almost eighty on the gravel, the truck fishtailing, and when it got worse I had to let off the gas a second, though, there, up ahead, was the other truck now, but on the opposite side, the width of marsh between us, copper in my headlights, its windshield lit up, fractured web patterns, but it could have been anybody's, the driver hunched down over the wheel, so I could only get a glimpse of his face, his black hair flying out the window, and just when I gave my truck one last kick, and shot ahead—

I just *had* to see—

the truck across the marsh braked hard, skidding, and I turned, looked: a face—

—something burst phosphorus white in the corner of my eye, up ahead. A sign. An arrow. Left.

I spun around, threw the wheel hard left, hit the gas, so the truck was sliding sideways, a big oak looming up, a sign nailed to it, and three white crosses with plastic roses, missed the tree by inches, and crashed through sumac, the thick, beaded heads pounding on the windshield, cracked through basswood and nettles, and came to rest on a sandy hummock, heard the car that had tailed me out from the Rambler's spin around and head south, then chase up the east fork.

And in the truck? It hadn't been Napoleon at the wheel.

I told myself, it had been a boy. Just a boy.

Still, I knew what I'd seen.

My heart was right in my throat. I had that peculiar sense of timelessness you get during an accident and after, as if you're in orbit, inside yourself.

But I was doubly shocked now.

I opened the door of the truck so the cab light came on, turned the rearview mirror down, looked at my eyes. My father and I have distinctive canthus, the fold at the corner of the eyes, where the lids meet. The top lid comes over the bottom, but in the outer corners of ours, hooks up slightly, making us look a bit wide-eyed. Nita, my grandfather, had had it, too.

One woman, a guest, had said years ago, when those things happened in the boats, or on islands when I was guiding,

Your eyes . . . kind of smile, she said. You have bedroom eyes, you know?

That's what I saw as I shot by that sedan. My eyes, my father's eyes.

Nita's, my grandfather's, eyes.

In a *girl's* face, a face I thought I'd never seen, but recognized instantly. A girl of about fifteen. And then I corrected myself.

She'd be sixteen, his girl with the long past lover's face, and my eyes. And then I thought, no. That was crazy thinking, pure and simple. I was just imagining it all, and I put my mind to what her being at the Rambler's window like that was all about.

She'd come in for Napoleon, had made a bid to meet me, but I was being followed. Had been, all that time. She'd— Or *was it* a boy?

But no matter how I tried to talk that image out of my head, it still shocked me.

BACK AT OUR cabin, on the island, I lay in the dark, trying to talk myself out of what I'd seen.

"What is it?" Gwen said.

"How's Hugh doing?"

"He won't quit before the season's over, if that's what you mean."

She lay with her back to me. I wanted to tell her that I'd nearly gotten hold of Napoleon, but I was too upset to talk about it.

"Charlie called," she said.

I nodded and yanked the pillow hard under my head.

ALL THAT NIGHT I had strange dreams, a boy, or girl, crying, in some abandoned hotel. I went up one corridor, then another, looking, woke time and again, startled, and when I couldn't go back to it, rose and got coffee and had another go at that ball of sinew.

"LURPS," CHARLIE SAID, his voice slightly slurred.

I had a mug of coffee, the phone pressed between my shoulder and ear; Mardine was giving me nastly looks from the stove.

"Yeah, right," I said. I had something more caustic in mind. "Lurps to you, too, buddy. Late night snack didn't agree with you or something?" I was thinking *liquid* snack.

Charlie coughed. "Special forces."

"Somehow I'm not getting this."

"That cop that just happened to be out there on the Angle havin' a fistfight with Eugene? LURPS."

"So what?" I said. "Half those cops are vets, you know that."

I stared into the answering machine. The small red light was blinking. Messages.

"Listen, this guy's got a clean sheet," Charlie said. "I mean, *too* clean. I called up some friends of mine, people in St. Paul, who'll still talk to me. They looked into this Bozo. See? I mean, I read them the riot act. They couldn't come up with anything, except that he's moved around a lot. Always works in 'sensitive areas.' Remember that fall when they built that new spur in from 313?"

Did I? Bobby had died that fall. Everything in those months was etched into me with the sharpness of grief. Just the mention of it still brought it all back, made my mouth dry, my eyes burn.

"I'm sorry," Charlie said.

I wanted to say, Charlie, bad as things are, you've still got a chance.

"So, listen," he said. "Remember that LaShapelle kid, what he did then? Kind of like. . . . Christ, I'm just gonna tell it how I see it, okay?"

I said, "Fine, Charlie."

"Happened down at Rice Lake, right?"

I told him that was right.

"Just like that," Charlie said, "he goes crazy after some church meeting where they're all conveniently stoned out of their minds on drugs—"

"Peyote. Not the same thing, Charlie. And he was hardly a kid. He was twenty-two."

"Well, *whatever.* Anyway, he leaves the meeting early, he says just to walk around in the woods by himself," and here Charlie paused—in the past he'd have said, bitterly, to see the big fucking boohoo and all, have his guardian come out of the stars and all that— "and when his family comes back, he pops 'em one at a time from a hillside. Found the gun with his prints on it, shells there and every- thing. You remember that?"

I told Charlie I did.

I'd known Stanley and his family for years. And then that odd connection hit me: Stanley'd gotten a job with the state highway commission earlier that summer, a real feather in his cap, had worked all over Minnesota, even up on the Angle.

I wrapped the phone cord around my finger, pulled it so tight my finger turned white.

"Guess *who* was at Rice Lake, doing some roadwork, snoopin' around for the BCA just then?"

"Our cop, who went for a swim."

"Bingo," Charlie said.

"Think Stanley'd talk to me?" I asked.

Charlie huffed into the phone. "He's refused to talk to anybody all these years. Even lawyers. Why should he talk to you?"

"I'll try to think of some reason," I said, and hung up, then made a call to George.

"YEAH, SHIT. I know who Stanley LaShapelle is," George said, cutting me off. "But what's he got to do with you?"

I told him what Charlie had put together. George didn't so much as address that.

"So you think because I've been in Stillwater I can just go visit old Stanley?" George said. "Say, hey there, Stan baby, how's it hangin'? Killed any more people lately? Gettin' your monthly issue of *Guns 'n' Ammo?*"

Mardine barged back into the kitchen, gave me a hard, sideways glance. She wanted me out of there, doing something else.

"It's George," I said.

Mardine's look just got all the harder.

"All right," George said, "I can set it up, even go in with you, TP—but I'll do the talking. Think you can handle that?"

SEVENTEEN

I got busy. Made trips into Pine Point to stock up, it was the least I could do, then dumped the whole works on Hugh. He wasn't happy for it, and I could see it only made things worse between us. He said, Yes, to standing in for me, but was just burning over it. I got Charlie to take our newest, biggest cabin— just until I got back I told him, Hugh'd take him into Pine Point mornings, and in that way, Charlie agreed to stand watch nights, but the irony of it didn't make him happy.

"I told Jimmy he'd be staying in the brand spanking new, hotsy totsy honeymoon suite with me. He was just *thrilled,*" Charlie said.

Gwen had her hands full, too. We had a church camp up, fifteen kids trying to be things they weren't and going nuts for it, and now, in a few weeks, the end of season guests were coming—big money, not people who fished so much as spent their time drinking, joking around, playing cards, taking potshots at each other, bankers, contractors, businessmen and their wives, a hard-driven bunch in their late forties or older, and we had to clean up for them.

Only Mardine got real with me:

"Leave me the keys to the gun safe," she said, and I did that.

We stood in the kitchen, Mardine in calico, braids bound in blue.

"Get out of here," she said, finally, and turned her back to me, but I knew what she meant.

"Thanks," I said.

IN STILLWATER THE following morning, I sat in George's car smoking while he went into a Dunkin' Donuts.

Looking out the windshield, I could see Stillwater, a town of about thirteen thousand, hadn't changed much. A main street of sandstone buildings bordered the river, some with false facades, small businesses behind them; above, on a bluff, were white frame houses and a high school off on one end, with a field there. In the middle of it, an iron bridge crossed over the St. Croix to Wisconsin. The prison was just south of town; signs leading there warned motorists, *Do Not Pick Up Hitchhikers.*

Now, people going by on the sidewalk gave me suspicious glances. I knew I looked rough. I hadn't been able to catch a flight with my pilot, so had driven all night and then some. George threw the driver's door open and got in. He held out an apple turnover.

"Here, have a gut buster," he said, "lubricate your heart," and turned the key in the ignition.

"Is it just me, or has that Ford been behind us all this time?" I said.

George glanced into the rearview mirror. He blinked, then threw the door open.

I was always surprised at him. I remembered him as big, but he was more than that. Six six, two hundred sixty pounds, in his green army jacket, braids bound in red, he strode up the steep street to the car, and as he approached it, the car spun its wheels, went around into an alley, and was gone.

"Government rig," he said, getting back in the car.

THE PLATE GLASS was bulletproof, speakers set head level at regular intervals across its width.

Six stations. On one side visitors, a handful of color in work clothes, quilted nylon, Raiders jackets, hair dyed all colors, and rough-looking girls waited, one a teenager in fishnet stockings, a red skirt up to here, and a too-tight T-shirt, an owl over the chest, so that the eyes were black O's in the word *HOOTERS*. The place smelled of stale cigarette smoke, cheap perfume, and a fusty body odor—a tired smell. On the other side of the glass, prisoners in orange monkey suits, most sunken-cheeked, hard-eyed, glowering, bent over a counter, smoking. Some, though, were pumped up, thick necks and hard smiles, winking, cajoling, jiving.

The chairs on the visitors side, twenty or so, folding metal ones, were all taken, so I stood with my back to the wall.

I nursed a coffee and smoked, George hulking there beside me. I couldn't tell whether I was still suffering the drive down, or if being in the prison was making me feel ill.

I'd bought a pack of gum to chew, hoping it would help me stay awake, driving at night. I pressed a stick into my mouth, offered George one.

"Wrigley's."

"No, thanks," he said. "That sugar gum rots your teeth."

Christ, I thought.

"You flossing?" he asked.

"What?"

He grinned, teeth white as porcelain. "Rembrandt. Got this whitening shit in it. You aughta use it. And floss—"

The door into the prisoners' side opened. Two hacks almost as big as George, in gray uniforms, swung an Indian prisoner in orange around and into the room by his arm. The bigger of the two hacks nodded, and they stepped through a side door.

"Showtime," George said.

"NIND ANIJITAM, NIND anawendjige!" Stanley said. George, in a low voice, gave me the gist of it, which I told him I didn't need, but he did it anyway.

(And I did need it, but would never have admitted it, not yet, anyway.)

I quit, I give up; Why'd you come here? Stanley'd said in the old language. They're gonna kill me now. And how the fuck is talking to TP gonna help me?

"Babapinwewin!" he said, What a joke!

My heart kicked, I sat up in my chair. George reached down and squeezed my thigh. Hard. It was obvious now that George had been here before, had taken some interest in Stanley.

Stanley glanced off to his left, worried his lower lip between his teeth.

"What can it hurt," George said. "See what he has to say."

Stanley glared at me. I didn't want to waste words, or come on too fast. Just like that, one name popped into my head.

"Does the name Vincent Chemical mean anything to you?" I said. "Or Ryder Geologic?"

Stanley's eyes narrowed, and then he smiled. "No," he said, and pointed to George with his chin.

George pinched my knee between his thumb and finger so hard my eyes nearly crossed at the pain.

Now Stanley and George were talking about the weather, *Niskadad,* bad weather. They were speaking dialect, and even then, in some patois that was all mixed up. I strained to understand. Five, ten minutes, I sat on the edge of my seat, could understand almost nothing. They were using up the whole visit. It made me furious. George glanced at the clock on the wall. Stanley shook his head.

The hacks came in, moved over toward Stanley.

"Who investigated your case?" I asked. I had to do that much.

"Guy named Michaels," Stanley said, and rising, shoved the

chair back.

"You could have gotten that out of the paper," he said, and glaring, added, "thanks so much, George."

GRAY CINDER-BLOCK walls, dank air, overhead lights in protective cages, doors, all gray, bolted, key codes, narrow hallways, George, ahead of me, massive, in front of George, one of the hacks, left, right, the hack punched a keypad back of a door, the door buzzed and we went through, then another series of hallways, and by doors with mesh-reinforced windows set head high in them; I imagined we were being watched, the corridors quiet, absorbing all sound, and then into a lobby, windows and sunlight, and outside, striding up the walkway to the car, just then happy to be outside, happy it was summer, happy to smell the St. Croix.

I wanted to go down and swim in it, wash the gray off me. Wash what had gotten to Stanley off me.

But it wasn't going to come off. Not then, not later.

We sat in the car in the parking lot, the windows open. Everything was green. Elms that late summer green, like life itself, threw the lot in verdant shade. It was late morning. A lawnmower puttered somewhere near.

"So, that's it," I said.

George put his keys in the ignition. He chuckled in a way that made blood rush to my head, made me dizzy, feel heavy in that seat.

"You don't want to be like Stanley, you'd better wise up, Paul," he said. And then, pulling into traffic, veering around a semi and flashing his lights at the sedan in front of us, and passing, he added, "I don't have to tell you, you owe Stanley, right?"

"Why?"

"You make sense out of this, you're going to do something for old Stanley."

"Like what?"

"Get him out of there," George said.

OUT ON 36, George glanced into the rearview mirror, then back at the road.

"They record all that, in visitation. You know that, right?"

I told him I assumed as much, which was a lie. I hadn't assumed anything.

"You think we were just talkin' about the weather, huh?"

I said I had no idea what that was all about.

"You aughta speak your own language, Paul," he said, "get with the program. You aughta know Nakewewin and Nishnaabemwin, at least."

I told him I did; sort of.

"Yeah, right," George said.

St. Paul was coming up, highways turning over highways, and where the Old High Bridge had been was a new concrete monster, under it brownstone factories, and back of the riverbanks, narrow cobbled streets and colorful Victorians, green and yellow and blue, stately, broad-limbed oaks in the yards.

I liked St. Paul, the old parts. But it was odd to be here now. Usually Gwen and I didn't come back down until late September, at the earliest, and my associations with the place were now autumnal, and of winter.

"He told me," George said, "he thinks they went after him because somebody outside did core samples, and they got the two Indians on the crew mixed up, stopped by one afternoon when the head engineer was gone, and gave Stanley a sheet with some kind of chemical analysis.

"They were 'assholes', he said, so when they got him confused with the other guy, who hadn't shown for work that morning, he didn't tell them different.

"So Stanley took this thing home, one silly sheet of paper, gave it to his old man, and they were all trying to figure out what it meant. Percentages and formulas and crap on it, Stanley said.

"It was a Friday. Stanley's old man goes and loses the thing.

"Monday, the guy they got Stanley confused with is back at work, and Stanley's shittin' bricks. But nobody on the survey team so much as mentions the men that stopped by. The boss noses in there, asking some vague questions and Stanley lies—says he has no idea what the chief engineer's talking about. They had the meeting of the Church in Rice Lake the end of that week."

George, at the wheel, shook his big head. "Ryder Geologic is just a new name for Vincent Chemical. Any reason I should know what that's about?"

"Just a name I saw down in Warroad, connected to all this road nonsense."

"That's it?"

GEORGE PULLED INTO the parking lot of the Selkirk Arms, a ratty hotel off Tenth in downtown St. Paul, the State Theater around the corner, warehouses, high and obscuring the sun, one with an old sign on the roof in red, *The Rossmore.* I'd left my car there, but didn't move to get into it.

Just before noon now, I wasn't looking forward to my drive back up north.

"So you gonna tell me what you're not telling me?" George said.

I was thinking about the sheet of paper I'd gotten from Eugene's. Even if I did tell George I had it, he wouldn't understand the figures. *I* didn't, for that matter.

(Now I ask myself, how could I have been so stubborn? So full of myself, as to not ask, right then, for George to make sense of it, what Eugene had written at the bottom of that sheet of paper; or what Edna, Elmer's mother, had drawn on the card I'd taken from her refrigerator—Or what was on the tape.

But I didn't.

Now, thinking back on that moment, I know fully well why I didn't. I didn't ask George, out of pride, or the possibility of humiliation. It was just like that between us. What, wasn't that your big *ace area* or something, chemistry and all that? George would say. Some chemist you are! I'd have to explain that I'd studied biochemistry, P-chem, genetics. The inorganic I'd taken was just to get to the other, more interesting work.

And I had other rationalizations:

Stanley's father hadn't lost the analysis, he'd given it to Eugene, a Waubunowin, so why didn't George know about it, since the Waubunowin helped each other out like that? I told myself he probably did.)

"I'm going to look into some things, and then I'll call you," I said, and got out of the car.

"It's your funeral," George said.

He tore out of the lot, and I went up and around the corner and into the mall there, all shiny glass and bright lights and shoppers, that piped-in one hundred and one strings kind of nonmusic, walking jaunty and feeling clever. At the Radio Shack I got a tape player, one that used microcassettes, the size of a pack of cigarettes, and shoved it in my shirt pocket.

I HIT THE highway out of the Twin Cities, aimed for Warroad, chewed gum until my jaws ached, drank coffee by the awful-tasting plastic thermosful. My heart got that too-much-caffeine tick-over, but I was still falling asleep. Three days without, and I wasn't worth much. A ten-hour drive down, it would be ten hours back, and even after I'd passed through Warroad, I had to cross the Angle to the Inlet, hop the launch, and by boat get to the lodge, another hour or so.

Still, just then, I grinned. I touched my shirt pocket, the player there, sluiced the truck up the road through tall, blue-green pines.

EIGHTEEN

I was on the last leg of the drive to the Inlet, the evening coming on, the radio playing, my right hand slung over the wheel, now rocky farmland as far as you could see, eighty-acre plots, undulating by.

I'd gotten gas in Warroad, stopped at the Red Owl Shopping Center. The centerline wove off to the left, lulling me into a near sleep, so that I rolled my window down, the wind buffeting my face.

A light rain started and I switched on my lights.

I crossed over the Canadian border and into Minnesota, on the right side of the road a sign riddled with bullet holes, *You Are Entering Upper Red Lake Reservation. NO HUNTING, FISHING, OR TRAPPING WITHOUT PERMIT.*

A car was following at a distance in the gloaming, without its lights on. I craned my head around, waking myself, sped up, seventy, eighty, the car behind me receding until it was gone.

I changed stations. Now some ragged blues out of Duluth. The rain came down in a persistent drizzle.

The groceries I'd picked up at the Red Owl were bouncing

around in the bed, and I worried that they'd get wet in back, wondered if I should stop and throw my tarp over. I didn't want to stop, though, and I gripped the wheel and held it at eighty.

There was a desolate stretch between the Canadian border I'd just crossed and Pine Point, not a house on it, this time of day hardly so much as another car, either. I glanced in the mirror again.

It was raining harder, and I had to turn on the windshield wipers. One of the cardboard boxes in back had broken, and my groceries had slid to the tailgate, a roll of paper toweling bumping around and going over the tailgate to hit the highway.

Now the road was straight, low, dark hills on either side. I reached under the seat. All I had there was a tire iron. For years, when I was younger, after I'd been beaten one night behind a bar in the Twin Cities, I'd kept a knife strapped to my calf. But I didn't do that now.

The rain kept on. The sky darkened. And then, the lights came on behind me.

But they didn't come closer. I looked at my odometer, fifteen miles to go. At eighty, how long could it take? I counted the telephone poles, the line sagging between them, my heart skipping beats.

Up ahead, in the rain, a car pulled onto 525, going north, its taillights making long red smears on the wet pavement. I hit the brakes, then turned the wheel to the left, to go around him, but another car pulled out from the opposite side, blocking the highway.

I bent my head around, slowing, heart kicking up, thinking I'd pull a U turn, and go by the car behind me, see if I could make it back into Canada.

These were Staties, I could see that now, patrol cars.

I thought to swing onto the shoulder, pass that way, but another car came from up ahead on the right.

All at once, they hit their lights. Two million candlepower of blue gumballs, highbeams, and a searchlight going right through the windshield and blinding me.

"Pull to the side of the road. You are under suspicion of armed

robbery," one of them said over a bullhorn. *"Do not get out of the car or we will be forced to shoot."*

Like that I was squeezed onto the shoulder, boxed in.

I stopped the truck but didn't kill the engine.

I wasn't afraid just then—no, I was near weeping with rage, at myself. I was alone. My father had taught me never to travel alone like I had now. Never without a CB, or some way to get some leverage.

Four of the officers in standard issue rain gear got out of their cruisers with shorty twelve gauges, and from twenty feet back or so, waited.

"Get out of the vehicle, place your hands on the roof, spread your legs wide.

"Any quick movements and we will be forced to shoot."

There was a moment when I thought I might really get out of the truck—I reached for the door handle, and one of the men in rain gear stepped closer. I couldn't see their faces, because the light was blinding, but when I looked down, I saw one thing.

A hand, along a trouser leg, with the three middle fingers missing.

My heart kicked double. I ducked, hit the gas, the truck screeching forward, smacked the bumper of the patrol car in front of me and ricocheted off the road and to the right. The side windows exploded. I was covered with glass.

I drove the car in a straight line, what I thought was paralleling the road.

A high-caliber bullet went through the back of the truck, smacking into the dashboard. Then another. I heard the roar of engines behind me. I lifted my head over the dashboard. There was a rise of land ahead, a deer trail up it, the hill slick as snot in the rain. I hit the hill, sideways, the cars roaring up behind me, and aimed down into a stand of poplars, hit the gas, and went by them, another shot going through the tailgate and out the front seat beside me with a loud—

Pock!

The sky opened up, rain so heavy the wipers couldn't keep it off the windshield, and I put my head out, my foot pressing the gas pedal to the floor. Up ahead was a crude road that went east off the highway and into the Red Lake Wildlife Area.

One of the cruisers loomed up behind me and I jammed on the brakes, the heavy, framed-mounted rear bumper of my truck tearing through the grill. I threw the steering wheel to the right, and the patrol car spun off the road to the left, hit a rock outcropping that nearly bent the car double.

Another car roared up, paralleling. The passenger door blew off to my right, before I knew I'd been hit. There was blood all over the cab.

Up ahead, in the rain, was the wildlife area. For years, I'd lost Charlie here, only one entrance, but one slough after another, and duck hunters leaving their boats in protected marshes.

A birch flashed up in my lights, and I hit it, and the truck broke it with a crack, but humped up the length of the tree and nearly rolled, the waist-high grass there for a second whipping across my face through the driver's door window, the truck up on its side, and I turned that direction as hard as I could, thumping down, and nearly missed the gate, the cruiser that had been paralleling me now just behind.

I aimed for what looked like an earth shelter. There was an expanse of water, Nokomis Slough, seventy-five feet wide, dividing the wildlife area, and the other side, a dump and access to the lake there.

I jammed my foot down, and gritting my teeth, the white-trunked birch going by, pulled my head in, could see nothing but rain on the windshield, dropped off the gas, and a half block back of that earth shelter mashed the gas to the floor, the engine pulling for all it was worth, and then I was pressed into the seat, the engine gave a deep roar, the drive wheels off the ground and spinning free, and I came up off the seat, the truck high over the cattails, and bulrushes, and the garbage dump on the other side under the truck, the hood angled almost vertical over me, but falling, and I watched it, coming down, and the rear of the truck hit first, my face smacking into the steering wheel, then the truck slammed down on the front wheels, hit hard, the back end almost coming over, my head smacking the back of the cab.

I swung wide of the old Pontiac nearly blocking the dump road, slid nearly sideways again, and driving fast, but catching my breath, heard the cars behind me, one gearing up. They were going to come across, just like I had, Goddammit! and I hit the gas again, the steering wheel slick with blood.

There was a rickety dock coming up. I was praying now, really praying. Laughed to myself, nearly in tears, Godalmighty. Godalmighty.

And there it was. A duck boat, battered engine on the back, an old Evinrude. I jammed the brakes on, jumped from the truck, and fell, I didn't know what was wrong with my leg.

I got hold of it and put my weight on it, flash of pain so bad I nearly passed out, got up the dock and dropped into the boat. Flat bottomed, water in it, I gave the gasoline bulb on the tank three big squeezes, a cry in my throat, yanked out the choke knob on the engine, and heaved at the starter rope.

Shitty fucking engine just puttered and died.

One of the cruisers banged down on the far side of the slough, crashed through the rushes, then swerved around the junk in the dump, then a second.

The engine kicked again, blue smoke, then died. The rain was coming down so hard I couldn't see.

I yanked again, and this time the engine popped and revved. I jammed it into reverse, then hit something and the boat stopped. I hadn't thrown off the bow rope, and I threw it off and backed farther out, swung the boat around. Lights were coming on, one of the cruisers skidding to a stop.

They fired, just at the sound of the engine, but I was already deep into the slough, bulrushes six, eight feet high on all sides, a green wall.

Like that, I cranked that tiny motor open and went into the labyrinth of the wildlife area.

I gave it ten minutes, then cut the engine and rowed.

It was raining so heavily the boat was sinking. I bailed, with the coffee can in the bottom, until my hands bled, the can cutting me time and again. Still, I was happy.

I was freezing, shaking almost uncontrollably. I was bleeding somehow, and was dizzy. At one point, I heard another boat start up, but then, I was rowing again.

The rain came down like that for hours, and then it was dark.

Gwen saw me first. I couldn't open the kitchen door, so sat in the rain on the stoop.

"Oh, Paul," she said. And then she said, her voice reedy, and sharp, "So help me God. I'm going to call the police now. Don't say no—"

I told her it was the police who'd done this to me—and that stopped all that.

LATER, I WENT back to the honeymoon suite.

"What happened to you?" Charlie said, blinking and holding the screen door open. "You look like fuckin' Harry Houdini."

He reached out to touch my head. I'd cut my scalp, probably needed stitches, but refused them. Gwen had wrapped me up with gauze.

"You going to let me in, or what?" I said.

At the alcove table, Charlie pulled out two chairs. He smelled of hair oil. But I was wise to that.

"Where's the kid?"

"In the back bedroom," Charlie said. "So what happened?"

I told him, then lit a cigarette and reached into my pocket, pulled out the recorder.

"Listen to this," I said.

I played the message for Charlie, watching him closely, his mouth puckered in concentration.

Market value is all it's worth.
Offer it, but don't hang things up with
waiting. Are we clear on that?

Our . . . Pawn, the man said, on the other end, and that conversation in Ottawa started up.

"No," Charlie said, "I don't get it. Am I supposed to recognize somebody, or what? I mean, since when did I ever know a word of—"

The woman laughed in that now familiar, and infuriating way, said, *Stop it, stop it, I'll wet myself.* Charlie glanced off, as if startled, and just as quickly shook his head, no—

"What," I said. "You recognize one these voices?"

There was that surprised, *"What?"* and I stopped the recorder.

"Back up," Charlie said. "Run it. Again."

I did that.

"Who's that woman talking to?" Charlie asked. "What have a couple of—" Charlie caught himself "—*locals* got to do with Skip King?"

I leaned across the table, watching him.

"Don't gimme that look," he said, "we both know he was up here earlier. What are they sayin', those two on the other end of the line?"

"I'm not sure, exactly," I said.

"What do you mean, 'not sure, *exactly*'?" Charlie said. "Do you understand it or not?"

"It's dialect," I said. "And the answer is no, I don't."

Charlie set his hands on his hips. "You gonna tell me what happened?"

"Was anybody in the station this afternoon?"

"Regular circus," Charlie said. "An assault and battery, a few council members grousin' about—"

"Who?"

"Walter, Truman— I mean, what does it matter?"

"You tell anybody where I'd gone?"

Charlie glowered at that, insulted. His son came out of the back of the cabin, rubbing the sleep from his eyes. He pulled up a chair, scratched at his nose ring.

"Your eye's twitchin' all over the place, you know that?" he said.

I stood and tucked the recorder in my pocket. The kid pointed to me, had his mouth open, and Charlie said,

"One word outta you and I'm not gonna be responsible for what happens, all right? Show some respect."

To the kid's credit, he did, long enough for me to get out of there.

NINETEEN

In our cabin I paced back of the bed, Gwen finally rising and dressing. I told her about the phone message and what I thought I could do about it.

I didn't say I'd decided to see Henry Selkirk, my old teacher, because any mention of Henry always brought out the worst in us, as it brought up our son, Bobby.

Still, she knew exactly who I meant, even if I hadn't used his name.

She spun around in the dark, her eyes hard and glassy.

"Don't use me as an excuse to wait," she said. "I can take care of myself."

I paused there a moment, then pulled on my jacket and went out.

OUT ON THE lake, steering the boat toward the Angle, and passing Magnuson's Island, big and high as an oceanliner, the sides of it twinkling with lightning bugs as if with living stars, and the water still, and cool, I felt as if I were dreaming. And it was a very dark dream, in it all that with the floater, Eugene, and Elmer, and, now, the policemen who'd come after me on my drive up from Warroad, with them the cop missing the fingers, blue-suited, and deadly. It surprised me, how I bent to the memory of it, hands hard on the wheel.

But I was past threat, I thought grimly, steering our launch up the lake in the dark. I was even past not wanting to go to Henry for help.

So I watched for other boats, in bays, or behind islands, but I was thinking of Henry.

THAT AFTERNOON BOBBY had been shot, I'd carried him to Henry's, and Henry had driven us into Pine Point, hadn't told me our boy was dead, even as he made pretenses of driving fast to get us there, had helped rush us into the hospital, had held me, crying in the lobby after one of the doctors told me what Henry had known the moment he'd seen me.

That was one reason I hadn't gone to see Henry. I was afraid seeing him would bring all that back, and I'd never thanked him for what he'd done. I hadn't been able to.

I just couldn't bear it.

And I hadn't visited Henry because I felt a certain uneasiness— at how far I'd gotten from what mattered up there; and at how, at least it must have seemed to him, I was unwilling to bear the burden of larger family, which filled me with a certain guilt.

Which made me, on the surface of it, angrily defensive. After all, what did they want from me?

But I hadn't wanted to see Henry because, maybe most of all, I'd failed him.

In those in-between years, long after I'd had the run-in with Father Prideaux and tried to put out my own lights, I'd studied with Henry. He was, in our area, one of the only eighth-degree members of the Midewiwin, the medicine society—though I found out later, it wasn't only up at Red Lake, but anywhere—and he didn't take just anybody on.

He'd refused a number of people I knew, and when my father asked if he'd teach me, Henry had accepted. Even back then, I was aware that I was some special case for Henry, but didn't know why.

I knew the least I could do to save face was just talk to him.

(In truth, I think, now, my father and Henry were trying to save me. I'd been working for Frank, the old owner of the lodge, was getting to be something of a drinker, and had quietly, and almost completely, cut myself off from anything having to do with the reservation, my family, or our people.

I did everything but cut my hair, and had been thinking of doing that, too.)

So I was honored, but quietly terrified about Henry. Everything was bullshit then, I thought. My life, tribal politics, religion—anybody's.

Bullshit. All of it.

But Henry scared me senseless. I couldn't have told you why then, but I know now it was because I was certain he would see right through me—that all that raging, and posturing, and toughing it out hid somebody who was barely holding it together. I was afraid he'd stick something in there that would just blow me apart.

And he did exactly that.

Even the first afternoon we met, at his cabin out in the Nin'-godonin'djigan.

We talked, sitting back of the lake, about the weather; it was October, the trees colorful, and that quiet having descended up there, the water calm, and the smell of parched wild rice everywhere.

"*Makade-mashkikiwaabo?*" Henry said. Coffee?

He took forever in his cabin, a one-room deal, black tarpaper tacked over with lath, Red Lake Tudor, I thought sarcastically to myself.

I was just going to joke myself through it.

Then Henry was back with the coffee, handed me a blue mug.

"Where is the blue in that mug?" he asked.

I knew it was a trick question. I couldn't think of the answer he wanted to hear.

"Drink up," he said, and I did, and he took the mug, and right there, smacked it on the lichen-covered stone we were sitting on. Broke it into umpteen pieces.

"Just one question, and I'll let you go. Huh? *Enh?*" Yes?

I'd meant to make some speech about why I wouldn't study with him; it was odd, how just then, I felt I'd lost something, something I'd thought I hadn't wanted.

I nodded.

Henry picked up one of the ceramic shards. "Now *where* is the blue?"

I didn't get it.

"What if we call it, *'ozhaawashko'?*" he said.

"It's still blue," I said.

"Yes," he said, "and *gaawiin,*" no. "If I say, *'ozhaawashko,'* what comes to mind—no, don't translate, what did you think?"

I said, *"Zhashagi, miinan, diindiisi."* Blue heron, blueberry, blue jay.

Henry smiled. "Now, *blue,*" he said.

And I said, "electrical insulator blue, teapot blue, Chevrolet Impala blue, blue plastic."

I remember sitting there, shocked at myself.

"So, *ozhaawashko,* and *blue*—the same thing, right?"

"No," I said.

"What's the difference?"

"What's attached to it." But I thought, no—*belongs* to it.

"Ah," Henry said, his eyes narrowing. "Attached. But you're not attached to anything, are you? Especially not your people or your language, huh?"

Right there, he had me all choked up. He put his arm around my shoulders.

The character of the people are in the naming, Nawaji, he taught me.

Pay attention to the names.

It was Henry who taught me how to listen, to see, again. The world, at Henry's, came alive again. Henry taught me about the thunderers, the grandfathers, how stones talked.

He brought Nita, my grandfather, back to me, and those good years, before the BIA ruined my father.

The world will speak to you, if you listen, Nawaji, Henry said. Enh? Yes?

I BECAME AN uneasy student. Spoke the old language with Henry, paid attention to the names, as Henry was always reminding me to. There was a big-eyed and lovely girl I'd run into, who worked afternoons at the government docks bait shop, Gilby, and I was stuck on her. There was something broken, or sad, in her that I was drawn to.

Speechless, I fell headlong into it. And there was this, complicating things:

I was skittish. After all those years, someone came around asking after Father Prideaux, and I could barely sit still. Even there with Henry, I wouldn't say what was tearing me apart. But he knew.

He *saw* me.

My last afternoon with him, he knew what I was going to do. And in his own subtle way, I know now, he said good-bye.

"So, do you believe in some things now?" he asked.

"Enh," I told him, yes. "I believe in what I know."

"And you know yourself," he said.

I grinned for him, bone sick. Felt, just then, almost . . .

"There's the daylight me," I said, "and there's all that is . . . *agawateshin,*" in shadow. *Shadow,* in Ojibwemowin, is a powerful and dark word.

Henry got to his feet, his head turned so I couldn't see his face.

"Watch what you feed your shadow," he said, and touching my shoulder, went into his cabin.

THE WEEK I ran, I was initiated into the Midewiwin.

I believed, then, in none of it. Fifteen or twenty people I knew were there, the Streaked Clouds, the Morrisons, Strong Grounds, Selkirks.

Night, back of the lodge they'd erected, I shuffled my feet on the flinty ground. I was going to go through with the whole thing, out of fear of public embarrassment, so as not to seem to have thrown away a prize others coveted.

But mostly to show respect for Henry.

So I stood outside the makeshift lodge, thirty or so feet long, and all of them inside, waiting for me.

They were singing inside. I went in with the rice and tobacco and blanket Henry had told me to bring, wrapped as gifts for the singers. There was a kind of solemnity to it that made me want to laugh, but it wasn't funny. People made speeches, honoring me, the initiate, which both embarrassed me and made me worry I'd disappoint them, or show them the fake I was.

I was called on to be upright, to uphold the ideals of the society. Sobriety, integrity, forthrightness, kindness, and charity.

The man Henry had called to be the *ne'mita'maun* stood. My whole body felt strange and energized. Tingled.

Then the *ne'mita'maun* stepped in front of me, and shot me. Blew through the shell in his mouth, so that feeling his breath in my face, my whole body lurched.

I was supposed to fall on my back, arms outstretched.

Henry jabbed me, and my legs buckled, so that I fell just as he'd told me I would.

Think of it as hypnotism, he'd said earlier.

But it *wasn't* like that. (And he'd known it wouldn't be.)

Whatever it was sunk right down into me; whether it was my thinking it had, or whether it really had, didn't make a difference. It was as if something rolled over inside me, awakened.

So that after, in Pine Point, walking in the dark, when I couldn't go home to my father, who'd be nearly comatose with drink, I went in circles, something talking inside of me, set loose, and my face would flush, and this voice would talk to me, out of my paralyzed, but animated mouth.

Everything was—vivid, electrical, glowed with some animating spirit, just then, laid bare.

I was in some ecstasy, like I'd read saints had, or dja'sakid, and it terrified me. Truly.

That thing in me told me what I was going to become.

A healer, it said.

Me. I laughed at that, tears wet and cold on my face, crazy, ululating laughter.

CAN I SAY, I panicked? Completely.

All that burst in me, the middle of that night, like some bubble, and I was back, only *not,* not really, I knew I would never be the same, but I was trying to be, and I went for Gilby.

I stole a car at the government docks, a bottle from the bait shop, and drinking, and driving, and stopping, along the way, the radio on, so loud the speakers in the doors crackled, Gilby and I tore at each other, and I had to have it again, dirt, or my body, sex, filth, I wanted to smear myself with dirt, anything to wash away what had come out of me—

had terrified me, was *in* me

I had to *inhabit* my body, so—

—again, all hot skin, and this insane hunger in me, so that, boyish me, had her again, and again, each time trying to turn inside-out what was in me, until getting to the cities, late, we went to an old friend's at the projects on Cedar, the Little Earth Projects, where I drank myself comatose, and we lived there, month after month, and I loved Gilby, long-legged Gilby, her breasts, her mouth, her loveliness, her blue-black hair, her sex, but it was this hunger.

I wanted to escape through her, and she'd see me look at her, and we lost hours, but out of it we argued, couldn't do anything but argue.

We had no money, we'd spent the last of what I'd earned at Frank's resort, guiding. I worked at a body shop on Cedar. They needed somebody to weld, toss ho-jo, do lead work on wrecks, repair engines.

Dirty, difficult, awful work. Chemicals, spray paint, rosin from welding rod, dust. Oil, and gasoline, and raw metal. And hard cases working with me, half of them having finished stints at Stillwater, or Leavenworth, and back up in the Twin Cities.

And Gilby, big-eyed, sad Gilby, waitressed tables at the Rainbow Cafe.

Nights, we worked the magic on each other, she got through the door, or I did, and there was all that bittersweet wonder, and release, but it was all wrong somehow, I didn't know how.

I felt like I was being devoured, by myself, by the Cities, by life.

I'd had no experience like that, falling into someone, and trying to stop, and still falling. Did I love her? Was that love? I wanted to make the world go away through her, and huffing, and panting, and yearning, it did, for hours, an afternoon, a day.

All that I'd felt after my initiation, I tried to erase.

Gilby was part of how I did it. And the rest? I was stealing cars for the body shop, and drinking when Gilby wasn't around, and reading.

I read everything I could get my hands on. I disappeared into books, books on ethics, or history, or philosophy. What I didn't know was, I was bored stiff, and dying.

I'd heard Dr. Piper was trying to reach me. So was Henry Selkirk.

The names. Pay attention to the names.

I tried to tell Gilby about it, what had happened that night, and why, maybe, we should go somewhere, anywhere else. But that only seemed to make her, just then, completely crazy. We were in this downward spiral. A cousin Doden, was staying with us, worked with me days at the body shop. Gilby and I didn't take precautions, as if fate, or biology, would fashion a life for us, tailor made, just put in the ingredients and stir. An instant life on Franklin Avenue. We were going to parties where people shot each other, were driving a stolen car, discovered meth one night. It was a rush I took to, and it scared me.

The morning after, feeling like I'd fallen into a hole I could never climb out of, Henry'd spoken to me. And I'd listened.

Don't feed your shadow, Nawaji. It'll pass you by, then turn and devour you.

"Why do you complicate things the way you do?" Gilby said. "Why do you have to make everything so hard?"

She was padding around our Little Earth apartment, always eating. Quiet, sullen, something almost like a grin on her face. Something secret there.

And then, one night late that spring, it all came to a violent and swift end, my cousin, tipped off to what the men running the body shop had planned for us, breaking out and taking us with him. And when we ran, Gilby disappeared. Into the Dakotas, someone at the projects told me, they'd seen her leave.

I'd gone back to our apartment to wait for her, an almost suicidal thing to do.

And again, circumstance saved my life. Before daylight, Dr. Piper just happened to swing by—I was standing in the wreck of the apartment, holes in the walls, our furniture overturned, a blood stain under my feet in the green carpet. He was driving to Red Lake, did I want to ride up with him?

So I'd packed my bags, right then and there, never asked how any of that had come about; and when Dr. Piper set up all that with the school out east, I went, the same way, packed up and went, ignorant, just followed my feet and what seemed to be moving me here, or there.

I had an angel, it seemed, and that was true:

Dr. Piper. But on his deathbed, at Fairview, he insisted on telling me something he'd been sworn not to; I told him, No, don't then.

"Listen," he'd said, squeezing my hand. "I did what I could for you, son, but it was Henry who sent me down there that week. He knew you wouldn't listen to him. We go way back, Henry and me. I though you should know. Say hi, will you?"

BUT I NEVER once went over to Henry's, and if I saw him coming at me down the street in Pine Point, I crossed the street to the other side. And I did that even when I was with Gwen, after I'd brought her to live with me out at Frank's. Gwen, who set me free in some way, beautiful Gwen who I set free.

Was I a coward? Or was it, I didn't want her knowing any of what had happened all those years back? Didn't want to be tied into it, in the same way she didn't want to be tied to what had torn her up so badly.

And Gilby? After that night I'd tried to find her, but couldn't. And then, years later, out of nowhere, there she was. She never did tell me where she'd gone, but there was always something sad in her when I'd run into her in Pine Point. She was always smoking, her fingernails painted, and she was as beautiful as ever, but something that made me cry inside, though I couldn't tell her.

She'd gotten hard. Or was it, she'd lost the ability to want something for herself?

Or believe in anything.

And always, when I was back in Pine Point, in town, there was Henry, those dark, hooded eyes, aware of me, always, in my thinking, condemnation there.

Sometimes, he called out, cheerfully, "Boo shoo, Nawaji," which made my heart kick, and I'd veer off from him, full of burning shame.

HE WAS THERE, to the side, overlooking the lake, smoking, when I strode up his rutted, weedy drive in the dark from the lake. Sitting, waiting, just as he'd been all those years ago, in another lifetime it seemed.

"You're late," he said, chuckling.

"How'd you know I was coming?" I said, trying to sound jaunty.

"Wife called on the telephone."

"Ah," I said, and sat beside him.

Henry did not have a telephone. He had a pot of coffee on the coals at his feet, offered me a mug. A blue mug. Did he remember? Had he done that on purpose?

Of course.

"So, what did you find out all these years you been gone?" he said.

I didn't know what to say. What are fifteen years in anyone's life? (And, I was relieved he'd left our meeting the afternoon of Bobby's death out of it.)

"I've prayed for you," he said.

Reaching for my cigarettes, I avoided having to respond to that, couldn't for the burning in my throat. I got one lit, and hit it hard.

"I don't deserve it," I told him.

"Doesn't matter. You were always my favorite, my Doubting Thomas. Your grandfather saw it, too. You're the one who'll take the lost causes. I knew you would. Our own St. Jude of the Lake."

I had to laugh at that. "You got me all wrong," I said, "I'm just an apple businessman trying to run a resort and not make too many waves."

Henry smiled, a warmth in it like sunshine. It was the highest form of praise. I felt like that boy I'd been all over again. Ridiculous, and hopelessly transparent.

"So what is it?" he said.

TWENTY

Just as I had for Charlie, I played the tape.

Henry wanted a cigarette and I gave him one, held out my lighter.

"You said, those two, that woman and the man there, they were talking Ottawa. That's wrong. The dialect he and the woman are using is *Anishininiimowin,* Saskatchewan. That's high plains, but west, more like Cree."

I was feeling stupid, and from his seeming lack of response to it, also feeling—

"*Miinawaa,*" he said. Again.

I did that, the crickets chirring, the night full dark and the lake making a dull, rhythmic plashing on his rowboat below us. The voices, Skip King's, the woman's, and that third voice, seemed disembodied, odd there.

"*—our Pawn,*" the man said, and the woman laughed, "*Stop it, stop it, I'll wet myself.*"

Henry chuckled now, too. It was just a big laugh, at my expense.

All that trouble to find out what was on the tape and it was just some business down in Minneapolis. I felt my face go hot at it.

"So it isn't anything," I said.

"Shhhhh," Henry said, staring into the dark, then laughing to himself.

"You don't know this dialect?"

"No, I know it very well," Henry said. "They're punning, and that one talking to the woman, he's got a pretty thick tongue. He grew up speaking Anishininiimowin, but he's been away forever." Henry chuckled again, nodding to himself. "Clever."

"But it isn't anything," I said again, hoping he'd agree.

"No. You were right to bring it here."

I shoved the recorder in my pocket.

"You'd better be careful with that," he said, "You'll need it later."

I was getting tired of it.

"Still as impatient as ever," Henry said. He crushed his cigarette out.

"All right," he said.

HE TOLD ME, first of all, the man talking to the woman had caught himself in saying something he didn't want to say, and turned it into a pun.

"What?"

"*Pawn.*"

"How is that a pun?"

Henry, in the dark, turned his big, battered face to me. "Think about it."

"They're just going to use somebody for—"

"No."

"What then?"

"It's *you*, Paul."

I asked him how he knew that.

"You've been away from the language too long— You already know. It's simple."

"Not for me," I said, but even as I did, something came together powerfully in my thinking. There is no "L" in *any* dialect of Ojibwemowin, and never has been. "Paun. He was going to say, 'Our Paul,' wasn't he. But he made a joke of it."

And the word *Paun?* As the speaker had used it? I had to give him credit—he'd made a triple pun: *puan* meant something like weird foreigner. Or implied what the woman said, laughing behind him, *Pawen,* asleep, or sleepwalking. Or, what Skip King heard, in English, what I'd heard: *Pawn.*

Henry pursed his mouth. "Get it back out," he said.

I did that.

"Play it." Henry nodded, listening to Skip King, and then, when the man started, *Kopadisiwin,*

Henry translated—

"He's so stupid . . . he'll be sure it's about the road. Can't you just see him? All . . . bluster and *doonoo,* bullshit. He'll make all sorts of noise—like a . . . a . . . *badakidoon gookoosh*—a stuck pig—"

The man now made a noise I hadn't understood before, imitated a pig, in some death paroxysm.

Henry lifted his hand, held the recorder to his ear.

"It'll look like his own people . . . *bigishkizh* cut him to pieces. All we gotta . . ." Henry hesitated, then nodded to himself, "all we gotta do is . . . give a couple yanks on his . . . your . . . *nendo-nag*

"He was making a pun again," Henry said. "Pull on your . . . your begger. Yah, that's it," Henry said, and I stopped the player.

I SMOKED ANOTHER cigarette. The recorder, small as it was, felt heavy in my pocket.

"You're dealing with someone who grew up with the language, somewhere in Saskatchewan. But he's an outsider, or is now, anyway. Has been for a long time, you can tell because his . . . his place names are all wrong, but he's still connected. He's . . ." Henry had to consider what he wanted to say. *"Tawag*—his ear. He's been away so long he's losing his ear, but he knows it."

"If you heard him, could you identify him?"

Henry looked at me askance, long-suffering. "But, Nawaji," he said, "this one, he'd never speak the old language around *waibish,"* whites.

"Why?" I said.

"Could look like anybody," Henry said. "I know this, though. He's a mixed blood passing for white, got some Canadian in his speech. But he knows who you are, that's for sure. And he's . . . *gi-inaa*—*chi,"* sharp, "—especially so. But I'll show you how to catch him. Where he messed up. Play that first part."

I ran the tape back, played it.

"Right here," Henry said. "Listen."

"—our Pawn," the man said, and the woman laughed, said what, I still couldn't make out, and the man, laughing, replied, *"Ka, Binishi-angoshkabay!"*

"Stop," Henry said. "You get it?"

"What?"

"Run it back."

We listened to it a third time.

"The woman there," Henry said, "she's saying something about you, and he says, 'No,'—" Henry laughed. " '—*our pawn* . . . of *Binishi*-Angoshka Bay.' "

I bit down on my cigarette, at the end of my patience. Henry slapped my back, amused.

"It's another pun. He's got that old name stuck in his head. *Binishinuk* Bay. Made a pun on it."

"What's the pun mean?"

"Binishi-angoshka—Falls apart. Falls apart Bay."

I grinned, for Henry. "Lovely."

"I never liked that Saskatchewan dialect," Henry said. "Sounds like somebody talkin' through a mouthful of rocks. *Binishinuk.* Just remember that. He won't ever let loose in Anishininiimowin, but he'll trip up. He can't help it. For sure he already has. It's the guy who asks to be taken to places *nobody* ever heard of. Or *did* ask."

Even then, I thought of those surveys in Warroad. But who'd put them together?

"I'll poke around," I said. "It's in the names, right?"

Henry smiled, a real pleasure there. No, even pride. I meant to shake his hand, but embraced him. Old Henry, gone to gray now, and me no longer a boy.

"Yah," he said, "me, too, Nawaji."

TWENTY-ONE

Just before eight, it was already hot out. I sat in my sister's little tomato-soup-red Toyota, waiting for the Rambler's grocery to open, cursing myself for not having gone out to get my truck, the thought of which just made me nervous all over again.

Always, waiting, I made lists, and did that now, taking tugs from my thermos, hot coffee, which had me sweating.

5 lb. bacon, ched chs, chips
6 cs beer/1 lt//20 lb. burg
Marg/20 lb. Chick/SnB/

But it wasn't just the coffee that had me sweating, or the thought of the policemen who'd come after me, and what could have happened out there. It was that when I'd dropped Charlie off at the Pine Point station on the way in, and he'd said he'd call me later, to see if I wanted him back at the lodge, asked if Jimmy could stay with us for the night either way, had some things he wanted to check out at the Rambler's later, I'd told him sure, whatever, trying to be cavalier about it all. Don't trouble yourself trying to get back out, I'd said. I got a handle on it.

Gegibadisid, I thought, writing. Fool.

I shifted in the seat behind the wheel, wrestling with my imagination. I could hardly fit in that crappy little car. It had been Larissa's, just to get into town. She'd given it to me when she went to the university down in the Twin Cities, to St. Kate's. It was so rusted and worn out I didn't dare drive it very far, but it was reassuring, even in daylight now, to slide down in the seat, invisible.

I glanced over to my right, just then amused.

It was one of those ironies that my old friend's, Clark's, Jaguar, the hood open a crack, was parked in front, too, as it had been for weeks.

Dead battery, Dexter'd told me. But hey, it makes the place look classy, don't it?

Then here came Dexter, gray-green pants, chambray shirt, boots, laces undone and slapping around every which way.

AT THE REGISTER, over my boxes, Dexter rang up the groceries.

"Business okay?" I said.

He'd hung that Twins baseball cap over the peak of the coatrack opposite the door, had something for me, but he wasn't in any hurry to say what it was.

"It'd be great if Michaels weren't hanging around nights," Dexter said. "Got half the usual crowd now. Puts a dent in the register, know what I mean?"

I said I did, and we squared all that with the groceries, and I pushed a twenty across the counter, and he slipped it into his pocket, waited, looking out through the front windows at nothing.

"A girl, about fifteen, came in."

"Who?"

"Kinda pretty, wouldn't turn so I could get a good look at her."

I stood at the register, suddenly very clear and sharp. It couldn't be—and anyway, I'd convinced myself by then what I'd seen that night was a young boy.

"Wanted me to promise you got it," Dexter said. "So here—"

He stuffed something into one of the boxes, and I carried the boxes out, then drove to the docks, loaded the launch, and not until I was out on the water, and far from Pine Point, did I stop to see what it was.

I WENT TO the Rambler's that evening. I wanted to run into Charlie, and to try to pick up more on what the girl had passed on to me. I knew there was something crucial in it, it could identify someone. Place someone somewhere. But who? And where?

I waited in Larissa's car, up a dirt road a block or so from the Rambler's, hoping if somebody came after me I'd see him first, watched the action in the parking lot crowd, wild hair and silly fishing hats, women dressed in L.L. Bean gear, or the native look, jean jacket and fancy shirt, loggers in plaid, some going inside, only to bang through the door and outside minutes later, a pitcher and frosty mugs in hand.

What Henry had told me came at me time and again:

Could look like anybody.

But this was a public place, they wouldn't do anything here, I told myself. I was exhausted and trying to rise to it, Never problems, Only solutions, Frank, the old owner of the lodge, had always said.

My eyes fixed on the Rambler's lot, those neon lights buzzing almost obscenely, I drummed out a 49'er on the steering wheel, my hands palsied with fear.

I had that knife on my mind again, what Michaels might do with it, and there was nothing for it.

And there was Gwen on my mind now, too. When I'd left, Gwen was bristling with resentment. I'd told her Charlie had promised to come back out. I'd tried to catch him at the Pine Point station, twist his arm, but he'd gone out on some call, so I'd given Mardine a sideways glance, and she'd frowned, eyes angry slits, on guard again.

It was that frown that had decided bringing Charlie back whatever it took.

Now Vern Stronghold lurched up the road toward the car, not as big as George, but he was walleyed, which gave him a certain unpredictable look, like a dog that could just as easily as not lunge at you from his chain.

"What are you doin' out here," he said, "playing pocket pool?"

"Waiting for somebody."

Vern spun around and kicked the front fender of the car and a piece of trim tinkled off.

"Thanks there, Bruce Lee," I said.

"Rice burner," Vern said, disgusted, then set his hands on my door and put his head in, whiskey breath that'd curdle milk. "You're wasting your time if you're waitin' for Charlie."

I had a trailer hitch ball, about a pound and a half of solid steel, in my palm. My neck had swelled, and my arms felt tight.

If he touched me, I'd put the ball through his forehead.

Vern stepped back from the car, set his hands on his hips and laughed.

"Man, you are one crazy chingus—" weasel.

"So where's Charlie?"

Vern let his head drop back, the stars overhead lovely in the black sky. "He was pokin' around earlier, but he got a phone call and tore outta here like a raped ape. Never seen old lardo move like that."

"He have his lights on?"

Vern looked surprised at that. "No. Why?"

Nothing, I told him.

"They're out to get cha," Vern said, then lurched on up the road, and when I called after him, "Who?" he laughed in the dark, "Somebody."

I started the car, eased up the road, intending to drive back to the island, but then pulled off to the side again. Maybe Michaels, without Charlie to hold him back, would give something up. He'd been working this case for months, after all.

I smoked another cigarette, waiting.

Then, out of the dark, here came Michaels.

HE WAS TALKING to Truman Wheeler in the corner. That corner, where the man who'd come after me two years before, the night of the boat accident, had sat making deals under that very same swarm of Christmas lights. Truman had glared that evening, I'd thought, a coconspirator, though it turned out I'd been wrong about that.

Not so now, I thought.

Wheeler, though, unshaven and rumpled, shot me a look of pure relief. I couldn't make sense of it. He slid a chair around, making a place for me to sit. He'd been pushing this whole road thing all along and I'd assumed he was dirty, wanted to take me down, but, grinning, over a beer, he caught my eye, time and again now, as if I were to save him there.

I wanted to go up to the bar, to talk to Dexter. He'd hung the Twins baseball cap over the jackelope's horns, but I sat beside Truman.

"He pumpin' you for dirt, Truman?" I said.

"We're talking business," Michaels said, "which is of no concern to you."

"If it has anything to do with Eugene's murder, I'd say it has to do with me." I leaned in closer, could smell his aftershave, lime, said to Truman, *"Maamakaaj, izhinaagwad . . . wiisigine,"* I'm surprised, you got this look about you—like you're in pain. Truman took a sip of his beer and smiled. *"Gabaanazha,"* he said, tell him to get off my back.

Michaels gave Truman an irritated stare, then turned to me.

"I don't have to speak the language to get inside," he said.

There was something false in that, or in the way he said it, but I wasn't sure which, so asked,

"You find what you were looking for down in Warroad, at the DOT?"

"Who told you I was at the DOT?"

"Charlie," I lied.

"He said that, did he?" Michaels said.

"If you got that case all wrapped up, the way Charlie tells me you have, what's keeping you here?"

"Official business."

"So, that's it?" I said.

Michaels turned in his chair, his back to me. When it became apparent I wasn't leaving the table, he nodded to Wheeler, said,

"I'll see you around."

He stood and headed toward the door. And that's when it struck me to do it. Mess with him. Truly. I reached into my pocket, carefully got out the leather sachet the girl had left.

Under the dim light, I removed the fetish inside, held it out in my palm.

"This mean anything to you?" I said, in a voice so sharp it cut right through that place.

Michaels glanced back over his shoulder, a near convulsion twisting his face; he blinked once, but it was enough. He bent closer, between the door and table, his face first coloring, then livid.

The fetish glowed, as if alive. A rosette that had been on a belt, or a necklace—I knew from the work my mother had done. About the size of a silver dollar, one side beaded yellow and black, the other red and blue. On each side, dividing the two colors, in black seed beads, a feather.

It was a hundred years old, or older, and it felt hot in my palm.

"So?" I said.

"No idea," Michaels said, and with a quick toss of his shoulders, he went out.

It wasn't what I'd expected, and it sent a buzz all the way through me. Fury that quiet, I knew, meant business. Michaels couldn't hide that, how his face had given him away, even in that poor light.

Flashing that rosette around had tripped some switch in him. But whose was it, and where had it come from, before the girl had dropped it off?

"Do *you* know what this is?" I said to Truman.

Truman, across the table, still had his eyes on the door, but the artery in his neck was throbbing, his lip curled the slightest, almost a sneer. Then Truman swung around, tossed his head back and laughed, so hard his belly shook.

"Hell no," he said. "But thanks for tossin' that Michaels off. You sure did it!" he said, and slapping my shoulder, laughed again.

Truman's cronies, Isaac Kills in Sight and Jim Bailey came out the dark, filled the booth with a kind of animation I dreaded. *Memangishe!* Truman said, glancing at the door, where Michaels had just ducked out. What an ass! All of them laughed, Truman tossing his hand up, little finger and thumb out, so that Dexter, at the bar, sent over two pitchers.

"Sure looked serious to me!" I laughed, reminded of the man who'd been with Michaels earlier, who'd come after me up from Warroad.

"Doesn't that Michaels just kill ya?" Truman said, pouring from the pitcher, spilling in my direction, so I jumped up, knocking my chair over.

They meant for me to leave, which I was all too happy to oblige them.

I SLIPPED A bill across the bar and Dexter snatched it up. He went down the length of the bar, pouring drinks, hawking peanuts and popcorn, and cigarettes, sharing a joke, so that when he came by, passed me, once, twice, and finally a third time, I thought he'd ripped me off.

So I waited there, fuming.

Red, green, blue lights. That Santa in the corner, Truman behind me, laughing. I nursed another 7UP, followed the game on Dexter's TV.

The Twins were sinking themselves further in the American League, bright green field, blue and red hats. It was so loud in there, I couldn't hear myself think. The dancing crowd had come in. I was sure Dexter was waiting to pull one of his stunts. Kill the works—lights, music, the crazy Santa—so that it would take a minute or two for the roar to reach full tilt again, in which time, when the music was going again, he'd come over and give me another bottle and say what he had to say, and, if I knew Dexter, he'd expect me to have another bill to pass across.

But he didn't do that. He stayed at the end opposite. And, what I did then was, give the place a hard look in that mirror. A shudder ran up my back. I always felt it before I knew what it was about.

Michaels was back, talking with some loggers in a far, dark corner.

Dexter wasn't coming over, and wouldn't now. I drank from my bottle of 7UP, set it down, and that's when I realized what Dexter had done.

The bottle had not come down with that solid glass on wood feel. He'd put a coaster under it, which stuck to the bottle. I slid the coaster off the bottle and into my shirt pocket.

TWENTY-TWO

Outside, in Larissa's car, I studied the coaster.

I realize now, I shouldn't have done that. Held it up in the moonlight, wanting to see what was on it. I couldn't wait, couldn't see inside the car—the dome light was burned out, and so were the instrument lights—so held it under the windshield, trying to make out what Dexter had penned there.

They must have seen it on my face.

All that I gave away, sitting in the car, a block back of the Rambler's.

I was almost ecstatic.

I had to find Charlie, I thought. But then, I wondered what had taken him away from the Rambler's like that, why he hadn't used his lights.

Thinking where Charlie might be, I tore that coaster into pieces, absentmindedly tossed the whole mess on the passenger side seat. A thought went through my head. Pick it up. But who could make sense of it, much less torn into pieces?

And even if they could, would they understand?

Michaels came out the door. Cocked his head to one side, motioned me over. I reluctantly got out of the car, and in the parking lot, was drawn into some nonsense talk about Eugene's rifles. How many he'd had, what caliber, what manufacture. How many had been on the wall that afternoon Charlie and I had gone over to his place.

It just went on and on.

Still, even then, it couldn't break my elation.

ON THE ROAD back up to the Inlet, to the launch, I reveled at my good fortune. I tried the radio, Larry King on AM was all I could get, something about the stock market, so turned it off. Put my arm out the window, hummed "The Girl from Impanema." I steered my car up the sandy road, the long way around to the government docks, a car behind me, which followed for a time, then turned off to the side. It was after one o'clock, and there was nothing to it, that car— somebody calling it a night I thought.

I made a wing of my hand, the night air cool. I had time. I'd pack, take the south route through Sabaskong Bay, then motor north to Whitefish, and find Napoleon in the Sioux Narrows. I had a whole day on them, at least. Could leave the boat at the Narrows, get a car from family on the road out to 71.

Free and clear—with Napoleon.

Have Charlie meet me, later, at the Pine Point station. Safe.

I felt a kind of grace there, a resurrection, all things coming to an end I could live with. My hand slung over the wheel, I congratulated myself on getting the dirt on Napoleon, and cutting free like this, everything on my side. And Charlie? I'd bring him up to speed when we got back, fill him in on what I got, first, from Napoleon.

All that was a happy lie, I know that now.

(Why, otherwise, hadn't I thought to take Charlie with me? I was worried he was caught up in it, maneuvering around the way he was, not the usual lights and cop procedure—or maybe it was

Michaels putting the squeeze on Charlie, but either way, I wanted some distance when I found out just who'd been out on the Angle that night.)

I passed Oshogay's Gas, at the intersection of Highway 525, there bright, blue-white floodlights, and cyclone fence. Just for seconds, the car lit up, as if by lightning, and went dark again.

I jammed on the brakes, the car skidding to a stop. In the dark I scrabbled at the passenger seat, then thrust my hands down to the floor, the carpet coarse and dirty, let go a relieved breath—almost.

Felt the coaster pieces under my hands.

I'd left the coaster pieces on the seat. But had they slid off the seat when I'd braked?

I told myself they had. But what had I seen then, when I passed Oshogay's?

They *hadn't* been on the seat then—or had they?

(And could it have been Michaels, I thought, pulling that old ruse, distracting me with that nonsense at the Rambler's? No. It was unlikely anyone had touched them. *Impossible,* I told myself.)

Still, I got that little car moving up the road, the wheels out of round and the steering wheel shuddering so badly I could hardly hang on to it. Slid to a stop at the government docks and had the launch up and running and full throttle took it east.

AT THE LODGE, Mardine was on the front stoop, overlooking the lake. She'd thrown on a sweater over her gingham dress. She was sipping a cup of coffee, even though it was early morning now.

"Anybody come in?" I said. I was breathing hard from having come up the hill.

"Somebody in a real rush came close," she said, "but went on around north."

I tried to look blank about that, turned one direction and then the other, almost beside myself with the mistake I'd made. I had to pack, get food, get the boat packed. Mardine was watching me. She was a big woman, and when she folded her arms over her chest, the red wool of her sweater bulged up, giving the appearance she might explode.

"You expecting someone?"

"Maybe Charlie."

"*Ikwabe,*" she said, and patted the wooden plank beside her. Sit beside. I did that.

"Look at you," she said, eyeing me down the end of her nose. "You'd like me to think you've got your shoulders all rucked up and hands all clenched from the chill on the lake. You can barely sit still and your eyes are set on what you think's out there, all owlish and skittery. I can read you like bird sign."

"I didn't pay attention," I said. "I assumed things, goddammit."

Mardine tugged her sweater over her shoulders.

"They've got about an hour or so on you."

I was angry now, mostly at myself, but turned it on Mardine.

"So *why* are you making me sit here?" I said.

Mardine smiled that old smile of hers.

"Because," she said, "I know the only way you can beat them over there."

TWENTY-THREE

packed the canoe. Two, four-gallon tanks of gasoline at the rear, up front, a Duluth pack, in it, a rainproof nylon tarp, food, compass, maps, heavy boots, and rain gear. In the bottom of the canoe, in canvas bags, I stowed my short-barreled Remington twelve gauge, and shells—buckshot and deer slugs. When it was all done, I lit a cigarette.

I'd have taken my automatic, but it hadn't been in the gun case. I knew who had it, though.

Mardine. She came down through the birch along the water, then up the dock.

"You'll explain this to Gwen," I said.

"*Memendige,*" she said, and nodded. Of course.

I paddled a good part of an hour. Passed the buoys, then Snow-bank, finally eased the small three-horsepower Seahorse down over the transom and started it, even that tiny, well-muffled engine making a pillow of sound on the water, a rattling chutter.

I wanted a breeze, some chop that would cut the sound, make it impossible to locate me. But I didn't get that. Hour after hour, the air on the water was more dense. My jacket first glistened, then was sopping wet, so that I shook with cold, and I ached for a cigarette, and finally did smoke, hunched down, my hand cupped over the end.

Island after island loomed up in the water, grew higher, and darker, the silhouettes of trees high and black on the cobalt, star-studded sky.

I was following the tail of Ojeeg Anuung, The Fisher, or the Big Dipper. South, southeast.

North of me was the Aulneau Peninsula, but the shore was so varied it was easy to mistake parts of it for smaller islands, and each time I passed another offshoot of it, my heart sank with what I worried was the mistake that would end things.

And I had barely enough gas. The engine puttered, the throttle shaking in my hand. The canoe would hydroplane, but when it did, it became unsteady, and there were deadheads, floating stumps, to think about, and rock ledges that could break off the engine's propeller. At one point, the engine slowed, and I cursed it, then lifted the gearcase and propeller out the water, which was now tangled in weeds. Clouds as dense and dark as lead slid over the lake from the north.

I pushed a headwind. It wasn't much more than fifty degrees down on the water, and I was bone chilled, and lit another cigarette.

Then I passed through a high, block-wide chute of columnar granite, cedars growing right out of the cracks in it, and the water dipping down over a ridge, which emptied on the other side into a lake, so wide across I couldn't see the shore.

This was the route they did not take, which bought me an hour, or even two.

I cut the engine and coasted. The water was flat, and calm, and now I could see, through the steam on the water, another chute up ahead.

I opened the bag Mardine had given me. Almonds. Roast beef. A piece of dense bread. I ate it in handfuls, the boat gliding in a light northwest wind. The northern lights danced neon red and green and blue overhead. I lifted my thermos. Drank the hot, bitter coffee.

Mardine. Triple strength. My heart jumped at it, I felt sharper.

If I were to get lost, truly lost, it would be up ahead.

Even back of it, I could see, into the distance, layer after layer of tree, point, water that ended in another smaller peninsula, going back into fold of green after fold of green until the low cloud cover became a wall of gray fog.

I'D COME TO the end of the water. I'd followed Mardine's directions, but with the ground fog, and counting the islands in, ten, fifteen, and finally turning hard left, and guiding due north, I couldn't tell for sure where I'd cut into the Aulneau Peninsula.

Mardine had said there would be a rock spire, with petroglyphs on it, just offshore.

And then I found it, and the opening up the high and lichen-covered stone face back of it. Here there was a path up through the trees. I told myself it was too dark to see the petroglyphs so didn't look.

I rucked everything onto shore, then turned the Duluth pack inside out. I carefully arranged the still full gas tank so the cap was on the high end and the tank couldn't spill, and rode flat against my back.

I slung the tiny engine on a nylon strap across my chest, my shotgun opposite.

Then I reached down for the canoe, and bending my knees, in one motion swung the canoe over my head and down, so the carry pads set squarely on my shoulders.

I straightened my legs. My right hip began to burn right there.

I was carrying about a hundred pounds.

I stretched my right arm out along the gunnel to balance the canoe, then tilting the canoe back, climbed up that narrow path through the rocks, a hundred fifty feet up to the trees, and there took the path east.

THE GAS SLOSHED in the tank on my back. My legs quivered at the load, but I was making good time. The portage was a mile or so long, and only at one point did I slip and smack my forehead on the seat stay so badly I saw stars.

It seemed I had that canoe on my back for an eternity. I told myself it was just the weight.

I checked my watch finally. It was after four now.

I'd taken the earlier spur, I realized with pure dread, and had just cut in where I should have started.

FASTER. I HAD to move faster. I nearly ran, my lungs heaving. I did run. It was only a mile more, and I could catch up. I was jogging now, block after block, the path only a foot wide, and just when I'd settled into a rhythm that kept the engine on my chest and the gas on my back slapping at me in a way that didn't throw my balance off, I fell.

I pitched, with that gear, over something, and fell what seemed forever, to smack down hard on the bottom of the canoe.

The canoe absorbed my fall, but the keel cut my cheek.

On my back, I could see the clouds passing overhead, trees, growing up the granite face of the shoreline I'd fallen down.

I had to have fallen thirty feet.

The canoe had a dent in the bottom the size of my chest. I smelled water. I carefully lifted myself from the canoe. Stretched one arm, and then the other. Stood and brushed my hands down my legs.

I turned around.

Water. Lovely, blue-black water. And only a few bruises for it.

THE CANOE WAS pulling badly to the left, but I was happy. I motored up the east shore. Here were more inlets, but I was looking now for one that opened wide to the east, had a bridge spanning it, where Highway 71 went over.

Sioux Narrows. Named for an ambush that had taken place at that spot more than a century before. I checked my watch, I had no time at all.

I knew the place Napoleon had run to, could find it now without the stars.

I just had to get there.

LONG AGO, THERE'D been a logging camp in the woods of Sioux Narrows. As a boy, I'd played there with Clark, or with Al Eagle, and one night Gilby and I had spent the night there, in that interminable, lustful, and melancholy period we'd been together.

There were mills like Stump's all over the lake, but Stump's only we Indians knew about, or visited, for any number of reasons.

Dickerson's Mill was its other name.

We knew it as Stump's Place, though—*Gish'kanakad abinass,* what Dexter had written on the coaster.

My father had worked there, and so had Mardine's, Dexter's, and Al Eagle's, in the late 1940s, right after they'd come back from the war. The manager of Dickerson's had been an unusually short, heavy man, with a disproportionately large temper, a man all the loggers had come to hate.

His nickname, of course, had been Stump, and long after he'd died, and the place had gone to rot, it was still called Stump's Place, but only by the elders who'd worked there, and then it seemed the name had been forgotten altogether.

I wondered, thinking about that, if the names the surveyors had used on that preliminary map I'd seen in Warroad were no more than what we had here at Stump's, just old names, long forgotten. Just so much legend.

Now, coming across the lake, all that marked the mill was a

broad opening in the trees near shore where the logs had been hauled down on horse-driven wagons.

I lay my shotgun across my knees. Fed five deer slugs into it. Stopped the engine, a mile back at least, even though I was down-wind. I coasted across the glass smooth, blue water.

Listened—the lake was too beautiful just then—but for what?

A mallard burst out of rushes near shore, wings whistling as it went by overheard.

I nearly jumped out of the canoe at it.

I slipped the paddle into the water, drew it back and flared it. Glided across the lake, knowing, if someone were waiting, I would never hear the shot before it hit me. That echo you hear with a high-powered rifle is a tiny, sonic boom, the bullet far out in front of it, in that equation, acceleration the deciding factor. Insubstantial mass, but at that velocity, a 30.06, even at a thousand feet, would blow a ragged hole the size of a fist in just about anything.

So I came across the lake, feeling like one of those yellow, bob-bing ducks in a shooting gallery.

Each stroke took me closer. Which was no relief, whatsoever.

I STRODE UP the old skidbed, my legs threatening to collapse under me.

Just up through the trees was the dark outline of the old mill. High, rough-wooded sides and broken windows, machinery humped around it, band saws, and lathes, and routers, and old and massive engines to drive them.

My foot slipped off something slick, and there was a glassy clat-ter, and I was sure someone bolted out the back, but ran so quickly I thought it must be deer, drinking from the pond off to the side.

There was that definitive, *sher-clack,* of a bolt action rifle behind me.

I froze there, my shotgun hanging from my hand, useless.

I set it on the ground, and slowly turned.

Black silhouette, behind him the lake liquid with early morning pink and rose, my heart beating like crazy, I saw a flash of light, heard a report and felt myself kicked back, but only in that instant. And when that didn't happen, and he didn't move—no, he was looking at me, big-eyed and baleful, I said,

"Napoleon. It's me, Paul."

He fell to his knees right there. Put his hand to his forehead, and just let go.

TWENTY-FOUR

We went into the old mill, the roof rotted, twenty-five, thirty feet overhead, enormous, rough-hewn beams bracing the walls, remnants of Minnesota's first-stand pine. Pigeons were just beginning to rustle in the morning light, the bats swinging back in. While he ate what I'd brought along, I looked around for signs that the girl had been with him.

Against one wall was an oversize sleeping bag. He'd wired tin cans around the perimeter and through the trees and across the path in. Still, he was so jittery he could barely get the food in his mouth, the torn and soil-blackened sleeve of his denim shirt getting in the way every time he reached into the bag of almonds.

By one of the largest support beams, he'd set up a Coleman one-burner stove. He'd thought he'd fish, but he hadn't done that. He'd eaten a few of the pigeons. But then I saw what the problem was. He'd run out of gas and he'd been too afraid to start a fire.

I kicked around on the floor, pigeon droppings, bat guano.

The place was thick with the smell of time, exactly what we didn't have. Ghosts were yammering. Saws turned. Men drank. Cars from the twenties to the late forties pulled into the yard. Seventy men worked here. A forty-foot launch docked to ease the packets of logs, each log three feet or larger in diameter, out onto Whitefish Bay.

I found an elastic hair band. Yellow, with a rhinestone on it.

"This hers?" I asked.

Napoleon stared into the floor, wrestling with something.

"They're out there," I said. "We're gonna have to get moving."

"I *shot* that guy," Napoleon said.

I didn't want him to get into it right then, they'd be coming any time now, but I had to ask.

"Eugene—"

"No," he said, craning his head up to look at me, just then boy-ish, and stunned at himself. "One of the others. The one who drowned. I *shot* him, closer than you are to me. We snuck in there to steal the engine off the compacter they had, maybe lift something else. A truck or something, but Eugene was there, arguing with some-body. They were telling Eugene how much money was in it, and this guy said they'd all be rich if nobody let it out. Old Eugene, he said he didn't give a shit.

"It got ugly, this guy knocking Eugene down and kicking him, and the one in charge, shouting in some blanketass dialect, one I didn't even know. All nasalized and run together."

"Could you identify him?" I asked.

"It was dark. I couldn't see him, the one talking. Only, Eugene knew what he was saying, and Elmer did, too, and that's when I saw it was all going to go the way it did. By the way Elmer got spooked, and just like that, he walks right in there, shoutin'.

"The one doing the talking, he sees Elmer, doesn't so much as take a breath, turns and point-blank shoots Eugene in the chest—just like that, Eugene kinda kneeling there, holding his chest.

"The one who'd been kickin' Eugene, he came on fast, and I knew that he meant to kill El and me. I didn't think, just ran. I mean, shit. We took off running down the path to the lake, and Eugene's makin' all kinds of noise, and that guy just kept comin' on, so I stopped there . . . lifted the rifle I'd brought, but he just kept on . . .

"and I *shot* him."

Remembering, Napoleon's eyes went wide. We had to go, but I couldn't cut him off.

"And he *got up,* just kept on comin', blood all over—and we ran downshore, and Elmer took Eugene's boat—

"I made him take it, it was faster, and I started the other boat, the one they'd come in, and sent it off, out onto the lake, nobody in it, so the blond guy, would go after, using our crummy Lund, and he did, too—

"Only, when he saw I wasn't in it, he spun around back into shore, came up the creekbed after me. I was running, and running, but he followed, just *kept coming on."*

His mouth twisted, Napoleon looked up at me, blinking at it.

"I wanted to go back for Eugene, I just *couldn't* leave him like that, the guy stayed behind was hurtin' him something awful, and Eugene shouted—he was tryin' not to, and, god *dammit all,* it just made it all the worse.

"I couldn't outrun that guy after me in the trees, just *couldn't.* So I went upshore, just back of the bluffs, fell hard and lost my rifle. It was dark, and there wasn't time for anything, I was on my hands and knees, in the brush, and he was breathing hard, but he couldn't see me.

"I was trying to find that rifle. And he was closer, and coughing, and just when he leaned in right over me, I had my hand on it, and put the barrel right under his chin, pulled the trigger and god—something hit me, and I thought it was him, until nothing happened, and when I looked, I saw he'd gone right off the Spire, into the lake."

I knew what had hit him, but wasn't about to say so, not right then.

"So what'd you do?" I asked.

"The boat was on shore, where he'd left it," Napoleon said. "That's how I got away, used our Lund to get back to the lodge, tied it to the backside dock, right where we'd got it, so you wouldn't see we'd been out."

"Elmer—"

"Elmer *didn't do anything* but run."

Napoleon, staring into the near dark, lifted a hand, his fingers splayed, made a fist.

"It's that . . . guy speaks Nakawiwin or whatever the hell it is, and who knows who else. I mean, they had it all out there. Lasers, GPS, some kind of thing to make core samples. We *saw* all that, comin' into that clearing where Eugene was givin' them the what for."

"My knife," I said.

"I told Elmer not to mess with that goddamn knife. Told me it just showed up in his tacklebox and his knife there broken, thought I'd done it, so thanks me, and I told him don't fuckin' thank me. Put that thing back where you got it, but sure as shit he loses it."

"Out fishing."

"Nah—it was the afternoon that cop showed up, pokin' around and givin' us shit." I knew he meant Michaels. "That knife never made it off the fuckin' island."

"That cop, he talked to you?"

Napoleon laughed, a sharp, hard laugh. I was already in the door to go, we'd leave everything, take a fireroad I knew down to 71.

"He talked *at* us. Hugh told him to get the hell out unless he had something to say."

I swung my shotgun over my shoulder, gave Napoleon a hand-up, and moved off toward the fireroad, hidden in heavy sumac, then stopped, looked back.

"So what were you doing at the Rambler's that afternoon, after?" I said.

Napoleon had picked his gun up, but it hung from his hand, loosely, the barrel resting on the rocky ground. He turned his head away.

"Before I took the boat back, I went after Eugene. Eugene was *nowhere*, the other guy, he was gone, too. But I found a— I didn't know *what* it was."

I craned my head around, almost afraid to say it. It wasn't possible, was it?

"A fetish, a red and black one."

His eyes went wide. *"You* have it."

I said I did. "So why the Rambler's? Why were you there that afternoon with Elmer?"

I turned my watch up, wanting to get Napoleon moving, but he didn't take the hint.

"I had to find somebody who'd know what it was," he said, looking up sharply, "but wouldn't blather it all over the place we'd found it. El's mother said she'd come out, like she was havin' lunch or something, used to do beadwork.

"She took one look at it, sent El off in her station wagon, and me and my buddies from Our Lady walked Edna to my car and drove her to a friend's."

So it was Edna I'd seen that afternoon at the Rambler's. Napoleon raked his hand through his hair, pulled roughly at it, hurt, just a boy all over again.

"We didn't mean any harm," Napoleon said, almost pleading. *"I* didn't—and Eugene tryin' not to cry out. They shouldn't've done that, what they did. It was them that did El, wasn't it—he *wasn't* any dumbass huffer!

"Why didn't you look into it, why didn't you *do* something? You had Eugene's boat there and all, and then you even got the fetish that guy must've been carrying, that he lost out there."

I reached for his arm, swung him through the sumac onto the fireroad, in front of me. Up that old road, at a near run, trees reaching cathedral high over us in the rose light, I said the only thing I could.

"I *am* doing something, Napoleon. Believe me."

BACK OF A breakfast place with a huge fiberglass walleye on the roof, I hot-wired a car. We'd wasted too much time at Stump's to go to my cousin's, and I'd heard a boat out on the lake behind us.

We drove south, toward Nestor Falls, doing a good clip. A Cadillac, the car was warm and quiet, smelled pleasantly of cigar smoke and leather. A shriner's scimitar was fixed on the dashboard, like a gold quarter moon.

"I don't want you getting any ideas," I told Napoleon.

"Oh, I know all about you," he said.

"What do you know?"

"I know you shouldn't be tellin' me not to do things you did plenty yourself at my age."

I had to think about that, glancing now and then in the rearview mirror.

Up ahead, a car was approaching, its lights on. When I saw it was a police car, I bent over the seat, scrabbled in the back, for the hats I'd seen there, but came up with a blue-haired wig, and a straw boater with a red white and blue band around the brim.

I shoved on the boater and, hunched over the wheel, handed Napoleon the wig.

"I'm not gonna—"

"Put it on," I said.

Napoleon did that, held the map on the seat over his face. When the police cruiser got closer, I lifted my index finger from the steering wheel, and the RCMP flashed his lights in return.

The cruiser fwopped by in a quick wash of air, and I reached over and held Napoleon's hand down. He looked at me in that wig, and his face lit up, and he was laughing, and I laughed at him.

"How does she drive, *Cap?*" he said.

"Like herding a goddamn gaggle of geese down the highway, *Maybelle,*" I shot back.

Napoleon laughed, even harder, and then he started to choke, and hiccup, threw the wig off his head, gritting his teeth and breathing through his nose.

He turned his head away, watched the road off to the right, all over again, distraught. I gave him a minute, set the boater on the seat in back.

"So tell me what Elmer's mother said when you showed her the fetish."

Napoleon got even smaller, it seemed. "She told us *never* to show it to *anybody*—not for any reason, not ever."

"Why?"

He set his forehead against the glass, a fog of condensation forming from his breath.

"It's an Okitsita fetish," he said. "They're mercenaries—used to be anyway—killed people and stuff. She said we showed it around, whoever lost it would show up, and it wouldn't be to give a reward. I told her, they pretty much had to know we had it already. Or El did, anyway. The way he'd gone in there they'd gotten a good look at him. She told us to run, right then. I didn't believe her. She was always kinda paranoid, like El's old man was out to get her and all kinds of shit. So El took her car, was supposed to meet me back at the lodge, but got spooked—bolted. How could I know the dumb kid pulled that stunt with Hugh, he'd packed his stuff up already?"

He coughed, hunched up against the window, miserable.

"Jesus, I *got El killed,* didn't I?"

"It wasn't your fault. Don't think that for a second," I said. But I had an idea of how he felt.

I thought of the girl, dropping the fetish off at the Rambler's.

I thought to ask about her, and just then, Napoleon might have told me. He was barely holding it all in, head pressed against the glass, sucking in short breaths through his teeth, but it just wasn't in me to do it.

LATER, HE TOLD me the girl was somebody his mother'd put to the job. By then he had his story straight, and there was no poking holes in it, or anything else we'd agreed on in that car, for one, we'd tell no one Napoleon knew about the fetish.

Even if someone like Michaels came prying.

I STOPPED THE car back of a fishery, an aluminum-sided affair bordered by breeding pools behind cyclone fence, where my uncle, Victor, worked, opened the passenger door for Napoleon.

"Let's go," I said.

Victor came around to the car, half again my size, with a face only George Stronghold's could rival, jaw like an anchor, eyes that positively burned. He smiled to see me, then took in Napoleon.

"What is it?" Victor said.

I told him we needed a boat ride over to the lodge, something to cover the kid with, could he report the car stolen when he got back?

"A tarp do it?" He didn't ask anything else, and I didn't explain.

TWENTY-FIVE

Back at the lodge, Charlie still hadn't so much as called. I tried to reach him at the Pine Point station, but only got the girl, Darilyn.

Charlie had left a message on the machine that he'd be out all day, she said.

I put Napoleon in the cabin with Charlie's son.

When they came in for dinner that evening, Jimmy was sporting a black eye, and Napoleon had his hands balled into fists at his sides, walking like some bantam middleweight on his toes.

Still, they sat at the same table across from each other. Ate like two civilized kids.

I watched, as they went back for seconds, smoking, now my third cigarette, the nub of the second smouldering in the ashtray by my elbow.

We only had hours of daylight. I'd meant to get hold of Charlie and drive Napoleon down to Bemidji. I put out my cigarette, talked to the other guests, the Engles, the Lavenders, the Hughes and Elkins, having dinner. Judy Elkin asked me if the Minnesota Senate decision on development had affected us, here on the lake. I told her no, and left it at that. Hugh was waiting tables. He'd taken over and was very nearly flawlessly giving the appearance of calm.

When he passed me by the desk, where I was using the phone, he said, "End of this month, I quit."

I always gave staff a bonus, which was why, if they made it through the middle, they'd stay on the last few weeks: it paid to do it.

"Fine," I said.

All afternoon, I'd been making calls to that school out east, trying to get hold of a professor I'd studied under.

I had some vague notion gnawing at me and wanted to see if he could make something of it.

I went into the kitchen. Mardine was at the stove, Gwen playing with Claire, Claire laughing when Gwen hid her head under her arm, then showed her face again, smiling.

I sat with them, a plate on my knees. Took Claire, fed her, and when she slept, left her with Mardine, who put her in a hammock she'd made out of a blanket, which she strung right across the back of the kitchen, like a huge, green garland.

I reached for Gwen's hand. With a gesture, languidly setting her hand on the small of her back, and bending closer to the recipe she'd been reading, she told me where things stood between us.

"Gwen," I said, almost unable to get it out, and when that moment passed, I felt a kind of hunger.

I turned to go, and Gwen caught me in the doorway, one of those peculiar embraces, her hand pressed over my heart, holding us separate, but together.

"If you don't intend to take care of things here on the island, don't make promises," she said. "Otherwise—"

"Have to kill me to get me away now," I said, and went out.

Still later, I paced in the lodge, the guests all in their cabins. Charlie still hadn't called back. We needed him, and where was he? I'd sit up all night with Mardine, and god so help me, I'd shoot anyone that stepped foot on the island who didn't belong on it. In the kitchen, I pumped up deer slugs in the Remington.

I went down to the cabin, where Gwen was in her nightgown, and Claire was already asleep in her crib.

"They wouldn't try anything here," she said, "do you think?"

I told her I wasn't going to take any chances, now that Napoleon was with us.

I SAT ON the porch, until every light went out, and the cabins were quiet. I smoked a cigarette, then another. A blanket of quiet as dense as wool made me sleepy, there with the gun across my knees.

Hours passed, and it was early morning.

I told myself, no one had seen me come in with Napoleon. I saw myself there as ridiculous. I wouldn't sleep all night.

So why not do something?

I SKIDDED DOWN the hillside to the boathouse, paused at the threshold, the door open, reached inside for the light switch, and snapped it up.

Nothing. Shit, I thought.

I wondered if I should go up to the lodge and check the fuses. The new appliances used almost more power than our old, cloth-covered wire could handle, and the fuses were forever burning out. I'd warned Mardine, I couldn't think how many times, not to have more than two or three on at a time, but there it was.

I stepped inside. I'd light the Coleman lantern, and work by that, I thought. I heard a sliding, abrasive sound. It occurred to me some-one was in there, even as I was kicked from behind, so hard that I was carried through the door and banged into the tank with Hugh's engine on it.

Now a flashlight came on, but from the far corner, so I was blinded.

I could only see them in silhouette.

"I wouldn't run," the bigger of the two said. "There's someone up by your cabin."

I was suddenly and painfully awake.

"What's it all about?" I said.

"Why don't you tell us?"

I held my forearm over my face, trying to get my eyes to adjust to the light. Someone sniffed, loudly, and I thought there had to be a third person, behind me, and I was right about that, but not about what made me think it.

"What's to say I don't yell?"

"Try it and see," the taller said.

"What do you want?"

"What did Stanley LaShapelle have to say?"

That surprised me: I thought they'd grill me about Napoleon, who was, even then, hidden away in the attic of one of the cabins up-shore.

"Who are you, anyway?" I said.

If I turned my eyes from the light I could make them out better. One was a head taller than the other, held a handgun at his hip.

"It would be a whole lot easier for everybody concerned if you just told us what LaShapelle had to say."

I needed time, even seconds. I had to think, but my mind was a hot blank—I had nothing, or did I?

"You can fuck yourself," I said.

"So you're not going to be reasonable," the tall one said.

"Why not just shoot me?"

"You know why not."

"You tell me why not."

"We're not here to argue with you, Mr. Na'joi'se."

They hadn't so much as touched me. I wondered why? The answer that came to me caught my breath up. And the short one, he'd come out into the light now, so I could see him, but they wanted that, his face a patchwork of grafts, badly sewn together.

"So—where is the kid?" he said.

"Where's who?"

"You tell us," the tall one said, "or we'll go through your cabin—maybe the wifey knows? Or your little girl."

I felt my face heat, my eyes adjust to the light, and something certain was, even then, taking shape in that part of me that acts.

"Take off your boots," the tall one said.

"No," I said.

"Think of me as your 'Tall Friend,'" the big one said. "I'm going to make it painless. Take off your boots."

"No," I said.

"You could tell us, and we'd go away."

"Tell you what?"

"You know very well what it's all about."

"Right."

"He told you everything, didn't he. Stanley. We got it on tape."

Stanley. George could have told me any fucking old thing. I needed just a little more time, I thought, all that in me calculating.

"He said there was this casino deal, and old money coming in and—"

"Larry," my Tall Friend said, "help Mr. Na'joi'se make up his mind."

The short one stepped closer; he had wide-spaced, tiny eyes, a double chin. His fingers were thick and muscular, his fingernails blue underneath.

There was something in their calm, their patience, that nearly got to me.

"The boots," the tall one said. "Off."

"You can shove my boots up your ass," I said. I knew they wouldn't touch me. Not hit me, anyway. They wouldn't want marks on my body.

"You're sure now," my Tall Friend said.

I said, "You can—"

An arm, thick as my thigh, came up under my right armpit, the hand reaching across the back of my neck, pulling my head to the side so sharply a blackness swam up at me. He pinned my left hand under my shoulder.

"Don't break his arm. Just give him *more* . . . you know," my Tall Friend said.

I thought my joints would split. I was twisted so my leg went off under the bench and boxes of parts there, hit something soft. I yanked my foot back. Just then, I realized what had made that snuffling earlier.

"You've had a hip problem the last few years, haven't you," my Tall Friend said. "Since the accident."

I had my right leg pulled up and my foot bent in, the pain so bad, I cried out,

"God!"

"Just say 'stop,' and we'll stop," my Tall Friend said.

They worked on me a bit more, but one at a time, and all the while I waited. Finally, I was about to vomit, when my Tall Friend said,

"Stop! We don't want that. They'll get the wrong idea."

"It's impossible," the shorter said.

"Take his boots off, Larry."

The short one, milk-pale skin and those puckered grafts, got in front of me, reached for my right boot and I kicked him so hard he fell on his back, the man behind me twisting my arm so violently I thought, surely, he'd break it.

Then my Tall Friend squeezed my neck between his hands, until I started to black out, and like that he sat on my thighs, pinning me there.

I felt my boot come off, saw, off to the side, the short man reach into his shirt pocket and pull out a syringe with a green cap.

He carefully filled the syringe from an ampule, bubbles rising in some clear liquid.

My Tall Friend smiled in my face. There was spearmint on his breath.

"Hey, lover," he said, "you gonna tell us now, or will we have to ask the wifey and kid after you're down?"

The short man stooped to jab the needle into my foot.

"What do you say?"

Here it was, last call. My heart was racing, my whole body tight as a fist. I put my face right into my Tall Friend's, said clearly, and loudly—

"BEAUTIFUL."

My Tall Friend grinned, on his face pure, amused contempt.

Beautiful burst out from under the bench, one hundred pounds of snarling, sharp-toothed bulldog fury.

My Tall Friend kicked back, eyes wide, knocked over the short one. The man behind me let go to hammer at Beautiful, who'd gotten her teeth into his leg and was shaking him with such rage he stumbled, fell into the dark where I couldn't see him.

I leaped up. Reached for Hugh's engine, swung it out of the tank, yanked the rope starter, even as the light hit me. The engine roared to life, razor-sharp brass propeller spinning, an arm-length blue flame shooting out the exhaust pipe. The short one jabbed at me with that syringe. I grazed him with the propeller, ran it up his shoulder, a scream, spray of blood. My Tall Friend caught him at the waist, hurled him through the boathouse door and went after with the light, out onto the dock.

I spun around. The big man who'd been behind me was hiding in one of the corners—behind the life preservers, or by the bait tank, I couldn't tell where.

I turned the engine in a wide arc. The blue flame coming out of the exhaust lit the room, the walls blood spattered and flickering. Beautiful, teeth barred, pulled herself across the floor, lunged toward the bait tank. I ran around it with the engine, and the big man jumped up, bolted for the door.

I went after him outside. He ran for all he was worth up the dock. A boat burbled at the end and he arched his back sprinting for it.

I gave one last jab, caught him between the shoulder blades, even as he leaped, the boat pulling away, and I heaved the engine after, spinning full throttle, so it landed in the boat and they nearly went over the side, the biggest knocking it into the lake.

The boat lifted powerfully out of the water, and hydroplaning, veered to the left.

I stood there in the moonlight, shaking, one foot bare, the pain in my hip so intense I held my stomach, then paced up and back, until the nausea subsided. I was laughing, then crying, or was it still laughing? I was alive, we were all still here.

The moon rode silver and bright in the dark sky. A breeze whooshed in the pines.

They hadn't hurt Gwen or Claire.

But at that thought, I charged up the bank to the cabin. It was dark, but I could see Gwen through the window, sleeping in her blue gown.

She'd kicked off the sheets, had Claire held against her.

I ran back down to the boathouse, my legs trembling and this lark in my chest, nearly singing. I was happy, in an almost sick way. They had faces now. The short one and my Tall Friend. I knew how they'd killed Elmer.

They'd messed up now, left themselves open to a whole world of trouble, and I meant to be the one to give it to them.

IT WAS BEDLAM in the lodge kitchen. I got Mardine up and carried the dog in.

She took one look at both of us, and her eyes went wide.

"Look at yourself in the mirror," she said.

I didn't want to leave the dog, she was barely breathing. I'd gotten more than a little attached to that dog, after all.

"Go on," Mardine said.

I stood in front of the mirror. I reached for the light. Hit it. Blinked again, my eyes smarting. I was covered from head to foot with blood, as if I'd been sprayed with it.

I grinned. The blood made my teeth seem all the whiter. Standing there, I looked *Giiwanadizi,* crazy, like Trickster at an abattoir.

"Get out of here," Mardine said. "One of the guests comes and sees you we're gonna have a mess on our hands, we'll lose our goddamn business," and glaring, she added, "You shower, and then you get your foolish ass back here."

Gwen sat up blinking when I came in.

"What are you doing?" she said.

I flipped on the bathroom light, and then she saw my face, my clothes, and she got out of bed.

TWENTY-SIX

Just after first light, Gwen was drinking coffee with me in the lodge, Claire behind us in Mardine's hammock, when Charlie and George came striding up from the lake, Charlie mad enough to spit nails, but something else there, too. Excitement. He had something.

I still wondered if he was messing with me, caught in his own trouble now and trying to slip free.

He threw the screen door open, nodded politely to Gwen, who blushed, something awful, so much so, I think he got it, that we had our suspicions. Turning to me, he said,

"You ask me to *stick my fucking neck out,* look into things way the hell out in the middle of nowhere, say you're gonna meet me. I wait there, would've been out there the whole goddamn night if it hadn't been for George, and first thing we get back, Mardine calls and says, get out here, now, says you been on the island the whole time. So explain this to me. What is it I'm not getting here?"

I went for the pot of coffee, poured for Charlie. Either it was a good act, or he meant it.

"George?"

"Gives me acid stomach," he said. "Makes my teeth yellow, you know?"

I pulled out a chair and sat. Acid stomach. Yellow teeth. Christ.

"What's with you," Charlie said, "you're walkin' like you did after your accident. Like some fuckin' gimp. So what's your excuse?"

Mardine was putting together the sticky buns, in two large tins. Gwen, beside her, prepping the dough with cinnamon and sugar, gave me that look over her shoulder, nodded.

"All of it," she said. "Tell him."

I did. First of all, that I hadn't left any message for him.

"BUT WHY'D THEY go after you? Why not go right for Napoleon?" Charlie said.

I lit a cigarette and studied George there; he had his knife out, almost daintily trimmed his nails.

"All right," Charlie said. "Here's what it looks like to me. Your kid, Elmer, he becomes a target—both your kids—after they witness this murder. Elmer runs, and they get to him. Would've been the same with Napoleon, but him they didn't get a good look at. But it's all the rest of it, too. Not just who was out there, but what they were doin' that made 'em jump in the first place. And it isn't any . . . *coincidence* that cop who shot Eugene happened to be around for that murder at Rice Lake."

"Napoleon," I said, "told me it wasn't *that cop* who shot Eugene. It was the other guy with him. And down at Rice Lake—"

"Stanley *didn't* do it," George said.

Charlie took a tug on his cigarette. "I don't think he did either. I did back then, but I don't at all now."

"And why's that, Charlie?" I said, a little meanly.

"I know some things—" Charlie tapped his cigarette over the ashtray, and in a quieter voice, said "—things I should've known before, okay? But look, here's Michaels, poking around, internal affairs. But what's he *really* doing? The BCA tells me he's pretty much finished. But that's all they'll tell me. Nobody'll say *why* he's still here. We know things didn't happen out there the way Michaels has put it together.

"You say, if we get a postmortem on Elmer we're gonna find some puncture in his foot, right? Or some kind of poison in him. You even got the syringe, with residue in it, but it's something you could buy anywhere, Plastipak disposable U-80 insulin syringe. You got fingerprints, maybe—"

But I could see, in Charlie's expression, he didn't think we'd have to go far to get to the person who was behind it all.

"Roads down in Rice lake, and now up here," he said. "Same picture. Only Stanley didn't come home that night, so they didn't get to him. That's what went wrong for them back then."

I glanced over at George. Red canvas shirt, something like the beginning of a Fu Man Chu beard; right then he looked like two hundred sixty pounds of pure mean.

"Is that right?" I said.

George nodded, angling his thumb one way, then the other, trimming still.

"What else did Stanley say when we were down in Stillwater, that you *haven't* told me?"

George rapped his knuckles on the table; he wasn't happy with things at all.

"He said they were supposed to be running centerline for one road, but did preliminaries for all kinds of roads. He said they were sworn not to tell anybody, that it had something to do with property values around the resorts, and what would happen to business if the development buzz got around. They were afraid people'd pull out, the white resort owners. Come to bum-fuck resort, where you can see the highway right from your porch, that kind of thing. Stanley said that cop had been hanging around most of that spring, poking into all kinds of stuff wasn't his business."

I lit another cigarette. "Tell Charlie about the core sample they had done," I said, "how Stanley got it."

I wanted Charlie to understand, what was going on here wasn't about a road. All of what was out in the open was just some diversion. George let go a disgusted breath, said,

"Stanley got it by mistake, showed it to his old man, who lost it, or so he said. Stanley told me, down at Stillwater, the last word on all that was, they just needed a compaction survey—had to know how much clay there was in the soil, so they could drain if they had to. You know how those clay roads turn to snot in the rain? End of that week, Stanley shoots his old man and family. And just like that, the whole road deal there drops dead, and the company that won the bid for construction pulls out."

Charlie rubbed his cheek, making a rough, hollow scratching. "And it was just the cop, who took a swim later, and the other guy, and Eugene, when the kids bumbled in—"

"According to Napoleon," I said.

"So who do you think lost that . . . whatever you call it— *rosette?*"

"Wasn't Eugene," I said, "he wouldn't wear something like that."

"A *white* cop wouldn't be wearing something like that," Charlie shot back. "So—"

"The other guy," I said.

George scowled. He'd made a mess of one of his fingernails, pressed his now bleeding index finger into the tabletop.

"He doesn't have to be the one," George said, "somebody could've put it there."

"Okay, okay. But it *looks* like that," Charlie said. "But what I still don't get, though, is *why* would they go after Paul?"

George's raisin eyes wrinkled; he lifted his finger, jabbed it into the ashtray, then pointed it, bloody, ash-blackened, at me.

"Paul's the college-educated boy, and at that world-renowned fancy school. Our pilot fish. He's got more acres than anybody up here, and all over the place. He's supposed to have some edge on things, only he never knows shit."

He gave me a hooded, angry look. "Do you, Paul? That's the fuckin' joke of it. Let's hear it, Paul. What do you know?"

"Thanks for the vote of confidence, George," I said.

He pointed to my cigarettes and I shucked one up for him.

"The nail in the coffin of that road business," George said, taking a tug on the cigarette, *"should've* been that none of that land is tax-exempt. Anybody interested in development on the Angle, even if they *could* get Indian owners to go along with it, would have to kick out more bucks than they would say . . . down at Fond Du Lac, or Nett Lake, Leech Lake, anywhere you could use dummy owners—-" George grinned "—Indians with original allotment land. Tax free, see? You name it, a factory, casino, retail store outlet, like one of those cinder-block monsters they park along highways, whatever. That's what you gotta have to make money runnin' a business up here, tax-exempt status, and they don't have that on the Angle."

Charlie lifted his head to look out the back window, muttered something.

"What?" I said.

George raised an eyebrow, studied Charlie until he cleared his throat.

"So why up here now?" Charlie said. "Screwin' around, if there's no money in it?"

"There's no money *on the face of it,"* George said. "But people are hungry."

I startled at that. Hungry. Something Nita'd said came to me like a small explosion: Everything in life is speaking, Nawaji, he said. You just miss it because you think it should come in one language.

"Wegonen?" George said, what?

I took a bottle of Walker out of our cabinet and poured a jelly glass, put it in front of Charlie. I wanted him to give up what he was hiding. I'd had it.

"Just to grease the wheels," I said.

"Get that the hell away from me," Charlie said. "I want another cup, black as you can make it."

I poured, set the mug in front of him. Still, I'd made myself clear.

"I broke into Michaels' room," Charlie said. "Down in Warroad, that night you came over to my house."

I felt a sharp turning in my stomach, all that with Michaels and Father Prideaux's knife coming back to me, my stomach clenching at it. Charlie and George turned slightly away from each other, but I saw it well enough, they'd been working on something together.

"He had survey maps," Charlie said, "minutes of sites all over the Angle. Sound familiar? But the one they seem to have worked out, connects with 313, *not* 525, where Truman wants it. There was survey equipment in his room, lots of it. A theodolite. Hundred-foot tape. Some blasting caps, but no explosive, and it was all bagged and numbered, like he'd already taken it from some crime scene. Got pictures of that cop that drowned, Peterson, and that guy, Jenkins, missing the fingers. All arranged, Michaels making a case. Very meticulous, this Michaels."

"Who did it look like he was after?" I said.

"He could make a case on any of us here. Me, you—especially George, since then." Charlie bent over his mug, took a sip, gave George a somber look. "But more than anybody, he had the works on Truman, night I broke in. Notes on Truman's whereabouts, records of phone calls he'd made—"

"So what's it all come to?" I said. "What are you getting at?"

George poured a finger of Walker in his coffee cup, pointed to Charlie. Charlie kicked his chair around, sat with his arms hung over the back.

For a moment, he seemed to be wondering how to put it, then said,

"Lookin' at those calls Michaels got records of, I saw Truman hadn't phoned *anywhere* off reservation, so I got suspicious. How could that be, you know?"

"And?" I said.

"I followed him to the Perkins there on 525, where he eats breakfast Fridays. Sat it out one morning, called Ma Bell right after he did. Got the receiving from them. Minneapolis. Asked how many times that number'd been called from the phone there. *Fifteen times over the last month.*"

I asked why he hadn't told me.

"Wouldn't've meant anything if I had. Any of it. See, *that's* what I was waiting for—to find out from a friend of mine, works for Ma Bell, whose place it was. And he found out, that's for sure. A Carol Herbst."

I shrugged.

"Not important, right? So I had George here follow her."

George looked across the table at me, then back down at his hands, tore the skin he'd cut from his finger with a quick jerk.

"It's ugly, but—*shit, it isn't murder,*" George said.

Charlie nodded. "Tell him."

"This woman," George said, "Carol Herbst, she went down to CES, that's Community Emergency Service, some wino shelter on Hennipen. Hefted a few bags of groceries out and delivered 'em to houses on Franklin Avenue. Then, at the Nicollet Mall, went shopping, some fancy red understuff, Victoria's Secret kind of thing, hell I don't know—"

He blushed a little, did know. Or was it he was embarrassed at something else?

"Anyway, same thing pretty much the next day, I mean, the CES deal, and delivering food on Franklin, and wandering around. Lives right there on Lake Street, on the west end, at the Calhoun Beach Club. I'd try to talk to the people she delivered to, and they'd shut the door in my face. And the ones I knew, it was like I was a living, breathing pile of shit stink. So I got all their names, wasn't hard, looked them up in the band rolls, and *hey—*"

I got up, went to the stove, freshened my cup. Gwen was outside talking to Mardine.

"They all had land on the Angle," I said.

George gave a curt nod. "Yup. But I wanted to see where the money was coming from," George said. "I mean, this . . . *Carol* wasn't pluckin' it out of trees. Checked banks, talked to people pushin' the road deal. But most of all went after this Carol, sat up one night, behind her place, got heart palpitations from smoking and two jugs of coffee, and right around four in the morning, a car eases around the back. I mean, what are the chances it has anything to do with this woman? The following day, Charlie runs the plate.

"The car," Charlie said, "was *registered* to this Carol. A woman who lives at the Calhoun Beach Club—I mean, is that swanky or what?—but ends up in Tonto Town on Franklin three days a week, handing out bribes to people got land on the Angle. She isn't on anybody's map. No credit card, income tax, nothing. So, a dead end, right?"

Charlie lit a cigarette, tugged at it with a certain relish.

"*Then* I figure, after I was pokin' around the Rambler's last night, I'd try one more thing. I mean, I've already had the plate run for violations, but—"

"Try Canada," I said.

"*Bingo!* Guess *where* and *when?*"

"South of the Sioux Narrows," I said. "Yesterday, right when I came down from Stump's, around dawn."

"*Bingo* again."

"Who got the citation?"

Charlie lay the piece of paper he was holding flat on the table, as though it were a card in a poker hand. He spun the sheet around. RCMP, Royal Canadian Mounted Police, on the Ontario side.

The time, date, and location fit.

The car was clocked at ninety-five miles per hour headed south on Highway 71. The driver:

Wheeler, Truman A.

The policeman who'd passed Napoleon and me on 71, it occurred to me, had flashed his lights, must have been the one to write the ticket.

Charlie tugged a brown paper bag from his jacket, spilled its contents on the table. A few guineas, a surveyor's eyepiece with a level in it, and syringes, opaque plastic, black rubber plunger, green needle guard, the needle inside, sharp silver.

"Got the bag out of Truman's car parked behind the Rambler's," Charlie said, spreading what was there out, a royal flush.

"I was gonna come back out to the island," Charlie said, bunching his face up, "show you, but my girl, Darilyn, calls, says she got this message I'm supposed to meet you down in Warroad, out front of the DOT. I called George, and he made it there in—"

"Just under five hours," George said. "We wanted to catch Truman before he ran."

"But we were waitin' for you," Charlie said. "Since you'd said you were gonna meet us there after closing, and it had to be in Warroad."

"Never said a word of it," I said.

TWENTY-SEVEN

I felt absolutely gut-sick, daylight coming on. I had the phantom image of all that had been in Truman's car staring me in the face, but it wasn't that it added up to Truman Wheeler that had me upset, it was that Truman *didn't* fit.

All I had to go on, just then, was pure, gut instinct, and Charlie wasn't buying it.

In the new cabin, the honeymoon suite, I tried to convince Charlie to wait, to snoop around a bit more. See if we could come up with something more substantial.

"Why?" Charlie said. "So Truman can get wise to it all and run?" Charlie bent over his suitcase, jammed a shirt in, punched it into a corner with his fist. He looked at me over his shoulder. "Remember, after the boat accident? I told you they'd be back. So what if Truman's doin' all he can to push that road except walk around St. Paul with some sandwich board on him? I told you he was dirty then, and I'm tellin' you that now."

I sat at the table, worrying the watch in my pocket. Jimmy was glaring at me from the loft, where he'd slept this last week, a wannabe tough kid in pants so ill-fitting, the crotch at his knees, if he ever had to move fast he'd trip all over himself.

"When are we going?" he said.

"Right *now*," Charlie said, and turning to me, added. "If that's all right with you."

"No, it's not," I said.

"What do you mean it's *not*."

"If Truman has no reason to think you've pegged him, he won't bolt. So why the rush?"

Charlie set his thick hands on his hips. Stood over the suitcase. Then, in a voice so quiet Jimmy wouldn't hear, he said,

"Look, I didn't want to have to say it. It's my job if I don't wrap this one up. Some crap about . . . conflict of interest, and my service record up here, and those complaints I got years ago. They're gonna hang me if I don't make good on this."

"Michaels—"

"No, it started earlier. He's just the one to do it. All this came at me in April, before you were up. Some shitheels came in with that senator of yours, Skip King. Cops, too."

"King was up before opening?"

"It's just more of the fucking pot callin' the kettle black," Charlie said. "Skippy promises some favors over at that Council Office, and hey, suddenly he's a friend to all you people up here. And someone wants me gone, see?"

"And how's this supposed to happen?" I said.

"Wheeler and some council people'll sing for old Skippy, every bad thing I ever done or said up here, and they get this road—or least a promise of development money—and King looks like some hero for the election in November."

Charlie turned his back to me, packing, broad heavy shoulders, thick arms.

"Give me three days," I said. "I'll force them to come out."

"What've you got?"

"I can do it."

Charlie searched my face, saw I was dead serious, pressed his hand to his forehead.

"We're outta here," Jimmy said, dragging his suitcase, clunking, down the loft ladder.

"Put it back," Charlie said. "You heard me."

"Make up your fuckin' mind," Jimmy said, and when we didn't jump to his cause, he dropped the suitcase so it thumped heavily on the floor and went out.

Charlie set his hands on his belt, turned around slowly, a pained expression on his face.

"Listen," I said, "I want you to take Gwen and Claire and Napoleon, and Jimmy, down to Bemidji, tomorrow, and keep them in the station there—I don't care if you have to raise hell to do it. Right after breakfast, after it's light out. Have Napoleon sit in front—slouch down."

I handed Charlie my cap—orange and black, the only Orioles cap on the lake, as far as I knew.

"You think I can get Napoleon to wear this?" Charlie said.

"Tell him it's that, or he gets to ride in the trunk."

I told him the rest of it: I'd go into Pine Point with him, we'd make a big stink of leaving, so people in town would see us, I'd ride to the highway, and get out there, hike to the lake where George would just happen to be waiting with his boat.

Charlie would stop in the small towns on the way down, potter around, make sure they'd see Napoleon slouched in my seat, an Indian wearing an Orioles cap, who they'd assume was me.

Once they thought we were gone, they'd come off the lake and through the trees, down from the point, but this time, I'd have George with me.

I was pretty sure of what they'd be looking for: that Okitsita fetish.

"You tell Michaels what you had in mind?" I asked.

Charlie snorted. "I had my secretary leave a message. I told him, me and you'd go down to Bemidji, get a warrant, then drive back and pick up Truman. Take my car, make it official. That was the plan. Fuckin' prick, doesn't so much as call me back. I mean, the guy's been riding me for dirt on Truman for weeks, but now that I got the evidence that'll put Truman away first, the prick just up and disappears."

Somehow, none of that sat well with me. Why wasn't Michaels swooping down to jerk the investigation out from under Charlie's feet, since it seemed he'd been trying to do that from the first? I felt sick at it, but what could I do but shrug it off? Michaels was out of the loop now anyway, wasn't he?

TWENTY-EIGHT

It was late, after eleven, and we were settling in. George came up from the docks, took a seat in the lodge kitchen, a breeze carrying the scent of wild rose through the back window, a grasshopper mechanically rasping, as if in code. We went over all the evidence against Truman again, just George and me.

"And lots of people saw Truman and old Skippy getting friendly," George said, a kind of offering.

"But is Truman *really* that stupid?"

"If looks had anything to do with it, I'd say so."

I wasn't amused. I told George how I'd seen Truman take that envelope from Michaels in the parking lot of the Rambler's, all those weeks earlier. How Truman reacted in the Rambler's, when I got out the fetish, more shocked, it seemed, at me showing it around the way I had, to Michaels, or anyone, than at my having it.

If Truman was behind it, would he have done all that, out in the open?

Michaels was just going about his job, George assured me, and why wouldn't Michaels, for whatever reason, threaten Truman with what he'd picked up snooping around.

He pointed out how Truman had the right connections, the motivation, to front some double-sided development deal.

"Hell," George said, "everybody knows Truman's in bed with timber, and look how he's been sucking up to the council, even Walter, who hates his guts."

"Okay, but why?" I said. "Why would someone go to all the trouble, all the way to the state senate to push this thing if there's no money in building something out there, can you tell me that?"

George laughed, those mean raisin eyes hot.

"Get real, Paul. For whoever's running this show, it goes right, they get page one and a big headline. *State-Sponsored Development a Success.* It goes wrong, we get page 86 between the Firestone tire ad and the Maaco paint your car for $69.99 special.

"Reservation Altercation Kills Three."

I lit a cigarette. It didn't taste good, and it smouldered there in my hands.

"All right," I said. "So why hasn't Michaels taken Truman in?"

"I've seen tons of pricks like Michaels," George said. "Especially down there at Stillwater. What he's after is a TKO, see? He's got promotion written all over him. You think he'd let himself get caught up in some tangle that might get ugly?

"They're setting Charlie up for a very clean little crucifixion. He'll look like the model bad cop. Bad procedure and everything. And just when the case is gridlocked, Michaels'll swing in from the wings with all the right evidence. I'm sure somebody's all set to bail Truman out. Why else would he run his mouth the way he has? Even *if* he's done it, he's got alibis, witnesses, all on his side. The question is, who's behind it all."

I was shocked at his saying it. "So, if you got your doubts like I do," I said, "why are you letting Charlie go on the way he is?"

George motioned for a cigarette. He lit it, and just then smiled. It was the kind of smile you'd never want to see, unless it was on your side, a smile twisted with singular intent.

Harm was too soft a word for it.

"It'll never go that far, can't," George said, pointing the cigarette at me. "Those people, stand to make the money? They're gonna come now. You can bet on it. And we're—no, *I'm* gonna be waiting."

"So who do you think it is?" I said.

George just smiled all the more; teeth like those in a jack-o'-lantern.

"We'll see," he said.

I SKIDDED DOWN the hillside, the moon high in the trees, looked the docks over, saw the light on in the boathouse, figured I'd find Charlie there.

I wanted to talk to him before he left, alone.

I stepped through the door and Charlie stooped down, and even as I tried to figure what he was doing, he quickly stood, pressed a heavy automatic to the side of my head, cold steel.

"Don't move," he said, crazily.

I smelled things I hadn't smelled in that boathouse in years. A mint smell, from a cleaner I'd used at one time on the floor. Mothballs. White gas, for the lantern.

"What are you doing, Charlie?" I said.

His mouth was set in a frown, the wings of his nose flared. Here was a Charlie I hadn't seen. I thought right then he'd shoot me.

"This *isn't* like what happened two years ago. You're not messin' around with slow movers this time, Paul," he said. He shoved the gun harder into the side of my head. "They catch you dozing, you aren't going to have time to so much as think 'what's this all about?' You won't have time to blink."

He pulled the gun from my head, tossed it to the side and the carrier snapped back. He held it in front of me, so I could look down into the handgrip, said,

"Empty in the well," turned it so I could look down its length, "Empty in the barrel."

He handed the gun to me. I swallowed hard, my heart still pounding in my neck. It was a heavy pistol, the grip cross-hatched.

"Smith and Wesson 659. I had it overseas."

I didn't ask him if he'd used it. There was all that in the feel of it, the business of what he'd done overseas. He pulled his pants leg up, there, around his ankle, a sturdy leather holster.

"Where's the clip?"

"Magazine," Charlie corrected. "That's the surprise—I mean, besides the ankle holster."

"Nine shots or ten?"

Charlie took the magazine out of his pocket. It was black, narrow, finely machined.

"See, the bullets go side by side, in steps. That's the difference between a clip and magazine. You got seventeen bullets. All .38s."

It was quiet in the boathouse, oppressive. Charlie set the gun and magazine on the workbench.

"I fed a line of shit right to George. Told him I was going through Warroad, down to Bemidji. Somebody at the station there in Warroad called to find out when I was passin' through, three, four hours after we talked, asked me to stop and see 'em. So, either he's in it, or somebody he knows is." He set his hands on his hips. "He called somebody, from in the kitchen, didn't he?"

I said he had.

"Listen," Charlie said. "Even the BCA's dirty on this one. That's why they got Michaels out here, to look into what that cop was doing on the Angle when Eugene got shot. And they got connections, whoever these guys are. *Cop* connections. I looked into that ticket Truman got, after all that in the kitchen."

"What about it?"

"I talked to the officer who wrote out the citation," he said. "The driver, he tells me, was a *Caucasian male, between forty and forty-five,* five ten, one fifty-five, to one sixty."

"What?"

"It *wasn't* Truman. But to pull that kind of stunt, cut information going into a station's records, they had to have someone inside. See?"

"So, you don't want to go tomorrow?"

"That isn't it. It's the best thing now, to get Gwen, your kid, mine, Napoleon, outta here. See, this next time, they're not gonna fool around with phony accidents these people, they're gonna just blow you to fucking kingdom come and hope they can sidestep it." Charlie glared. "Your old pal George is deep in shit you don't even know about. Maybe *he* doesn't know about.

"They didn't plan for that to happen with Elmer, only it did. Or for you to poke around down in Warroad, at Edna's place. Didn't think you'd go down to Stillwater, talk to Stanley with George along, or find Napoleon before they did.

"They're on full tilt, Paul. We're a cunt hair from knowing who they are and they know it. It's the whole deal, for them, one way or the other.

"George looks bad. They could do you, and blame it on him, or, hell, fifteen different people. You got development that hates your guts—people are talking threats you made—and Michaels was making a case on us."

Charlie glanced off into a corner of the boathouse, turned quickly to face me, his eyes narrowed.

"You only need one of them, see? Whoever comes out, *keep him breathing.*"

I turned the gun in my hand, got a sudden heavy, sinking feeling, said,

"You're just trying to save your own ass now, aren't you? It's your big chance, isn't it? And if it goes wrong?"

I slid the gun across the bench at him. I didn't trust using it.

"Keep it, I've got my own," I said, but that was only half true. Mardine had my .357.

Charlie's face colored, he grabbed me by my shirt, put his face in mine.

"Sometimes I don't like you," Charlie said, "your insinuations, and insults. Surprise, huh? But you listen now. They fuck with me, it's one thing," Charlie said. "They fuck with people I'm supposed to watch out for—especially family or friends—try to do it *through me*, and my *job*, they're gonna be sorry they ever saw my face. *That's* a promise."

TWENTY-NINE

Five in the morning, Hugh knocked on the cabin door. I tossed on my clothes, jeans, work boots, khaki shirt, and still blinking, steered myself up to the lodge. Mardine was in the kitchen, red skirt and blouse so dark red as to be almost black.

I got a cup of coffee from the urn to the right of Mardine. She nudged me, glared, and I got a second mug for Hugh.

He followed me out to the stoop, his teeth set on edge, bristling with all of it.

I listened to him, just as Mardine had wanted. Every last bit, as the sky was going pink in the trees to the east, the lake mirror smooth and lovely. Thirty people up. Where the hell had I been? He'd been doing it all. In and out of Pine Point. Repairs. Delbert, this new kid, just screwing around unless Hugh got on his case, which got Delbert all pissed off.

Hugh was too proud to say he was tired. I hadn't ever given in to that either.

"What are you gonna do about it?" Hugh said.

It was going to be *sign on,* or *cut and run.* I knew it. But I should have given him the benefit of the doubt the year before, anyway.

"I'm going to be busy for a day or two, got things to take care of with George."

I put my hands on my knees, pushed myself up, stretched. Either I'd made the worst business decision of my life, or?

"That's *fucking impossible,*" Hugh blurted. "Who's gonna—"

"Hire somebody, another kid," I said. "Hire a few for that matter, just don't bust the bank."

I put my hand out, and it all dawned on Hugh. He got right up off that stoop. He was boyish suddenly, smiling and his legs coltish, and I had a moment of misgiving, but then he shook himself into it, too hard now, almost military, in his khakis. What face was he going to wear?

I could see he wanted to ask what to do first. I'm glad he didn't.

"Can you take Jimmy with you?" he said. "I'll rent that cabin, or move somebody from one of the smaller cabins, somebody wants a bigger place."

I lit a cigarette. "It's up to you," I said.

"I got some calls to make," he said, and bursting with it, ran inside.

I sat on the stoop, watching the light come up through the trees. A bass jumped, making a circle in the water.

My hands were cold, a touch of fall chill in the air, and I shoved one hand into my pocket, melancholy.

I'd imagined this moment, since I'd been a boy, guiding for Frank. Then, it had been a ridiculous dream, owning the place, and I'd dreamed I'd hire a part-time manager, later, when I'd sorted out the mess the resort was, and now I had, just like that.

All of it had come true, after a fashion.

But now, here, just when I was more deeply into all that I'd tried to stay clear of than I'd ever been—just as Frank, the old owner, had intimated I'd be.

"You'll see," he'd said, with a certain dark irony in his voice, "how you win things later on."

Somehow, just then I did.

I WENT DOWN to the dock. George was there, barrel chest in a green T-shirt, braids in blue cloth.

I got out a cigarette, broke it in my palm, sprinkled it on the water.

Just let me get through this, I thought. I laughed, amused at my-self. Spirit had its own plans, but I could always hope they were something like mine.

"So, George," I said. "You get anything?"

"I called around this morning. Nobody's seen anybody coming in, not out on the lake, or up 313 or 525."

"So?"

"Just means they're already set."

AT THE PINE Point station, gray cinder block and green awning over the stoop, I followed Charlie inside. He poked his knuckle into the answering machine on his desk, scrabbled in a cabinet for some pa-pers while the machine rewound. I stood at the window, shielding my eyes against the sun. A phone call from a Donna, *Call me, Lover,* she said. Someone from the *St. Paul Pioneer Press,* and then, a voice I recognized, doubly, it seemed just then. I couldn't think why.

"My secretary," Charlie said.

—so, after this morning, I knew,
just speaking for myself, I knew
that had to be the end of it,
and when you wouldn't stop,
just went on and

Charlie glared, and I nodded and stepped outside. None of my business, his personal life, I thought.

I waited with Gwen, Claire in her arms in a blanket, Jimmy and Napoleon giving each other wary glances at the pumps. Napoleon kicked at the broken pavement, gouged out a piece of blacktop and tossed it at the LP tank to the right of Charlie's cruiser, but hit the cruiser, the rusty fender clonging, green paint rusted through, the once jaunty dual exhaust pipes below the bumper knocked down in different directions, cockeyed.

The car was riding low, I thought, I was going to mention it to Charlie.

Then Charlie came out, skipped down the stoop, that sawed-off pump twelve gauge over his forearm. He popped the trunk lid and reached inside. Four Delco batteries, jumper cables, a length of chain, packed in so tight the trunk lid barely closed, and I thought, that's what it was, making the car ride low.

That and old leaf springs.

"Gimme a hand here, Paul," he said.

We got all that out and locked in the station, loaded the luggage. Jamming in Gwen's blue Samsonite, I smelled something chemical.

I said, "Why's it smell like—" I thought fuel oil, but that couldn't be right.

"Darilyn filled it up this morning," Charlie said. "She didn't want to tell me, but she started with *diesel*—we got it there for the snowplows—and when she saw what'd she done she pulled the hose out and got it all over everything."

Charlie grinned meanly, held his hands up.

"But why should I complain? Last time she put the oil in the radiator. I mean, Christ! But, hell, what difference does it make? She *quit* just now—I chewed her out yesterday—couldn't do it to my face, so left a message on the machine, so, what's the difference?"

He slammed the trunk shut.

"Well?"

UP A NOWHERE logging road, just a mile or so from the Angle shore-line, Charlie stopped the car.

We all got out.

I threw my arms around Gwen, Claire in her arms, just then re-assuringly substantial, rose scent and talcum and soft warm skin. I kissed Gwen, and she kissed me back, hardly a kiss at all, her eyes glassed up.

"This time," she said, "don't try to do everything yourself, all right?"

I nodded, turning away, and she pulled me back, kissed me, hard.

"You be careful, goddammit," she said.

"All right," Charlie said.

Napoleon swung around to the front, got in, pulling the door shut, then put on the cap and slouched sullenly, his head against the window, as if asleep.

There was some argument there, Jimmy saying who knew what, until Charlie took a poke at him, and like Gwen, he disappeared.

Charlie rolled his window down.

"Watch your hindside," he said, and drove off.

IN THE BOAT, headed back to the island, George had the wheel. I sat beside him trying to make sense of this feeling I had that I'd missed something. But here on the lake was late August perfection. The sun rose high over the pines, and the water was glassy smooth and calm. It was so hot already that when we slowed, approaching the dock, the cicadas were chirring.

A premonition of autumn.

Hugh had a number of guests out, others were in the water, swimming. Fluorescent swimsuits this year, bright as candied fruit. Lime, magenta, orange.

I waved to them going up the hillside to the kitchen.

Mardine threw plates together, and George and I stood eating back of the stove.

I kept glancing up at the clock, not seeing the time.

That's what bothered me. It wasn't that forty minutes had gone by since we'd left the station in Pine Point, or that I hadn't touched my food now, for minutes, glancing up yet again, checking the clock, but never seeing what time it was.

It was the clock itself.

"You're gonna make me lose it if you don't eat that there," George said.

"Oh, don't go blowin' up on us over nothing," Mardine said, at the stove.

Something hot shot from my stomach, ran up my spine, sat sputtering on my head, a lit fuse. I handed George my plate.

"Be my guest," I said.

I ran to the cabin, got the recorder, charged up the hillside to the lodge, and in the lodge office, got out the tape. I forwarded through everything, went by what I wanted, then rewound.

I pressed the play button, so hard I nearly broke the recorder.

There was that last bit of Anishininiimowin, and the woman, laughing. Had she masked her voice here, or was it just alcohol? Or another voice?

"Stop it, stop it, I'll wet myself!"

Stop. The O rounded, just as it had been in the message she'd left for Charlie: St*awp!* I was sick at it, recognizing her.

Darilyn—Charlie's "new girl."

Now I saw it was no coincidence she'd quit just this morning, or that Charlie's cruiser had stunk of fuel oil. And what of George? His having been so keen on staying on the island with me? Maybe Charlie was right, he was caught up in it somehow.

George was in the kitchen joking with Mardine. I strode by them both.

"Come on, George," I said, and he came out with me.

THIRTY

The launch was insufferably slow. I hammered at the engine, nearly spit at it, I was so angry, trying to reset the air/fuel mixture—it was far too rich, puked out heavy, blue exhaust behind us.

A wrench in my hand, I had what Henry had told me running through my head. They'd make it look like my own people had gone after me. And it *would* look like that. Crude explosive, an idiot could have made it. The BCA would play right into it. All their assumptions, all their conclusions, about how things got done on the reservation.

And Michaels, a safe distance from real trouble, after the explosion, would appear on the scene to gather information and make his case stick, and in that way, the real perpetrators would remain as they had all along, invisible.

I got that engine to lean out and hum.

George at the wheel, we passed another island, and he swung close, a shortcut, he promised, banged over a submerged rock shelf, and I thought we broke the propeller. But it was just a shear pin, and

I had it fixed in minutes, and we were off again, but now even more minutes lost.

George cut between two islands, all lily pads and weed, and our engine stalled.

That did it, so when I bent over the transom and levered the engine's prop out of the water, I reached for the fishing gaff I kept there, but George was way ahead of me, grabbed my hair up in his fist, yanked back so hard my neck cracked.

"That asshole Charlie, or somebody, has bitched you on me," he said, behind me. "And I've had it. All right, I got you into this, but *goddammit,* they've fucked me over too. So help me god, you come clean on who's stickin' it to me, or I'll break your fuckin' neck, Paul."

"Let go," I said.

"Give it—"

"You've got all those connections down in the Cities, had time to do things—"

"What *things?*"

He pulled back harder yet. With my free hand, I got the fire extinguisher free from the transom, angled it up and over my shoulder, pulled the safety pin and squeezed the lever, let go a blast, right in George's face, and he stumbled back and fell. I had the gaff on him, jabbered almost incoherently.

About Darilyn. About the fuel oil I'd smelled in Charlie's trunk—even through the diesel Darilyn splashed around to mask it. How George had betrayed me.

"Oh, man," George said. "You are so totally fucked-up paranoid."

He towered over me, his face powdered white, red eyes glaring. He faked left, and when I jabbed, he tore the gaff out of my hands, threw it into the lake, caught me in a headlock.

"Don't *ever* do anything like that again," he said, squeezing.

It was like having the bumper of a car wrapped around my neck. "Okay?"

I nodded the best I could. George let go. He wiped at his face, which only worsened the effect, so now he looked like some demented bushman, or windigo.

"Let's get the fuck outta here," he said. "You might've just cost us the whole damn ball game."

"No," I said, but didn't explain.

GEORGE COULD HARDLY fit in the passenger seat of my sister's rickety Toyota. And it was slower with him in it. It hopped and jumped and shook over the uneven dirt road from the government dock. One of the struts in front broke in a pothole, and then the car was bouncing like a yo-yo, veering from one side of the road to the other, between trees big around as oil drums, and I was pleading there at that car's duct-taped steering wheel,

Oh please dammit, *please*—

We swung around the last stand of trees, across the reservation line into Pine Point, log cabins, then shacks, the woods on the left, and by god, it was still there, right in front of the Rambler's, beside it Dexter's car.

Clark's Jaguar. Funky rack on the roof and all.

WE HAD DEXTER'S battery in the car, and George had cut the rack off the roof, before Dexter made it out of the store. When he saw what we'd done, he charged at me, stopped in his tracks at George, who stepped menacingly in his direction, that Kay Bar in his hand, his face streaked white.

George grinned. Positively impressive.

"Don't tell me," Dexter said, and went back inside.

OUT ON 525 I opened it up. How long would my father's cheap fix on the radiator hold up? The car was thrumming, then there was a straight stretch, and George said,

"If we're gonna get it on, let's get it on."

Right around one thirty-five the car started to shudder. Wheel out of balance, or something.

"Faster," George shouted. "It'll get worse, or it'll get better."

The needle climbed up. One forty-five, one fifty, the tach needle hovering on the right, the radiator holding. We passed Tillotson Lake, and I slowed, but not enough, hit the long sweeper onto 308 there.

"Pump the fuckin' brakes!" George shouted.

I hit the brakes, then harder, and they locked up and the Jaguar was sliding sideways.

"Gas now!" George shouted.

I did that. We'd roll, I thought, I was sure of it, and as if that thing were on rails, it squatted down, so low the chassis scraped on something, and we shot off onto 308 and George shouted again,

"Don't give me this Sterling Moss shit. Just fuckin' floor it."

The car shuddered again, and the speedometer needle came around, just short of one fifty, and there was some tractor on the right, and I hit the horn and kept it on, and we blew right by him, and then another car, turning left, and I got around him on the shoulder.

Warroad was up ahead.

"Don't slow down," George said.

I didn't. We passed the outside of town and an unmarked turned onto the road after us and we didn't see it anymore. I glanced down at the gauges. My heart leapt, the heat gauge was nearly in the red— the gunk my father'd used on the radiator had plugged up more than the leaks.

I held the pedal down anyway, the mile markers flashing by as if snatched from behind, the dotted yellow line under the hood a blur. Ate up over a hundred miles in forty minutes, the leaping cat on the hood shining chrome and diamond bright in the sun.

Come on— come on— come on— I was chanting.

We were closing in. Snapped by another small town, and outside it, the radiator exploded under the hood, geysered hot green antifreeze onto the windshield. I turned the windshield wipers on but still couldn't see. I rolled down the window and put my head out and the wind pulled the skin on my face back, my cheeks flapping, my eyes watering so badly I was blinded.

George pressed something into my hand. Sunglasses.

I pulled my head in, stuck them on my face, slick with antifreeze, looked back out there. There were cars ahead of us, blue gumballs flashing like fireworks, and when they saw we weren't slowing at all, they got out of the way and we went by them and they pulled in after us. Charlie would take 89 though lower Red Lake. That's where they'd set it off.

Use some radio signal, but sure enough, it'd look like our own.

The engine had begun to stink of burned oil. My old pal Clark had loved this car, but I was going to use it up now, every bit of it, so I kept my foot on the floor.

We flashed by another town, almost hit a kid that was playing with a turtle on the highway at a bridge, and the car humped over it, airborne, and I saw that kid's face, his mouth open, and the car banged down, and then the others, a mile or so behind us, went over, and we were on a high, high hill, a sweeper and that green guck stopped geysering out of the radiator onto the windshield, but that was bad, and I clung to the steering wheel, and then, on the backside, coming down, I saw Charlie's car, and the lake beyond it, shimmering, and the town there, just outside it, a bridge and spillway.

It was the last town before Bemidji, and Charlie was driving slow, and the Jaguar was still pulling hard but some death rattle in it, and miles back, I started honking, honking like a crazy man, and George got up in the window, his hair torn back like a black rag, and was waving his arms, and Charlie hit the gas, idiot, began to pull away, but I lay on the horn, just had to get around him, and the car came up, Charlie hard at the wheel, and Napoleon, looking for all the world like me, that cap on his head, leaning against the passenger window, not a sign of the others, and we went by in a rush, and I hit the brakes and the wheels shuddered, then held, tires screeching and screeching and the car sliding to cross the highway, just ahead of the bridge and spillway, a car coming on the opposite direction now, from the south.

The Jaguar jerked to a stop, and George and I got out, and the car from the south skidded across the bridge, just short of us, and going into the ditch shearing off the No Shoulder sign there, so that the angle iron support caterwheeled up and fell with a loud clanking on the hard asphalt.

George went down after the car. I ran at Charlie, coming at me in his cruiser, shouting, waving my hands over my head,

"GET THE HELL OUT! GET THE FUCK OUT OF FOR GOD'S SAKE!"

Charlie veered to a sharp stop up the road, short of the bridge. Those patrol cars that had followed George and me down skidded to a halt a block or so back of Charlie, blue-suited police bursting from those three cars. Charlie pulled Gwen out of his cruiser, Claire in her arms, and they strode, Gwen with Claire, Jimmy, Napoleon, and Charlie, toward me.

An officer called from behind over his bullhorn,

"STOP! I ORDER YOU TO STOP!"

It was then Napoleon charged, sprinted toward me and the Jaguar for all he was worth.

An officer appeared up the road, behind the others, pulled an automatic from a shoulder holster, and with a motion I'd never seen, jacked up a shell, a left-handed operation, and sidled off and down into the ditch, coming toward us.

Charlie, a wide-eyed look on his face, seeing something in it I didn't, gave Gwen a shove, shouted—

"RUN!"

They ran to me, wide-eyed and moving fast. I took Gwen's arm and swung her around back of the Jaguar, and the others went with her.

Charlie backed toward the car, scrabbling at his ankle for the 659, glancing left, right, a look of alarm on his face. The policemen up the road threw the doors of their cars open and ducked behind them.

There was a second of seemingly absolute quiet, everyone hanging on the edge of what no one knew, and at that moment, Charlie's cruiser lit up, flash of white hot light, the car lifted off the pavement, bursting, the doors and hood spinning off, an explosion so powerful my shirt caught against my arms and chest, my heatbeat stopped in the thunderclap of it.

The cruiser turned over, high and burning, to crash upside down in the road, a ball of flame at the center, oily smoke billowing from it so thick it cut the highway in two, the car exploding again, smell of raw gasoline and burning rubber now.

Michaels climbed onto the bridge, over the spillway, from the lakeside.

Charlie turned toward him, on his face something like surprise, but something else—

a shot rang out and Charlie spun around, hit. He crawled toward me on his hands and knees, the cop I'd seen behind the others coming out of the ditch opposite Michaels, lowering the gun to fire a second time, but Charlie lay still already.

The cop and Michaels both looked up the road, where the flame raged, spewing out a wall of oily black smoke, the smoke carrying north, so that you could hear the police backing off in a screeching of tires and barking radios and shouts.

It was one of those moments. The length of a breath, but eternity in it. There were the four of us in the road, on the south side, cut off. Me. Michaels and this cop, who I recognized now, and Charlie sprawled facedown on the pavement just yards from the burning cruiser.

Michaels took a step toward me from the bridge. Was it Michaels? The cop missing the fingers? Or both, doing the killing? I moved away from the car, away from Gwen and Claire, and the others huddled behind it.

The cop followed, his movements slow and calculated, even as I swept up the angle iron that Michaels' car had torn free. Michaels, across the road, drew a bead on the cop, and I felt a kind of hope lift in me, bright as life itself. But then Michaels' eyes went wide. He pulled at his automatic, cursing.

The cop jacked up a shell, stepped closer to me, Michaels more frantic by the second behind him, the cop's eyes set on nothing, it seemed—and then, in a studied and sure move, the cop swung around and shot Michaels.

The first shot lifted Michaels off his feet, the second knocked him off the bridge, backward, so he fell what seemed forever.

The cop turned to me, and I lifted the angle iron, jaggedly sharp where it had been broken off, a bit longer than a baseball bat. But I was yards more distant from him than Michaels had been, and it was a short-barreled automatic the cop had, and he wanted to take no chances this time.

I was his ticket out, however he was caught up in this thing, I'd seen that the moment he'd drawn on Michaels. If I bolted, he might lose me, but if he stepped closer, and I charged him, and he didn't hit something vital? I'd take his head off with that angle iron if he didn't kill me first.

All that we knew in the space of a second, seized on each other, staring, feinting, left, right.

We knew each other now, all right, from that morning at the sinkhole, and I realized then, from the drawing on Edna's refrigerator door, too, the left-handed man with the rifle, Darilyn, that woman in it, and the other, shorter figure?

Michaels? But he was dead. This . . . *cop* had shot him.

I shifted my weight, ducking, bobbing on my feet, blood roaring in my ears, balancing the bar to swing it, or jab with it, for all I was worth, or bolt—I wanted him to think I might bolt.

If I went by Charlie's cruiser—but I wouldn't leave Gwen and the others behind.

The fire up the road made a sharp crackling and there were more muffled explosions—Charlie's ammo going off in his trunk, rounds of twelve gauge and .38s. I could feel the heat on the side of my face.

The cop kicked his feet down, trying to bring me on, but moved closer each time he did it.

He did it again now, scuffed at me, his gun set on his forearm, bluffing himself closer, lifted his foot to do it again, but in that moment, I saw, in the muscle that ridged across the back of his hand, he meant to do it this time, shoot me, and I bent to it, teeth clenched, a howl in my throat, the bar coming up and over my shoulder, my legs bowing to sprint, and I heard, as if from a distance—

a gunshot.

A bright rose puckered the cop's blue shirt, then a second, and a third, the cop's feet kicked out from under him, and he tumbled in a heap, just yards away.

Charlie stood up the road with that 659 in his hand; he smiled, then blinking and gulping at nothing, his knees buckled, and he collapsed on his side.

A blue suit charged through the smoke, let loose a shot that hit the back of the Jaguar.

"Paul!" Gwen cried. *"Please—"*

I stood out front, still holding that length of angle iron.

George climbed the ditch, onto the shoulder, had his arm around one of those BCA cop's necks, Charlie's shorty under his chin.

You could see the other cars up the road through the smoke now.

George said something to the patrolman, and they both got down on their knees.

"Call your people off, or you're gonna die right here," he said. "I'll do it, too."

THIRTY-ONE

I rode in the ambulance with Charlie, Gwen beside me, Claire crying in her arms. Charlie was "leaking," the medic said, was unconscious. They had his shirt off, and he would have looked pretty pathetic, that roll of fat around his middle, fish-belly white skin, but he had scars like I couldn't believe.

"This guy's seen some action," the medic said. "Jesus, look at that."

One exit wound scar on his chest was the size of a fist.

We waited in the Bemidji emergency room vestibule, by the big glowing red Coke machine. All that I hate in hospitals there, a centerless tension, some farm kid missing half his hand; a woman with her face burned black, the skin sliding from it, and doctors, all in white, self-important or not, rushing, the whiteness everywhere, not the loveliness of snow, blue-white cold water, but sick white, slick white, waxed white, death white, steel-legged stretchers, sick people everywhere, down a hallway, medics in blue-green tunics, running, as they had with Charlie.

He'd lost too much blood, and then, in some freak irony, he had to have some odd blood type, one they'd used the last of, just that morning on a family of Vietnamese who'd had a wreck on Highway 2 and had been helicoptered in from Shevlin. George hadn't brought Jimmy down, he'd refused to come, and then I remembered something my father had warned me.

"Put some aside in Pine Point," he'd said. I hadn't.

And I asked about that.

AT THE END of that week Jimmy visited. And he was not so full of himself, but he was still mean. He gave the appearance of being all bent out of shape at his having to spend time at the hospital while his old man recovered.

I spent a fair amount of time at the courthouse, had some attorney taking notes. It was a mess and a half. George was in jail. I was out on bond. I'd told them about the cop missing the fingers, but he hadn't been in any of the cars that had followed us down. I wondered how that could be? Where had he come from then?

It occurred to me he could have come in with Michaels, this Jenkins, to take me and Charlie out, but I'd seen him shoot Michaels.

Or had he been waiting there at the bridge to catch Michaels? Just that?

I turned all of it over in my mind, like poking at a sore tooth, until your tongue hurt worse than the tooth: Jenkins, the cop missing the fingers, sidling into the ditch behind the others, the car exploding. Michaels, pulling at the receiver of his automatic, the gun jammed. Then kicked off the bridge, backward.

A chest shot.

Napoleon told them what he knew and was released. Jimmy was sent down to his mother.

I SPENT MY days, anxious, nights curled up with Gwen at a Motel 6, in Bemidji, and we swam in the pool and doted on Claire. Those mornings, waking and stretching in the parking lot were enough, and having breakfast, Gwen dressed in red and black applique clothes Mardine had made for her, and Claire in a high chair, eating, and then playing with her food. Just then, the miracle of sensation was enough to put me in a state of near bliss.

We'd survived—somehow.

It didn't matter that I was spending money I didn't have. Or that Hugh was calling almost daily, panicked, or threatening to quit, even with the new kids he'd hired to share the brunt of it. It's insane, Hugh said. *Who are all these people?* When would I be back up? How could he have known what a circus the place was?

But there was no use driving north, since we were meeting with an attorney nearly every afternoon. He sent people up, from the Bureau of Tobacco and Firearms, now that the size of the mess was evident. They were calling it a conspiracy, but weren't naming names, searched Michaels' room at the Muskeg Motel for the evidence he'd assembled, but the room had been ransacked, went out to the lodge, which nearly put Hugh over the top, poked around in Pine Point and at the Rambler's, but got the usual stonewall.

All they had was Michaels' notebooks. What he'd written in them he'd directed at George, and at Charlie, and, not surprisingly, Truman Wheeler.

But most of all at me, it turned out.

Michaels had done his homework, and then some. He'd gotten a bill of sale from the agribusiness that sold me the blasting caps, the ones I'd used to excavate on the island the year before, caps like those used in the bomb that destroyed Charlie's cruiser. Had recorded my abortive trips out to Eugene's, all those weeks back. Had sworn statements that I'd made threats, had names of witnesses. All who'd conveniently disappeared. He had times and dates of phone calls I'd made, photographs of George and me down at Stillwater, talking to Stanley.

All of that my attorney poked holes in. After all, what motivation did I have? To kill not only my friend, a policeman, but my wife and child, and two boys?

And had they *not* been in the car—*I* would have been in it.

So I wasn't the bomber, and the threats I'd made? They were proven to be bogus.

They'd been through my safe, but when I asked about it, I was told a strong blow to the handle had opened the safe door before they'd gotten there.

How much money had I stored in it?

I checked the tab in my wallet. Two thousand, two hundred seventy-five. Grocery money. So who'd been in my safe? I asked. I'd expected a finger pointed at this . . . *Jenkins,* the cop missing the fingers. Or Darilyn, but no one mentioned her. Later, they looked for her, and for Carol Herbst, as well, who, of course, had never existed but in the phone book.

And Michaels, why had he been at the bridge and spillway, exactly then?

The officers in the other cars swore Michaels had simply responded to their call. Michaels had been just south, looking into a few informants, had heard the call on his radio, had radioed back, and had come out, maybe to block the road.

A real hero's end for him. In the smoke and confusion, shot by the cop missing the fingers, who, it turned out, had been sent up by a St. Paul division of the BCA to work with Michaels.

Something had gone wrong between them. But Michaels wasn't around to say what. Michaels, who'd gone off the bridge and into the lake, had to have taken a lungful and went under.

That was the official story.

The mud in the bay around the bridge, because the effluent from Calmenson Paper was ten, twelve feet deep—the only really dirty water up there—swallowed any and everything. Scuba divers were in the water nonstop, day after day, until they found one of Michaels' shoes a fair distance from shore, crepe-soled cordovan brogue, a sock not far from it.

That did it.

Jenkins, the cop missing the fingers, it turned out, had had difficulties with Michaels before, on an earlier case. Had been reprimanded even then for excessive use of force.

Why Michaels had requested him on this case they were not at liberty to discuss.

What Jenkins had been up to was anybody's guess.

They'd look into it.

So, for us, all around, a nice clean end.

THIRTY-TWO

At the hospital, shiny chrome, white uniforms, and lifesaving machines, and doctors working over Charlie, who lay unconscious on his back, I fell into a habit of speaking Ojibwemowin with an officer the BCA sent to stand guard, Tony Beaulieu, a great-grandson of Gus Beaulieu.

Gus, along with B. L. (Benjamin) Fairbanks, had been responsible for buying uneducated half-breeds' allotments for a song, turning around and selling to timber and mining interests, buying more land, and selling yet again, and in that way gave away more than half of the reservation up there. Gus and B. L. were anathema in reserve parlance. Names that had the power of swear words, used only sparingly.

It was a tough legacy to live down, and it gave Tony a kind of watchful quiet.

He wanted to know why I was so wrapped up in this white cop. And that rang a strange bell—I thought at first he meant the cop missing the fingers, Jenkins; and then it occurred to me—it had to have been Jenkins who'd come down 71, passed himself off as Truman Wheeler. But I'd looked at the report. Charlie, before the explosion and all that followed, asked that a photocopy be sent up.

No mention of missing fingers. Or tattoos.

Beshwaji, I told this Tony, nodding to Charlie in the bed.

Tony didn't joke at that, tell me I should look at who I was calling a friend.

The idea was, Tony would watch over Charlie until an official charge had been filed. Didn't want him leaping out of the bed and running off. He'd shot a fellow officer in the back, after all, and not just once.

(And what did they make of Charlie's protestations, that he'd been acting on our behalf? That Jenkins had intended to not only shoot Michaels, but me as well?

All that had been taken as the incoherent rambling of a desperate, and injured, man.)

But Tony, I could tell, had his suspicions.

So, afternoons, when the doctors or nurses were around, we spoke Ojibwemowin, and Charlie, when he came out from under the painkillers they'd put him on, saw us there at his beside and rolled his eyes.

"Jesus," he said. "I knew it. I died and I'm in hell."

But he reached for my hand, squeezed it, hard.

"I thought I was a goner," he said, "I mean, my blood's one of those odd ones."

He looked at me, big eyed, and all banged up. What could I tell him?

"They got it from the person closest to you, Charlie," I said.

From the look on his face, I knew I was going to pay for this one.

"Jimmy," he said.

What could I do, but nod?

He looked stunned, some resurrection taking place there. It was shocking, and though part of me knew it for the good thing it might be, there, with Charlie flat out on his back, I felt I'd done something almost—

Well, something unconscionable. Charlie got so choked up he wanted to be alone a minute.

I had something the size of an apple in my throat, too. All that with my boy, and losing him the way I had, came back in that hallway, Tony, the great grandson of one the biggest swindlers of all time, right beside me.

His uniform was steam pressed, starched. His badge was shiny, cleaned in vinegar, just the way they were supposed to clean them. His shoes were so shiny I could see a reflection of the hallway in them.

Tony reached for my arm, took hold of it where there were still bruises inside my elbow. Needle tracks. Even three days later I was dizzy.

He squeezed a little; I must have frowned.

"No," he said, "I don't want any bullshit. Any double talk. Don't tell me why you did it. Why you told him that about the blood. I want to know what's behind it."

He pressed his card into my hand.

"Anything comes up," he said. "Call me."

A WEEK WENT BY.

The bomb that had destroyed Charlie's cruiser fit the picture the BCA put together. That's the way it came out in the *Tribune,* too.

An internal conflict, involving only locals, the bomb nothing sophisticated.

Tony asked me about that, who'd know about the kind of explosive that was used, Charlie asleep there in his bed between us.

"It was the smell of fuel oil that tipped you off, wasn't it?" he said.

I told him it was. Anybody up there would know, I told Tony. I explained I'd used ANFO myself, when I had to excavate on the island. Tony said I shouldn't let on I was so familiar with all that, or I'd have more cops bothering me.

But the explosive. ANFO.

ANFO is an acronym for ammonium nitrate fuel oil.

You bought the ammonium nitrate in granules from farm suppliers, mixed it with fuel oil. Sixteen parts fertilizer, one part oil. The detonator was simple enough. Blasting caps, about the thickness of a pencil, maybe an inch, two inches long.

"Where'd they put it?" I asked.

Tony told me, in the report he'd read, they'd wedged the bomb up under the car between the gas tank and the rear seat, where nobody'd see it, so the gas tank would explode, too, make more smoke and fire, had used a Kmart windup clock to set it off.

They had the remains of the clock, the face of it, arms bent at the time of the explosion.

I said, "But you don't think it was the clock that did it, do you? Set it off."

Tony shook his head. He showed me the latest story in the *Tribune.* Already it had been relegated to the back of the paper and was referred to as *"Upper Red Lake Unrest."*

The *Tribune* stated that tracing the construction of a bomb such as that used in the attack was nearly impossible, given farmers in and around the area bought astronomical volumes of fertilizer every summer, blasting caps were in common use, and half the "underdeveloped reserve" still relied on fuel oil for heat.

Even the clock wasn't much to go on. Kmart's biggest seller. $9.95, on sale all summer for $6.00 at Blue Light discount. Warroad had them, and so did nearly every small-town Kmart within driving distance.

The case had been turned over to the FBI, the paper reported. The remains of the patrol car had been examined and were in police impound.

For a time I was questioned, and I told them what they wanted to hear.

The final word was that the bomb had been intended for me. And through me, Charlie. Politically motivated, was how they put it.

They were right about that much.

Simple people, simple conspiracy, they said. I didn't argue that, and Tony just grinned when I pointed to the conclusion of that article we read in Charlie's room.

The bombing, the BTF has concluded, is the work of an amateur. A suspect is in custody.

Nawaji, I heard Henry say, pay attention to the names.

An *amateur.* That was right, too. But not in the way they meant it. I took it for the older sense of the word—from the root, *amator*—a lover.

He was out there, I was sure of it. Who, after all, had broken into my safe? And that Mardine, it turned out, had emptied it before that happened?

That was just my good fortune.

But the investigators had nothing to go on, and my Tall Friend and the two others were nowhere to be found, had left not so much as a trace, making one investigator question their very existence.

So, for the time being, they turned all their attention on Truman.

And Charlie? He was let go. Lost his job, pension, the works.

THIRTY-THREE

When we came in after our last day in Bemidji, climbed the hill to the lodge, Hugh was shooing a shortish, dark-haired boy out onto the porch. The boy balanced a tray of drinks to our end of season crowd, bankers, insurance people, businessmen, contractors, lifted one drink off the tray after another, set the drinks down, the tray wobbling, so that I cringed a time or two—he messed up like that, he'd put a drink right in someone's lap.

But they weren't watching the kid. They were watching Gwen and me and were giving Claire, red-haired Claire, curious looks—some hadn't seen her before—but only for a moment.

Mardine, in black applique, came out and Claire let go a delighted squeal,

"*Ninoshe!*" auntie.

I set her down and she ran to Mardine.

Gwen reached behind her, and I took her hand. We climbed the last of it, Gwen's hair that blue black, heavy on her shoulders, and face beautiful, and stylishly dressed in gathered skirt, a blue the color of evening sky.

I fell in love with her all over again, something like life itself in the swinging of her hips, and the fluid way she moved right into it, ahead of me.

It was that kind of night, balmy, a breeze singing in the pines.

"It's good to see you," she said, to one guest after another, and I was drawn, almost seamlessly, back into my life. At least, on the surface.

And when Gwen nodded, after an hour or so, I got up, excused myself, and went around back. It was a Sunday, and most of them, these guests, would be staying on a week or two, so there wasn't that pressure to catch up.

Mardine had quail grilling on the fifty-gallon drums I'd put legs on. Was roasting potatoes, green beans. Marinated the quail with Cointreau and orange juice and tamari, brushed it on so they had a lightly darkened glaze.

Beautiful, the bulldog, was chained to a tree, and I went over and rubbed her head, and Mardine came out, Claire still cemented to her side.

Claire reached for me, and I took her up, and she kissed me, and then reached for the dog.

Hugh marched around from the front.

"Godalmighty," he said. "How do you do all of this? Those people eat and drink like crazy. No matter how often I go into Pine Point there's always something crappin' out or going short, or—"

He got out a list. Mardine had written it down for him, what needed to be done. He'd added to it, almost obsessively. I knew all too well what a worker guilt could make out of you, so tried to reassure him.

"How's that new kid doing?"

Hugh looked surprised. I laughed. "See? Jobs get done the way they're supposed to, you forget all about 'em. And that kid in diapers out there?"

"He's okay, but he's scared shitless . . . of people, I guess."

We both knew what he hadn't said—*waibish.* The kid had never been off the reserve, had never worked outside his family's business, logging.

"He'll be all right," I said, smiling.

One of the older guests, bald, oversize glasses, lots of jewelry, came around back, comically ducking, then squeezed Mardine at the barbecue, and she gave him a mock angry look.

"Artie," I said. "How's business suiting you?"

Artie ran an exclusive men's store in downtown Chicago.

"Bunch of stuffed shirts," he joked.

He snatched at my head. "Hey, what's this? A gray hair?"

I grinned for him.

"You know how it is," I joked. "You don't die, you get older, Artie. Huh?"

GWEN PUT HER head out the back, called me inside for the phone. I hadn't heard it ring.

"*Robert* something."

I was still cornered at the grill, now giving Mardine a hand, using a basting brush, hoping Artie would pick up on the hint.

"Tell him we won't have any cabins open until the second or third week of September," I said.

The screen door closed with a slap, Artie joking again, and Gwen called a second time.

"He's saying *you* called *him*," Gwen said.

Mardine nodded, confirming it. *"Dasing,"* she said, he's called many times.

I gave it up there, smiled for Artie, nodded to Mardine. Maybe she'd have better luck getting rid of Artie, would be more blunt.

"Dr. Underhill," this Robert something said, as if he needed no introduction.

I was drawing a complete blank until it hit me, and then I was suddenly uneasy.

"Bad time to call?" he said.

I said it wasn't, and explained how I'd been running a resort. In Minnesota? he asked. I didn't like what he was implying in that— that I'd run home, run back to the safe arms of family. Not true, but I couldn't tell him that, couldn't tell anyone.

So I told him that was right, and he laughed.

"I don't suppose an understanding of biochemistry is too useful up there, is it?" he said. "Or am I wrong about that?"

"Listen," I said. "I just wanted to run something by you."

"What's it all about?" He knew I wouldn't call him over nothing.

"We've got moraines all over the place here; what soil there is, is pretty poor," I said, "but somebody's been prospecting. I think."

"What do you mean, 'but'—but *what?*"

"What could somebody be looking for?"

"What's under the soil? Sedimentary? Or igneous?"

"Igneous. Granite, actually. Quartz, orthoclase, microcline, mica. Any market value there?"

"Ah, *market value. Now* we're talking. Somebody wants to sell something. Well, there was a market in mica, back in the twenties, but not now. Granite you can get anywhere, microcline, the same."

There was a hum on the line.

"You got any marshland?"

I wanted to tell him we'd gotten more than our share of it, in the Angle's central corridor acres.

"Yes," I said.

"It hasn't been dredged?"

"God no, nobody bothers with it. Up here we call it muskeg. Most of what's up here hasn't had anyone but us on it since the glacier receded, you know, eight, ten thousand years ago."

"Railroad near?"

I had to think about that. What kind of question was that?

"Somebody was pushing to build a new dock on the shore of the Angle. Commercial size. Outbuildings, machinery, some logging, all that, so they needed a substantial-sized road in, a highway really. It looked like they wanted the road into the dock to connect with the

Soo Line, or the Burlington Northern. Bring in cats and the rest of it on rail, needed a mining clause to make gravel. That was the pitch they threw us."

"But nothing grows on this . . . muskeg?"

"It's poor land," I said, "but brush grows so thick there you can't keep it off. Red willow, basswood, box elder—all worthless, just grows like crazy out there."

Out east, Dr. Underhill sighed.

"You there?"

"I'm here—" he said. "That's all you've got?"

I tried to think of something else. I drew a complete blank, glanced up and saw Mardine, big as a bear, digging in the refrigerator.

"How about another casino?" Dr. Underhill joked.

Mardine slipped a list of groceries on the door, under a magnet, a cow in grass dancing garb, and some connection struck me, so much so I felt my eyes widen at it:

Edna's drawing had been a warning about *who* was out there. Eugene's scrawl at the bottom of that page of compounds about *what*. A word sat in my mouth, round as a stone.

Bakade.

"I got a core sample someone ran up here, was supposed to be a compaction study for a road site, and on the bottom somebody wrote, 'Hungry'—could that mean anything?"

"Is there P205 on your core sample?"

I remembered there had been. "Yes," I said.

Dr. Underhill let go an amused breath. He'd loved puzzles and had liked that I'd broken most of those he'd given me. But I was in no mood for it now.

"You've got appatite," he said.

"What?"

"Phosphate, in stone. It's called appatite."

"Does it have any market value?" I said.

He asked me to give him a minute. I could hear him on the other phone in his office. He was excited. Listening, I felt an old, and deep discomfort, a sense of having, in some way, yet again, failed myself. I didn't even have the satisfaction of having finished out east.

I told myself, waiting there, what Nita, my grandfather, had told me, over and over when I was little, as if he knew exactly how these things in the larger world would come to haunt me—

Just because you *can* do something, Nawaji, doesn't mean you *should.*

"What's your percentage of P205?" he asked, back again.

I remembered the figure on the sheet of paper I'd found in Eugene's cabin. It was a guess, but I was almost certain the two sites would be similar, if not identical—why, otherwise, would they have bothered?

When things had blown up in their faces at Rice Lake, they'd moved north to the Angle, after all.

"Ten percent."

There was that conversation on the other line, the clunk of the receiver set down. A student knocked on Dr. Underhill's office door. "Run that through the spectrometer again, and see if you get a better yield," he said. The other phone rang in the office, and Dr. Underhill answered it.

I heard him say, on the other line, "Right, that's right. Ten percent." There was a long pause. "Oh, is that so." His voice had that cutting tone in it I was all too familiar with. "I'm sorry to hear that," he said. "Well, I'm at," and he named the school, "but we don't usually concern ourselves with that sort of thing. Right. Right, thank you," he said, hanging up. "Just on the phone with 3M."

"And?" I said.

Dr. Underhill gave one of his famous sighs. He'd done that in class, when a student hadn't been fast enough. Maybe there was nothing to it, after all?

"Talked to somebody you might remember—Jonathon Warwick."

"I remember," I said. He'd been one of my classmates, a loudmouth.

"We gave him that fellowship. What was it you said when I told you you'd won it? 'Better than being poked in the eye with a stick,' that was it."

There was that hollow, radio hum on the line. I thought of ten things to say to him but said none of it. He knew I wouldn't hang up now, since he had the answer to what I wanted to know.

So, I waited, fighting with myself.

Still, I wouldn't have it different. Living another's life is the worst mistake of all, whether you're good at it or not.

"Just tell me what Jonathon said."

"You could've made something of yourself if you'd wanted to. Why didn't you?"

"Wasn't in me," I said.

"Right," Dr. Underhill said. "Well— Jonathon's just south of you in the Twin Cities. Works metallurgy. Called him because geography's important with this stuff—the environmental loonies don't like how the processing affects the groundwater or that the mining's done open pit. He tells me eight percent appatite is a good find, ten percent's almost unheard of."

"Let's talk business," I said, "I'm not interested in theory right now."

Dr. Underhill laughed. "Business? But you were never interested in that, were you? *Business* was just too dirty for you."

"So what do they use it for?" I said.

"Processing aluminum, soaps, but primarily for fertilizer."

"Fertilizer."

In my mind, fertilizer and cow excrement were one in the same thing. But what did I know? No one in my family had ever farmed. We were Giwadiswin, trappers and hunters, and had never taken allotments through the BIA for "agricultural development."

"So all that acreage is pretty much worthless," I said. "I mean, for purposes of mining or whatever."

"Did I say that?" Dr. Underhill said. "No, it's *protected* land.

You people—" and he paused there "—won't do anything with it, that's what he said, so why even look into it? That's what your old rival told me."

I wanted to tell him that Jonathon had been no rival, and even then, he'd cheated. I wanted to tell him, if he had something to say to me, he shouldn't be hiding behind someone like Jonathon Warwick.

And I wanted to tell him, even after all the years that had gone by, that he shouldn't be taking the credit for what I'd accomplished back then.

It was insulting, or worse.

Only I didn't, because I wanted to get to the end of it.

"So how much would it be worth if you *could* excavate and move the stuff off the reservation?"

"Twenty, thirty . . ."

"What?" I said, exasperated. "What did he say? *Dollars per what.* Per ton? Per—"

"No, Paul," Dr. Underhill said. "With a railroad to move it out, and on the federal budget—there's BIA money in it, right?—it's almost pure profit. That appatite *would be* worth thirty, forty, who knows—fifty . . . and there's an international market, the developing countries are desperate—"

"Fifty *what?*"

"—*million.* Maybe more. If you've got substantial acreage, could be worth three times that."

It took my breath away. I'd hit pay dirt, and then some.

Appatite.

"You there?" he said.

"Thank you," I said, "for all your help." Then added, "And I can say now, Dr. Underhill, the disappointment goes both ways."

LATE THAT NIGHT, after the guests were all in, Gwen and I went down to the cabin, and lay in bed in the dark, and after a time, Gwen said,

"What is it?"

I told her how I'd failed, hadn't put what I'd found at Eugene's together with that warning Edna'd left, had missed everything, going right back to the boat coming in and circling, and the morning after, not pushing the boys, all moments when, had I acted, done something more decisive, all of it would have turned out differently.

"Oh, Paul," Gwen said, and pressed her head to my back, wrapped her arms around me.

But she knew. I needed, more than anything just then, to be connected. By blood, by skin, with everything in me, to rise up into our dream of life, again, which was life itself.

Gwen behind me, I lay in the dark, thinking about what the appatite had brought us.

There was a certain fascination in the numbers I didn't like— something in me keened to it all. How could it not? I'd been struggling all my life, at times, early on, hadn't so much as had shoes to wear, or a belt to cinch up my hand-me-down pants.

There was freedom in that kind of money, wasn't there?

But it wasn't mine anyway, I reminded myself, even if that appatite was on my land. My Angle land was on the reservation proper, and anything that came off it, from mining, or in timber, belonged to the Red Lake Band Chippewa, and not me. A business, that was different—we generated revenue, but taking things off reserve land? Even if a mining operation were up and running, the revenue would go right into the Red Lake Band's common fund. Divided by all. Unless—the land were privatized, leased, to a company, or, even—the State. Then, only a percentage of what was taken off the land went to the tribe, and the remainder?

Into whoever's pockets ran the operation.

So why not me? If I were just a little . . . crooked.

I had to laugh at myself, even considering, in the dark and quiet there, doing something like someone had tried to do now.

But then I sobered at rest of it—even angered.

No matter what the Angle was worth, it wasn't, not for so much as the blink of an eye, worth Eugene's life, or Elmer's, or Charlie's, which was, even then, spiraling into oblivion.

How could you put a value on all that? On so much as a friend's handshake?

You love a place, and its people, and your infinitesimally small time in it, like your very soul. After all, what else is there?

And so, with Claire asleep in the adjoining room, Gwen and I made love as we hadn't since that night earlier in the summer. No— maybe since that first night we'd spent together on the island, more than a decade before.

It scared me.

All too often, in my life, endings snuck up on me like that. In fire, and yearning, and need.

I WOKE LONG before sunrise, the remains of my dreams like malevolent presences in the room, Gwen tucked in beside me. I let my mind wander, hoping that at some point it would exhaust itself, and I'd sleep again.

But when I did, I dreamed of windigos and woke time and again in a sweat.

There was a whole cycle of stories anyone raised on the reservation knew, windigo stories, about men who, out of hunger, or greed, or envy, became cannibal giants, made of ice. They towered big as trees, killed and rampaged without remorse, one way to kill them, to become cold and ice yourself.

A cannibal for cannibals. That's what I was thinking about, lying there, and about the stories my grandfather, Nita, had told me.

In those stories, the hero had an accomplice somewhere, and after the hero had battled the windigos and beaten them, but now one himself, inhuman and ferocious, the accomplice would entice the hero to drink hot fat, which would melt him down to size.

No mean feat, getting a cannibal tall as a pine tree to drink hot fat.

Or, in other stories, the hero, instead of becoming a windigo himself, could keep moving, searching, and trust to the miraculous—

Which might appear in something as common as a pile of stones.

Windigos, the legend went, hid their hearts.

If you could find a windigo's heart, you could kill the windigo.

In one of Nita's stories, a boy so fat he couldn't walk, but rolled from place to place, did exactly that. Round As a Ball Boy, in deep woods, tracking the windigos who'd killed his father, tumbled down a hill, upsetting a piles of stones.

That was the clue: a pile of stones.

You see, windigos, being self-consumed, can't remember where they hide their hearts, and so, have to mark those spots. With stones, a mound of dirt, a broken branch. I never forgot, in Nita's telling of that story, how the least likely hero, Round As A Ball Boy, with a sliver of steel, pierced those windigos' hearts. And set his people free.

Sometimes, success was only a matter of knowing what to look for, Nita told me.

Just then, I had one, bright clue—the Okitsita fetish. And a voice on tape, voracious. A high-plains Chippewa, from around Saskatchewan, who spoke Anishininiimowin.

Just that.

Put them together and—*what?*

THIRTY-FOUR

I had my pilot fly Charlie up from Bemidji, met him there at the dock.

He'd lost a lot of blood, but the bullet had, almost miraculously, only broken a rib, and had missed his spine and lung, cleanly exiting his back, and hadn't done much worse. There'd been some infection, but they'd taken care of that, so released him.

He was mad as hell, sputtering and his arm in a sling, and white tape there under his shirt, his uniform, mustard stained, and dirty. They hadn't so much as washed it for him, yet he'd insisted on putting it on. Just to get back up to Pine Point.

"This is how they treat you," he said.

Gwen coaxed him into the lodge, and he made a good show with the guests, and not so much as one person asked him about the charges that had been leveled at him—wrongful death in the case of the cop missing the fingers, and a tangle of nonsense about his cruiser, and why George had had Charlie's shotgun, all harm coming to sit squarely on Charlie's shoulders.

I filed all that away. It was bold. That those running the show would use the truth that way, to attack the injured parties.

Thinking about it put me in a blue mood.

Which Gwen, touching my shoulder, warned me was showing.

We were in it. High season.

Here was the business of business. We had to look good now. Here were our most discerning guests. They were paying the highest rates of the year. They could be anywhere on the lake. Barney's Ball Lake, Northwest Outfitters, Whitefish Bay Lodge, Manitou Lodge, but they were here, and had been, since I'd begun guiding.

We were an odd sort of family. A mixed lot. Trendily dressed democrats, hip to jazz, and in from Barcelona, or Perugia, or Paris, all talk of books and politics; the old republican contingent, in tailored suits and dresses, the men in white bucks or tasseled shoes, relating golf games and indignation over taxes, the wives in stiff, swept-up hair, and bright lipstick, watching; and a few closet fascists, always in clothes somehow out of date, and oddly severe haircuts, like Owen Harnak, up again, even after I'd torn into him two years earlier.

So they were bearing with the sometimes dark presence of Charlie and George on the island, too.

I smiled through it all.

But when I thought I wasn't being watched, I felt a heaviness in my face, almost leaden.

If he was out there, he'd be coming. And he was no ordinary killer.

Still, in those moments, my forearms hardened, my hands balled into fists.

Come on, I said to no one, *Bring it on, you.*

FRIDAY NIGHT OF that week, Charlie was on the phone in the lodge after dinner. I was in the dining room, watching the clock, and trying to talk to Viki Nyberg, who, in her low-cut sweater, was causing something of a distraction. She'd had a few too many drinks, and when I'd rigidly kept my eyes on hers, and her fiancé ambled off "to the loo," a resigned but almost bitter grin on his face, she said,

"Go ahead and look—they'll be around my knees in a few years, and then what?"

I didn't look. I smiled, made some small talk, tried to move to another table, but she pressed my forearm.

Then the fiancé was back and, picking up his fork in his left hand, the tines inverted, and mashing peas against it with the knife in his right hand, he said,

"Golly, this is good. You do this all right on the island, do you?"

"He wants you to know he went to Choate," Viki said. "And then, where was it? Yale, that's right. But, *Golly,* I didn't go anywhere. Not that I stayed home, either. But he took one ogle at these and—"

The fiancé's face reddened. He gave me a look that presaged my leaving the table, said, to get me moving—

"Where might you have attended university, Mr.—"

I shrugged, smiled for both of them, kicked my chair back and stood.

"Didn't so much as finish high school," I said, which was the truth, then nodded, and polite as could be, let myself out.

CHARLIE WAS STARING at the wall in the kitchen. It was late, and I thought, that's it. Another night, and— But Charlie nodded, a grim look on his face, Mardine and Hugh there at the sink, and I went out with him.

Brought a dish for Beautiful, and she ate, happy to have company.

"So what is it?" I said.

"That Walter," he said, "is a naturalized citizen. Married some woman in Michigan, got divorced, worked in Detroit, in the worst of it. Got promoted, time, and time again. Faster than he should have—"

"I'm not getting you, Charlie."

"Before he came here, to Pine Point, he was a *cop,* in Detroit. *Walter,* Walter Davis, your council chairman. And never, on any of those forms, did he identify himself as a minority, not even when it would have done something for him. You gettin' it yet?"

"No," I said, frowning. I resented what he was implying, that Walter'd got where he had through favoritism. The handout.

There was a peal of laughter from the porch, all thirty or so of our guests drinking, playing cards, dancing, music of the early sixties playing, now Miller's hit, "King of the Road."

Walter was metis, of French-Chippewa descent, the French coming through his great-grandfather. Though it was obvious to us he was Chippewa, outside he could pass for white.

Charlie rolled his eyes. "Jesus, I didn't mean *that,*" he said. "I meant, only cops who play dirty get promoted like that, or awful damn lucky or good ones."

"So where was he before Detroit?" I asked.

I'd told Charlie that the Okitsita rosette was high plains, but nothing more.

"He went to school in Toronto, the university there."

I let go an almost relieved breath. "So he's from Ontario." East of us.

"No, you go back a little further, high school, he went to—" and Charlie had a snear on his face saying it, "—St. Mary of the Woods. In fuckin' *Moose Jaw, Saskatchewan.*"

I felt as if I were walking through glass wall after glass wall, all those things I'd assumed, that I'd been wrong about.

"Moose Jaw," I said.

"Somebody in the Twin Cities dug all that up on him. That mean anything?"

The night came in around us, darker. Charlie had put one damning thought in my mind: A *cop* was behind it. But a cop who *also* just happened to be a high-plains Chippewa. *And* could pass for white.

"I'd say Walter's in bed with Truman," Charlie said.

"Who looked into Walter's background?"

"Michaels."

"He just tell you back when, or what?"

Charlie lit a cigarette, crushed the match under his boot.

"You think for one second I'd take verbatim anything that had come out of that asshole's mouth? Jesus, what do you take me for? I mean, hell, the dumbshit's sent up here, some expert and all, and he doesn't even know the name of the lake he's lookin' for, Jesus!"

I felt my eye tick. I forced myself to take a slow, deep breath.

"What do you mean?" I said.

"When Michaels first came up, he pulls into the pumps behind the station, trying to pass as a tourist or something, got one of those geeky hats on with the lures hangin' from it, already, even then, screwin' with me, like I'm too stupid to notice he's in a car with government plates. So he wants directions, out to see you.

"I knew you'd been on a fly in, so asked him what bay, where it was he thought he was supposed to run into you. Wouldn't even look at me, the prick, says, *Binisho'hunk* or *Bohunk* or whatever, or some such shit."

I made a face, as though I were trying to recall something.

"What?" Charlie said, letting go a plume of smoke.

"Binishinuk."

"That's it," Charlie said, and for a second he looked confused, though now at the expression on my face, surprise, or even shock, there.

"I say something wrong?"

"You were telling me about Michaels," I said.

"I was saying that Michaels didn't know shit up here," Charlie said. "So—" He squinted over his cigarette. "Yesterday I had somebody owes me a favor look into copies of everything Michaels requested through the Warroad office. Few hours ago all this crap Michaels had on Walter comes through my fax. I mean, whaddaya think?"

I nodded, a plan already taking shape in my mind, a simple way to end the whole mess. Just me.

And the man responsible.

I slapped Charlie on the back, Charlie, who, though he was hurt in ways I could only imagine, was doing his best to keep moving. I was grateful, and then some.

I recalled what Charlie had said earlier. *Whoever comes out, keep him breathing.* I'd do that, but thinking of Elmer, and Eugene, and that afternoon they'd set the bomb off, the harm that could have come to Gwen, and Claire, and the rest of us, I wondered.

"It's him then, right?" Charlie said.

"Good as red-handed," I said, joking, just for Charlie.

GEORGE CAME IN around midnight. The party had moved out onto the slope in front of the lodge. Dancing, and laughing, and drunkenness of a benign, forgivable sort—after all, no one was going anywhere, just a short walk up to a cabin, and a bed Josette, or now Darius, had turned down earlier, Godiva chocolates on the pillow.

Going down through our guests, a handshake, and a good night, now Bobby Darrin on the stereo, to meet George, I caught Gwen's hand, embraced her.

"Be careful," she said, and let me go.

BUT HE DIDN'T come that night. Or the night after.

Gwen's parents were due up in five days, for the last week and the end of season dinner. It was Friday now, and the summer was winding down, you could feel it in the air, and already one birch on shore had gone to yellow.

Delbert ran guests out on the pontoon, but no one was fishing. Or they'd catch and release.

I'd fallen into the ritual of the resort, mornings now up and making lists, sometimes going into Pine Point with Hugh, and sometimes not.

But always, George was on the island, or Charlie, out of uniform, doing a poor job of looking like a guest, his agitated smoking and glancing around giving him away. But always, nights, both were up. Charlie on our cabin porch, George in the lodge, eating more than three guests, and trying to joke with Mardine, who was set against him no matter what he did.

But no one came.

And that got me to thinking. I'd have to do something, clearly provocative, whether it was dangerous or not. Because on the surface of it the whole business had gone cold. Truman had come up with alibis enough to put him in the clear, as we'd thought he would. The BCA, at least ostensibly, had pulled out. The new cop at Pine Point had settled in, even though he'd made plenty of enemies already by cracking down on underage drinkers at the Rambler's, and the road was in a permanent stall, it seemed.

Pine Point looked as it always had. The tall, brass statue of the Viking at the center of town, shining gold mornings. The end of the season traffic, more sedans now, Cadillacs, BMWs, Mercedes, than minivans and station wagons, signaling the arrival of the older, mon-eyed crowd, smell of cigars, and rough voices.

And what, I thought, would happen when my guests were gone?

He could come, then, any time, day or night. All that potential for mishap magnified ten times.

No one can be alert that long. Life takes over, the heart slows, the trembling in your limbs subsides, ritual, the old paths are just old paths, and the fear that kept you moving, alive?

Even my almost hourly shock at remembering my knife was still out there, and that someone could use it against me, didn't jar me now.

So I knew I had to push. I was a wreck. Night after night I sat on our cabin steps with Charlie, that shorty Remington twelve across my knees, the bulldog at my feet, her chain wrapped around a stack of empty tin cans. If she sprang up, even if we'd gotten sloppy, I'd have a shot at them. But I was just going through the motions.

All along I knew he wouldn't come, not with George and Charlie on the island.

So I sold Charlie and George on a plan to shake Walter out. To get him to show himself. It was a pack of lies on my part, but I justified it by telling myself I was the one who'd stay behind, take what came.

The rosette, I told Charlie, had to belong to Walter, that was clear now.

We'd hung on to it, hadn't told any of the investigators we had it, while George circulated Polaroids to all the northern lakes reservations. George had found, in Saskatchewan, people who knew what it was, but not who it belonged to, or, they weren't saying. I said it was time we stirred up the BCA with it.

"A bit like shoving a stick in a hornets' nest, isn't it?" George said.

"We won't tell them what it is," Charlie said. "The way to do it is to just give a few hints, see if whoever was working through them bites on it."

I had to agree.

EARLY AFTERNOON, CHARLIE called the BCA in Bemidji.

He told them he'd gotten some new evidence he'd like to present on the behalf of his case, evidence that would show who was behind the bombing, and that the cop who'd been killed, Jenkins, the cop missing the fingers, had been there *not* to protect and serve, but to knock off witnesses, including Michaels, take out those the explosion hadn't. Somebody who'd been around for Eugene's murder, too.

"Somebody you'd never figure, not even with bells on it, or waving checkered flags," Charlie said. "Somebody you haven't so much as looked at sideways."

"Uh-huh," the officer on duty told Charlie.

They told him it could wait until Monday, and Charlie threw a fit. He had an attorney, he said, and No, it couldn't wait. He wanted his job back. He harangued whoever it was, and they refused, until he told them, he had hard evidence.

This changed the whole picture.

What *kind* of hard evidence, they wanted to know.

Tapes, and something the conspirators had lost at the road site where the first agent was killed, earlier in the summer, Charlie told them, would identify the killer, proof positive.

You could be more specific, the officer said.

Charlie said not.

So they agreed to meet. In Bemidji.

Fine, Charlie said, which was exactly what I thought he'd say.

I told them to go, but I kept the fetish. I wasn't going to have them giving it to just anyone at the station in Bemidji, not, when it was clear now, there was at least one snake in that garden of blue suits.

So they took one of George's Polaroids.

THAT EVENING, RIGHT around dusk, Charlie and George drove down 525, stopped for coffee in Warroad, and in the Cafe made a scene—so much so that the proprietor called the police—then quickly got on Highway 5 south, headed for Bemidji.

Or it looked like that, Charlie and George in George's blue Pontiac sedan, behind them, limping along a mile or so back, on overweighted springs, a ratty looking tomato-soup-red Toyota, with one headlight, bobbing like some crazed kid's toy.

THIRTY-FIVE

We shut down at one in the morning. All the guests were saving it now for the big end of season dinner, and they turned in one after another, and as each left, sleepy, and ambling to a cabin, my stomach knotted, until there were just Gwen and Mardine on the porch, playing cards, as if it were any night of the week. I went inside and sat in the office. I had Charlie's 659 on a shelf under the desk.

The dog I'd left down in the bunkhouse. Didn't want her growling.

If he were alive, by now he had to know I had the fetish. The fetish proved he was at the sinkhole, had called the shots there, the third man, had shot Eugene, which alone was enough to put him away—forever.

I tried to do my books, couldn't push the buttons on my calculator for the shaking of my hands, each breath coming short, numbers adding up to nothing, and absolutely alone, and then, I felt, in me, or in the room, a kind of presence, palpable in stillness.

Wenjishid, a word old, and long forgotten, came to me.

Spirit.

That room started to breathe. I went to the window, where I'd watched the boys going up the hill all that time ago, arguing about a glass insulator.

I wanted the feeling to stay, so at my desk, I drew a song picture, of the kind that had been done on birch bark, and when it blossomed off the page, I was amazed that I remembered. Song pictures, and they came now off the pencil, one after another, with them memories so long pushed under, scent of lake, and duck grass, and rice, and my father, and Nita, singing, so I was as much hypnotized as listening, my heart a drum, one voice, distinct, and singular, and the songs drew me into myself, and the pencil moved, danced, and all that old life, and longing to live, and the beauty that was fast passing away, rose up in me, but seen now, as if at a distance, because to realize the beauty was to know you couldn't possess it, no matter how you wanted, and were only a lover, held in its grasp for a short while.

And as I was drawing that last song picture, I felt, more than heard, him in the room.

I looked up, heart ticking slowly in my neck.

I'd discussed this moment with Gwen and Mardine but hadn't told them why he'd come. If they saw him, they'd let him go by, but would stop talking on the porch. But they were still talking, and I heard the patter of Mardine shuffling cards.

But of course, he hadn't gone by them, and it wasn't Walter anyway.

It was Michaels, with his back to the door now.

He had an automatic, dull, blue-black, in his right hand. A cop, he was all ritual, a sweep of the room, then stepping through the vestibule and into the room itself.

With my boot, I pressed the button I'd taped to the floor, to start the recorder.

"I'm not wearing a bullet proof vest like you did," I said.

"You figured that out, did you?"

I set the pencil down, lay my hands flat on the desk. Michaels stepped closer, the gun trained on me, looking this way and that, until he was sure we were alone and stood an arm's length back of the desk, his dark brown eyes, I saw now, on mine.

"Why?" I said. "Why'd you do it?"

"You could never know."

"You think it was all so easy for me?"

He ran his thumb up the automatic's black rubber grip and back.

"That school you went to—all that, people giving you things, and you not even using them. Handouts. I know more about you than you'd ever imagine. How you just happened to be around to pick up this place."

"It's worthless," I said. "You should know that. Just rocks and water and trees. Except those acres on the Angle."

Michaels grimaced, his eyes narrowed against the light on my desk.

"If you'd just stayed out of it, back in February," he said, "none of it would have happened with the boy, or old Morreaseau—"

Eyes bloodshot and smelling of woodsmoke and stale clothing, he came closer, into the light. Green twill, now soot blackened. I had my hands pressed on the desktop, but was slowly pulling them back.

"But no, you didn't do that."

There was no way I could get the gun off the shelf in front of my knees now, or fire through the desk with any accuracy.

All that sunk in me, a kind of ashen gloom, and I decided, then, the least I could do was keep him talking, get him on tape.

Charlie would see to the rest of it.

The player was locked in the desk drawer, a remote speaker in my Orioles cap in front of me. Michaels might be able to disable the speaker when he found it, but he'd never get the player out of the desk without Gwen or Mardine hearing him—or unless I unlocked the drawer and got it out for him. That Hudson's Bay desk was that substantial, and they'd meant it to be.

"Give it," Michaels said. "What you've got. I know it's you that had Charlie call. And he's gone now. That wasn't too sharp, was it.

Not telling him you knew who it was."

He was stroking the back of the automatic with his thumb, more quickly now.

"Give it—"

"Why should I?"

He slowly lifted the automatic to my head, the cold steel touching my temple.

"It'll make too much noise," I said.

"It does, I'll take out your wife, and that fat old bitch Mardine. I'll be out of here before anybody has a light on to see. You know that as well as I do. And who'd guess, anyway?"

"What about Skip King?"

"What about him?"

"How's he involved?"

"You know what it's all about in Minneapolis, all those bleeding heart liberals. He's gotta look right, needed the boost, so promised a BIA go-ahead on the Angle, and we'd make him look good."

"So what's in it for you?"

"I'm going to take my life back."

"Ah," I said, as if that explained everything. "And how do you do that?"

It must have been the way I looked at him. I really wanted to hear it.

"You *make people pay*—"

"And what do they owe you?"

"About now, quite a lot. Put me up to things, and decided not to hold up their end."

"So it's money," I said. "That'll compensate—"

"More than you could imagine," Michaels said.

"I don't think so," I said. "What were they going to pay you, if you could keep things quiet up here, help force that road deal? Five percent? And you, off to— *Where* would you be, Michaels?"

He bent over me, so that I turned my head to the side. My closet was open, which I wondered about. Had I left it open? In the dark—

all those shirts, canvas jackets, rows of boots, corks, sorrels for winter, hats on a rack—something moved.

My Tall Friend and his pals? Was that why Michaels was coming at me like this?

It was just . . . a breeze, I told myself. The breeze had blown through that back window, luffing the curtains, had moved things in the closet. A shirt, maybe.

"I got you on tape," I said, "talking to Skip King and Charlie's secretary, Darilyn, about how you were going to fix things. What'd you do, give her a swimming lesson out there on the lake?"

Michaels' eyes darted. Of course, the fetish was his; but the tape?

"You're lying," he said. "There's no tape."

"You gave yourself away."

"I don't think so," he said.

"It was your joke—calling my place 'Falls Apart Bay'—that did it. *Binishi-angoshka* bay. A pun on *Binishinuk* Bay. You asked around earlier, trying to find us. Asked Charlie, for that matter, where Binishinuk Bay was. And it was you down in Warroad, at Edna's, and setting up excavation sites, using those DOT surveys and core samples. Used old, high-plains names, *Anishininiimowin* names, to confuse people, to protect your sites. Anybody looks into all that, finds out where you're from—what reservation was it up in Saskatchewan? Moosomin? Yorkton? Kansack?—they'll put you right in the middle of *all* of it. You and Skip King. I got you both on tape, discussing how you'd do it."

I'd inched my hand forward, toward the letter opener, but Michaels saw it.

"You had the blasting caps in your room, put the bomb together—"

Michaels had begun to shake, a fury coming over him, the automatic bobbing in his hand.

"And you did Stanley's family."

"I *didn't* do that," Michaels said.

"No, I suppose Larry—or your Tall Friend did. Or Peterson, the cop they pulled out of the lake, or Jenkins, missing the fingers, who put my knife in Eugene that morning at the sinkhole, after you'd gotten it from Elmer. You use people, like you used Stanley, or the people up here. Like you meant to use me. Only you made a mess of it, so you had to wrap things up, to protect yourself.

"Killed my kid, Elmer, didn't you? Blamed it on him. But your own people turned against you after that. So you used Jenkins, to disappear.

"I've got your knife, and Truman has photos," Michaels said, each word hard-bitten, threatening. "One of your own took pictures that evening you killed the priest."

Something fell in my stomach, leaden. "Self-defense," I said.

"The pictures would say something else. I think your keeping the knife would, too."

I took the fetish, slowly, from my shirt pocket, set it on the desktop.

"One of my guides, Napoleon, found this out there. Saw the whole thing. It's yours, isn't it. That's when it *really* came apart. You lost it, Michaels. When they came down the path, you didn't recognize them—and with all that they must have stolen, you didn't figure them for kids—and you panicked."

He'd backed away from me, but not much.

"One of them had a rifle, meant to use it."

"You're a liar, and I think a coward, too."

He swung his fisted hand around, struck me in the mouth. I tasted blood. He swept the fetish off the desk, jabbed it in his shirt pocket.

"Give it," he said, "the tape, all of it."

"Trade you the tape for the knife."

"You think I'd bring that knife here?" he said, but it was the tone in his voice that gave him away.

"You don't have it, do you?" I said, "you lost it when your place got ransacked."

Michaels jammed the automatic into my head so hard I felt the blood slick there, the barrel nearly sliding off for it, the blood running down my neck.

"Give me the tape."

"It's under the hat," I said.

He lifted the hat off the desk, the speaker and wire there.

"Say—'one, two, three, testing,'" I said. "See if the volume's right."

He carefully set the hat back down, then rammed the automatic into my windpipe, cutting off my breath.

"Open the desk."

"No."

"Sure as I killed the others, I'll kill you."

"Do it," I got out. "People'll see you, and it'll be over, Michaels."

"Hands on the desk," he said in that policeman's voice, and I did that, and he grabbed the hair on the top of my head, banged my face down into the desktop. Now there was blood all over. He jerked my head back, bent over me. *"Open the desk."*

"Fuck you, Michaels."

His eyes screwed around, his mouth set in a bitter, angry line. Hitting me again wouldn't do it. He was thinking there, and what it was coming to was not good. He took in the room, the open window. It might just work—he could shoot me, and go out that way, get down to the dock, and running, who would identify him?

But it wasn't that simple. He had to get into the desk now. And he'd have to shoot me to do it, and what could he use then, to pry open the drawers?

All he needed was seconds, a minute, or a key.

The phone rang on my desk. It rang, and rang, and I didn't pick it up.

Michaels lifted the gun from my neck, then, backhand, cracked it across my forehead, so that I nearly passed out at it.

"Pick it up."

"No," I said.

He put the gun in my face, but at the bridge of my nose. A threat to take off my face, but leave me breathing. It nearly undid me.

"*Pick— It— Up—*" he said.

I heard the recorder go on in the kitchen, on the other side of the wall.

There was a knock at the door.

Michaels stepped back from the desk, flattened himself against the far wall, the gun trained on me.

"Paul?" Gwen said.

Michaels' face lit up, and she came through the door, not waiting for an answer, Claire in her arms.

"Someone's on the telephone for you, says it can't wait until—"

Michaels got behind her, and Gwen's eyes went wide.

Michaels was blinking, sharp, quick blinks; he glanced, over his shoulder, back into the lodge. It was dark, echoed, woodenly empty, but was anyone out there?

"All right," Michaels said, "Give it, *now,* or I'll kill her."

"I give it to you, and *then* what?"

"I'm going to take her with me. You can fly in when I call, pick her up."

"No," I said.

"*Don't fuck around,*" he said.

There was a noise in the kitchen. Michaels turned to look back into the lodge again, and I had Charlie's 659 out and on the desk, behind my hat.

"Is someone out there?" he said.

"It's the compressor for the freezer," I said, "it's a big one and it shakes the counters."

Michaels stepped into the vestibule between the room and door. When he did, the shirts in my closet parted, and there was Charlie, with his shorty twelve gauge.

He ran the barrel of the shotgun down the wall, so it made a hollow rasping.

"I told you *don't move,*" Michaels said.

I told him I hadn't. Charlie did that with his gun again.

I saw, emerge out of the dark of the lodge, Mardine, her eyes bright and sharp.

Michaels backed farther out. I shook my head very slightly at Mardine. Took one deep breath.

Then nodded.

"*Hey!*" Mardine shouted.

Michaels craned his head around, I got the 659 in my hand, jammed back the receiver, Charlie swung around beside me, made a jabbing motion with his shotgun, Michaels saw him, lifted the automatic, and for one fatal second, aimed at Charlie, out of reflex, even as I reached across the desk, Michaels, too late, bringing the gun around to put under Gwen's chin, and I—

Squeezed—

Caught Michaels in the forehead, spray of blood on the doorjamb—Michaels' gun going off, the shot thonking into the ceiling, leaving an oval hole, Gwen holding her hand to her cheek where the bullet had grazed her, Claire bawling in her arms.

In the weak light from my lamp, plaster dust sprinkled down on them from that hole in the ceiling, just then, like so much stardust.

A SHORT WHILE later, I sat in one of the porch chairs, still shaking. It was dark yet, but the lake was coming alive with bird calls, and it would be light soon. Charlie apologized for what he'd done. It had been George who'd gotten Charlie to take the shotgun. After all, I'd had his 659.

"Once it all got going there, when he came in, I knew that gun was worthless," Charlie said. "The kind of cop he was, he'd've known it better than me. A shotgun, short barrel like that, I'd fired and I'd've taken *everybody* out."

"But you didn't really make that mistake, did you?" I said.

Charlie shook his head.

"I had deer slugs in it, but he didn't know. So, he was sure I wouldn't shoot, but I couldn't get at him, the way he had Gwen turned toward me anyway—and if you'd fired, and missed? He'd have stayed behind Gwen, shot you, then me, and Mardine, then dragged Gwen out; he could've done it, sure as were sittin' here." Charlie squinted, held up his thumb and index finger. "That close," he said.

"Why would he have taken Gwen?"

"He got in trouble, he'd always have some leverage. And who'd shoot at a woman carryin' a two-year-old?"

"And if he weren't followed?" I said.

"He would have killed both of them. He'd've had to. He'd have what he came for, and who'd know he was alive, otherwise, without Gwen around?"

I set my boots up on the porch railing, my knees trembling something awful, lit a cigarette, offered one to Charlie. We smoked in the dark, glow of cigarettes, a bird calling distant off the lake.

"Thanks," I said.

"It's me that aughta be thanking you," Charlie replied.

I craned my head around to look into the lodge. Gwen and Mardine were in the kitchen; their conversation carried out to us, just then, the most beautiful music.

"Go ahead, ask," Charlie said. He had a shiner coming up, his left eye nearly shut.

"What were you doing in my closet? How'd you get in?"

"Window was open."

"Ah," I said. "Explains everything."

"You're gonna like this part," Charlie said, leaning forward and setting his elbows on his knees, the cigarette glowing in his thick fist.

"All right," I said.

"It's dark, right, and George and me have just got onto Highway 1 there, on the west side of Red Lake. A Hi Po pulls ahead of us and signals us over. So we stop like that, both cars, theirs ahead. Tall guy, thinks he's the Terminator or something, gets out and comes back, while the cop riding shotgun up front is getting ready for the show. I mean, what do we know, they're cops, right? I'm digging into my pocket for my wallet when the Terminator hauls off and hits me, George got hold of his arm and was slammin' his head on the wheel, and this bug-eyed little freak dances out of the car in front with a nine millimeter, gonna cap us both."

"You left something out," I said, and took a tug on my cigarette.

"Nobody puts stock in a car like your sister's—and they didn't either. Who'd be drivin' a piece of shit like that anyway? So when it slid to the side of the road there, and George's brothers jumped out? It was—" Charlie shook his head and chuckled, grimly. "It was like when those clowns come poppin' out of one of those little cars at the circus—but *mean*. Man, they'd've blown those phony cops to kingdom come; and when they weren't too happy about givin' up what they were doin' out there, George persuaded 'em—he and old Simon—very creative what you can do with a gallon of gasoline and a Bic lighter."

"It was one of them called here earlier," I said, "had Mardine ask for somebody we'd never heard of."

Charlie nodded.

"He was in the lodge the whole time?"

"Yup," Charlie said. "I guess it was a kinda code they'd worked out, let Michaels know they'd fixed things with me and George."

"How were you so sure my Tall Friend wouldn't send Michaels running?"

"You kidding?" Charlie said. "Your Tall Friend had luck on his side. He could cop a plea and rat fuck the rest of 'em. He needed Michaels—knew Michaels had shot Eugene, could put him there, at the sinkhole, and who had anything on your Tall Friend but circumstantial evidence, for Elmer? And besides, he wasn't too keen on bein' a human torch."

I told Charlie he still hadn't answered my question.

He glanced away, almost embarrassed. He'd seen me at my desk, chanting.

"Had to do it. While everyone was dancing and drinking and all, I came down from the point, got in through the window, saw what you'd done with the recorder, and knew to wait. That bit with the recorder was smart," Charlie said. "Real clever."

"Could've turned out badly."

"Yeah," Charlie said, "but it didn't."

He crushed out his nub of cigarette, lit another, and holding it up, studied the smoke lifting and curling and turning back on itself over his hand.

"Tell me, how was all this supposed to work for them. I mean, I got an idea, but—"

"Oh, they had it all ready to go," I said. "Or, *almost* did." I shifted again, setting my hands on my knees, trying to stop the trembling in my legs. "I mean, from the start, it was a bait and switch. People like Truman were screamin' for a new road, so the State, after god knows how many years, just up and proposes one—right across the Angle, just happens to be a site that needs the heaviest equipment, so independents around the area won't even bother to bid on it, no Indian companies, I mean.

"So the State offers to buy up tracts, or lease, and fund the road with BIA money. Get the thing put through that way. A gift, or maybe just some politician, like Skippy, tryin' to look good."

Charlie poked his cigarette at me. "But you guys refused right-of-way."

"We stalled," I said. "I mean, you always look the gift horse in the mouth up here, and up his hind end, too. It all just looked too good. The pitch was, we'd get a road, a dock, and all the State wanted was some limited timber harvest, right? And, hell, there isn't anything to harvest out there, just scrub."

"So, I don't get it," Charlie said. "Why *not* let the State put itself out?"

"See," I said, "if they'd gotten us to bite on it, *their* building that road, and our selling leases to them, we'd have privatized the whole area—the central corridor acres, and whoever set up business, whatever they'd be taking off that land would be theirs. So some politicians were in bed with private enterprise, greasing the wheels. They figured, and rightly, too, once the decision to build the road was in place, we'd have sold peripheral leases, for drainage, even mining clauses in it—so they could make roadtop. They'd have got all that for nothing, since nobody figured there was anything out there worth mining anyway. And then, building that road, they'd find it."

Charlie nodded. "The appatite."

"Right. And the best sites would just happen to be—"

Charlie shook his head. "Right where the northern spur of the Burlington Northern rail came in—so they'd have a way to ship it out."

"You got it," I said. "McKennet would put in the highest bid, snap up those worthless acres and hundred-year leases, or better yet, get that land free and clear in a swap, and set to mining, would only have to kick back a percentage to the Red Lake Band, which would look small, since they'd give figures from the lowest yield site out there, and when the band accepted that deal, McKennet'd move in the works and—"

Charlie tapped the ash off his cigarette. "—they'd expand onto the sites you saw in the surveys, all six of 'em, rake off all the prof- its and give you people just enough not to complain. Or to shut up those that did. And somewhere in there—"

"You got it," I said, taking a tug on my cigarette. "Somebody'd juggle the books, and Michaels was going to get paid," and, I added, "I'm sure, Skip King, Darilyn, Peterson, that cop who drowned, Jenk- ins, our dryland lobster, and my Tall Friend and his pals."

"The whole crooked bunch," Charlie said.

We smoked there in the dark, sobered at the thought of the ex- tent of it, and something occurred to me.

"Does truth—exactly the truth, and only that—always serve jus- tice?" I said.

Charlie eyed me over his cigarette. "You think too much," he said. "Christ. Right about now, you aughta be countin' yourself lucky, with what you had up against you, and that's about it."

"No, I mean it."

"Justice's got in it fairness, and life isn't fair. So it's always some—the best you can do is *try,* see, and, I don't know. . . . What are you gettin' at?"

"Then does it matter *exactly* what happened back in that room?"

In the dark, I could see he was weighing what I'd said. In a few hours the BCA would be out, and all that had happened would be taken out of our hands, and for both of us, the result would be damning.

Charlie sat stock-still in his chair, as if afraid to so much as blink.

That he didn't ask me to made me do it.

"Let's go and talk to Gwen and Mardine," I said.

This time, in the kitchen, I did all the talking, put together what happened in the office, all of it true, but for one, significant detail.

THIRTY-SIX

We had the FBI up again. They came to investigate cases in which citizens not members of the Red Lake Band were killed or injured. Or, as they put it to us, time and again, any violation of the major crimes act was within the jurisdiction of the Federal Bureau of Investigation, which gave them the right to pry.

They had their work cut out for them. I was busy, too, with our end of season crowd.

And then those investigators were gone. Still—

I was all nerves, sure now that knife would appear, or had already, worried that maybe, just maybe, Truman had it, was waiting until the worst moment to take me down with it, get his road after all. Every morning, I woke early, and I prayed, up on the ridge. Left tobacco. Tried to breathe easy, but I couldn't.

I went into Pine Point, for supplies, and some mornings walked miles on back roads through sand and by trees now high again, second-growth pine, and tamarack, and spruce, the sumac going red, and milkweed pods bursting with silken seeds, and time and again,

I stopped to yank them from a brown pod and toss them into the wind, to see them lift away, diaphanous, light as air.

(Wouldn't it be great to be able to just fly? Elmer had said once. Up there in the clouds?)

But it was history I was thinking about most now, my own.

Or was it just Truman? If Truman wanted to ruin me, he had all he needed.

So, when I went into Pine Point, I invariably circled Truman's old place, a huge log cabin, which had been the second biggest on the Angle until the Crow place had burned thirty some years earlier, and here were Truman and his family, in and out day after day, battered Ford F-150s, turquoise, crayon red, an oily, royal blue, and Truman, in his hat, with the coins around the rim, working in his yard, or in town, his voice that big booming embarrassment.

SO HE WASN'T altogether surprised when I strode up his drive, that last morning before our big dinner. In fact, at first, he didn't so much as lift his head. Which made me all the more apprehensive. It was bright, the sun gone to yellow and the trees lit as if from inside, all green-gold and my life, I felt as if I were carrying it, corks heavy on Truman's long road in, all the more precious for the possibility it might change, become ugly again.

Truman sat on his stoop, a small fire going off to the left, brush they'd cut down and stacked, and it smelled good, cedar.

"Truman," I said.

"Boo shoo," he said, hello.

In the old language, I asked how it was going. He said fine, considering.

By this time, everyone had read about the mess in the *Tribune.*

If you could believe the paper, Charlie had broken the case. We'd wanted it that way. *I'd* wanted it that way, had gone to great lengths to paint Charlie as the man who'd made sense of it, single-handed.

I'd given him all I had, the tape with Michaels on it, now five seconds of it static, and the fetish, which Napoleon testified he found on the Angle that night, and which was identified as having belonged to Michaels.

Charlie, with the help of Beautiful, found Peterson's head on the Angle shoreline. Didn't move it, called the BCA. (What was I gonna do, Charlie said, joking in the Western, carry his head out of there in my bowling bag? Which, later, became a rumor, that he'd done just that, more Lake of the Woods apocrypha.)

Ballistics matched Charlie's gun to the bullet that killed Michaels, and no one so much as asked if I could have had the gun, done the shooting. They exhumed Elmer's body, and, sure enough, found the needle mark between his toes. And with the help of my Tall Friend, the BCA located the body of the man who'd worked me over so badly that night in the boathouse, prop scars on his back.

While my Tall Friend was saving himself, the short, pug-faced man tried to do the same.

And like that, the BCA sewed up the last of it. Tony Beaulieu dug the radio detonator out of Charlie's cruiser in the impound lot and identified Michaels' work by the wire he'd bought in the Twin Cities, odd for the strand of orange on the insulation. Edna, Elmer's mother, flew down from Sitka, Alaska, to testify against Darilyn, who, along with Michaels and Jenkins, had won Edna's confidence, and then used her to find Elmer, the guilty three on the fridge, I thought.

Darilyn the BCA picked up in the Dakotas.

I set the BCA after McKennet Mining, too, and pointed them toward Ryder Geologic. McKennet was sent packing, a heavy fine against them for illegal exploration on reservation land, and private use of State property and personnel. Were threatened with racketeering charges, so coughed up some compensation for the damage they'd caused. Ryder Geologic, under investigation, filed for bankruptcy and disappeared overnight.

And good to my promise, I made sure Stanley was released.

Only one person involved, that we knew of anyway, had run

free: Old Skippy.

When the finger of blame swung in Skip King's direction, he'd given evidence to prove his lack of involvement. How was he to be responsible for what these people he'd backed had done? What Skip said on the tape was circumstantial, the property deals he'd mentioned, on Penn and Nicollet Avenues, real, in Minneapolis, so had nothing to do with the Angle, or anything up at Red Lake, for that matter, and so he was cleared of any wrongdoing.

Special interest groups were a fact of political life, were they not?

So what that McKennet Mining and he'd had business relations in the past. He was an advocate of development, as was McKennet. And that McKennet had had a team of geologists out on the Angle, on his ticket?

That was their business what they'd done.

And out of all that exploration? Nothing out there, King testified, was there?

We all knew he was dirty, and that proved true, when, years later, he was killed up on the lake, but that is another story.

And Truman? I knew he was connected, if only through what I'd seen Michaels give him.

Just then, Truman was carving a length of willow. I lit a cigarette, watching him. He carefully notched the red bark, deftly removed a section of it, thin as paper, the knife exquisitely sharp, and his hands steady.

"Your grandfather, or father, ever show you how to carve a willow whistle?"

I said they had, Nita had, but that was long ago.

Nita's voice, as always, was there with me:

Nawaji, a man's worst enemy can't wish him what he thinks up for himself.

Just then, I tried to believe it.

"Here, finish this," Truman said, and handed me the knife, and went inside.

I looked up behind me. Three-story log cabin, a roof with hornets' gray paper nests tacked to the eaves, in the early fall air, the hornets lazily bumping up under the roof and swinging down on the dew-covered fields that spread out from the stoop.

When he came out, he had that manila envelope with him.

"It's all here. Negatives, too."

I wanted to say, *all?* I'd feared Truman had the knife, but now worried who did, if he didn't.

"Of course I looked," he said.

I nodded at that, my mind a white hot blank.

"Give me that," he said, and motioned for me to hand him the willow.

We sat there on his stoop, two old enemies, but just then, not.

"Why'd you get involved," I said. It was all I could think to say.

"Michaels said he could use some help, didn't tell me what it was about. Said he'd make sure that road got built and that dock. All I did was agree to look at what he had. Daughter inside's diabetic, needs a dialysis machine." He glanced up from the stick. "We're not the kind to put her picture on a jar beside a cash register, see?"

He shook his head—just then, another father.

"The money I've been tryin' to make isn't for me, Paul," he said. "See? And your sister wasn't the only one that priest bothered, did you know that? Church wouldn't take him back, and some had ideas what to do."

"Who had ideas?"

Truman notched the ends of the willow. Sighted up it. "Walter."

I felt my eyes go wide at that. "Walter was there that evening, when I went out with Father Prideaux?"

"No. But he sent his brother, couldn't make it that night, and his brother failed him entirely. Louis, that half-wit, was supposed to call you back if it was just you and Prideaux in the boat, but he didn't. Was to take pictures to make Father Prideaux think twice about doing anything in the first place. But Walter's brother was terrified of that priest, see, so when it got out of hand, he hid. Walter always felt guilty about that. We all did, about what happened to you out there, but Walter's idiot brother took the pictures, all right, and gave 'em to Walter."

"Walter's had them all these years?"

Truman nodded. I felt a pain at Walter's betrayal so sharp it nearly took my breath away, but then a certain confusion. Truman lifted his head from his carving.

"Michaels convinced Walter you were going to do something," he said. "All kinds of people did. Michaels had your receipts for the stuff to make explosives, and Walter was out there the first time you used 'em, to bust up that granite, remember? And I'll just say, Walter knew you could get outta whack, see, and he was worse than impressed at the hole your homemade explosives made in that solid granite."

"So why didn't Walter just come to me?"

"You're known around here for never, never having anything to do with council members. Walter thought you'd never listen, that it'd gone far beyond that already. I mean, you should have heard the rumors about you. According to a few of 'em, you were even gonna blow up the council office with everybody in it."

"That's crazy," I said.

Truman shook his head, made yet another notch in the length of red willow.

"So Walter just up and gave those pictures to Michaels?"

"No. It was a deal," Truman said, puckering his mouth. "Michaels was IA, it wasn't supposed to go no further. We didn't want any newspaper mess, attention that'd ruin that road deal. So, it was gonna be all inside, just us, and Michaels. He was gonna put the screws to you he said, you'd listen to a cop better'n anybody. Michaels said you'd back down if we convinced you the pictures looked like murder."

My heart caught in my throat, but I managed to get it out,

"Well, do they?"

Truman nodded. "Yup. They certainly do. But then, just overnight—and we all know what happened that night now— Michaels up and changes his mind, so the following day he says, Meet me at the Rambler's, and there in the lot, tells me, it'd be better if I did it, he's got something else on you. We'd come at you from both sides. So he gave me the pictures and I was supposed to do the hatchet job. You hated me already, so, you'd listen, wasn't no friendship holding me back and I wanted that road, bad, the way Michaels saw it, and Walter went along because he thought you might hurt somebody."

"So why didn't you? Come at me, I mean?"

"I didn't trust that Michaels for shit. I started to wonder if Michaels'd had something to do with those rumors about you, see? Was givin' all of us the runaround, had his own scam going. And when I didn't go up after you, he threatened me."

Truman's eyes hardened, and he nodded, to himself really.

"Bad move on his part. That's when I knew he was rotten. Followed him one night, when he left Pine Point. Drove all the way to St. Paul, and then, the jackass lost me, and that was that."

"But you had business down there anyway, didn't you," I said. "Wasn't altogether a wasted trip."

I thought about him bribing people down on Franklin Avenue. Truman craned his head around away from me, shook his head, I knew, at my combativeness. Or was it, to his way of thinking, just a lack of gratitude?

"What about Carol Herbst?" I said.

"That woman had *nothin'* to do with what went on up here. Had *nothin'* to do with McKennet mining; all *I* was pushin' was work, and a place to do it."

"So it was timber that fronted the money down in the Twin Cities?"

"Leave it alone now, all right? All that's over. I'll just say I had *nothin'* to do with Michaels."

"What if it'd gone wrong those photos?"

"Walter knew his brother could testify it was self-defense—he was there, after all, an eyewitness. He's just down the road, works on some farm."

Just then Truman looked tired; he let go a sigh, shook his big head.

"What would you say to *one* road in? We do it right, it'll pay for itself and then some."

I knew what he was implying: mining the appatite. He was testing me. Of course, everyone knew about the appatite by then.

"That new road'd help a lot of people. We'd build it ourselves and be beholden to *nobody,* put the dock there on shore, a big one, maybe a fishery to restock right from the Angle. Hire our own to do every last bit of it. There's gotta be a year of work there, hell maybe three, or more. God knows, you can't take on anybody. It'd pay for itself and then some. We'd even make it look nice."

"That's what Walter was trying to sell me on earlier?"

"He tried to talk to ya, didn't he? But you wouldn't listen—not back then, anyway."

Truman blew on that whistle. It made a light, airy sound. Walking out of his yard, I dropped the envelope into the fire.

I don't know if I just imagined it, or that paper set the whole thing to blazing. He blew on that whistle, and I turned, and nodded. My answer.

I could hear it all the way up the road, to the government docks. Willow whistle.

SATURDAY NIGHT OF that week, I watched, from a distance, out on the lake in the dark, with Charlie, as Gwen's parents came in, overdressed, Italian leather shoes, seasonal chic, right out of Nordstrom's, or Neiman Marcus, her mother regal, but wounded, though trying to shake herself out of it. Her father, stepping from our launch onto the dock, slapping his dinner jacket in place.

Hugh, in tuxedo, playing the part I had for nearly ten years, ushering them up the hill.

I sat on the gunnel of Charlie's boat—his new boat, an eight seater, with all the new gadgets, radio, cellular phone, GPS, sounder, electric winch for the anchor—wanting to go back in, but just then, not able to.

Charlie sat beside me, fiddling with his cigarette, clearing his throat now and then.

He'd been given a clean bill of health, got his job back, and there was a rumor that the promotion he'd banked on, had caused such ruin for him, might materialize. He'd gone on about it, steering me home from the government docks, and out onto our bay, where we'd been all this time, even as people continued to come in.

I was none too thrilled about going in and having to deal with Gwen's parents. But the island?

The island rose out of the liquid dark, magical now. We'd all helped to string the lights up, coils and coils of lights, and a star on the roof, so it all had the look of festivity.

Charlie tilted a can of Pepsi back. I sat with my elbows on my knees. We'd been waiting for Hugh to bring in Gwen's parents, and here it was, but still, neither of us moved.

"Here's to the in-laws," Charlie said. "You ready to make your grand entrance?"

"I'm going to give it a few," I said.

"Good," Charlie said, but he was even worse now, shifting his feet, and rubbing his neck.

Up the bank, Mardine was working at the grills, Gwen had Claire by the hand, Beautiful beside her, shaking with excitement and taking a scrap Mardine tossed her. Gwen's mother hoisted Claire up and kissed her, and Gwen's father bound them all up in a bear hug.

"Look at that," Charlie said.

What could I say? I wanted it all to just go on, my life, and this time, for life—maybe, for a while, please, I thought—be kind.

Be kind to the people I loved. Gwen was introducing George, who dwarfed Gwen's father, and George's . . . *girlfriend* we were calling her, a sturdy, but lovely woman who tied George all up in knots.

The older guests danced a slow one, good dancers, out of another time and place.

Charlie and I floated there, on the lake, just then distant as spirits.

I could have it all back, I thought, and that knife would take it away.

Charlie cleared his throat. I felt my face heat; I feared Charlie, catching me alone, would have to say something. After all, he'd been keeping me out here, and I'd just gone along with it, really. But I knew he would do it now.

"I appreciate what you did," he said, and then added, "for me."

"Hell," I said. "I didn't want the attention up here anyway. And besides, you were on to it before I was, up there on the Angle—and put me onto Michaels, and—"

"No," Charlie said. "I mean about the blood."

"Hell, Jimmy—"

"Goddammit, you liar."

He turned away from me. The stars were out. A bird warbled, far off on the lake. A peal of laughter carried to us from the island.

"Watch out," I joked. "You're gonna tan easier now—"

"What?" Charlie said.

I had to laugh at that. "You might find yourself in the middle of the night half-stepping, you know, or paddling, like in a canoe." I stood and made a paddling motion. "Or getting a godawful craving for fry bread."

"You're so full of it," he said.

"Same to you," I shot back, and we both laughed.

But there was something he wanted to do just then, and it was making him awfully nervous.

"Some people are gonna come out and ask more questions."

"Why?" I said.

In front of us, all that on the island hung in the dark like some miraculous, jeweled Fabergé egg, but alive.

"Some things Michaels did were sloppy," Charlie said. "Some of the stuff he got early on, meant to use, to twist your arm, he talked about. See? But he kept things in different places, and I got to thinking what places, went crazy looking, and finally hit on something. Found Darilyn had a deposit box in Warroad, didn't say boo about that when they got her statement, so I took a look, night when that bank's burglar alarm just happened to go off."

He held up a plastic bag in the dark.

"You said self-defense on that tape. I just want to hear it."

I took a deep breath, said,

"It's true."

He turned the bag over, and there was a watery plunk, and a second, heavier plunk, and I bent over the side, and the knife handle turned end over end, shining moon white, bone white in that dark water, and was gone. I turned my head away, throat burning, felt as if, just then, I were rising into that starry sky itself.

A bird, free, at last, my god!

"They come wondering about those things Michaels had," Charlie said. "Tell them to ask me."

My eyes fixed on the island, I nodded.

Everyone was out now, twenty-five, thirty people on the soft slope of the bank. Inside, Mardine, colorful in an apple-green applique dress, lit candles that flickered warm and inviting in the lodge windows, Mardine sharing a joke with a guest, tossing her head back and laughing. And here came old Joe Strong Rock, to sing the prayer for the year, and to play dew claws.

Hugh stood with a soda in his hand at the grills, directed Josette and Darius with plates. Napoleon dodged inside after them, wiping his forearm across his forehead. I'd kept Napoleon on, even knowing the trouble he'd be, for Napoleon's sake—we'd work on him, Gwen and me.

And I had another motive in it, too: sooner or later, the girl would come.

It wasn't just any girl that'd do what she'd done for him, stood by him like that, figure out how to get that fetish to me. But then her parents hadn't just been anybody either.

More boats were arriving. Finedays, Morrisons, people up from Barney's, gliding into shore, and tethering at the docks. Men and women climbed the hill to the lodge, the night August-balmy and a breeze whispering in the pines, the air redolent with sage, and cedar, and sweetgrass from the powwow going on just north of us.

Outside, Mardine rang the bell, signaling the start of dinner.

Gwen, in a flowing, rose-red gown, descended the bank to stand on shore; Claire, bundled in a green blanket, in her arms, peered into the dark.

Onto the lake.

Waiting.

"Hey," Charlie said, and put his hand on my shoulder, "will you look at that? Will you just look at that? Is that something, or what?"

"*Enh,*" I said, "Yes," and like that we went in.

THIRTY-SEVEN

OZO (TAIL)

And the message of Gwen's that morning so long ago, on the answering machine? It hadn't been from her parents, but from her obstetrician.

Good news.

That surprise, though, we'd have to wait on the better part of a year. All I could hope was, I was able, and the spirit watching over us, willing.

Nin deba'nagadon. But I've said enough.

Onwas—luck.

ABOUT THE AUTHOR

WAYNE JOHNSON text to come.